– The Sense of Things –

– *The Sense of Things* –

ALISON DYE

*to Ruth with all
good wishes –
Alison*

HEINEMANN : LONDON

First published in Great Britain 1994
by William Heinemann Ltd
an imprint of Reed Consumer Books Ltd
Michelin House, 81 Fulham Road, London SW3 6RB
and Auckland, Melbourne and Singapore

*Chapters one and two appeared in a slightly
different form in Stand Magazine, autumn 1989.*

A CIP catalogue record for this title
is available from the British Library
ISBN 0 434 21194 X

Phototypeset by Intype, London
Printed and bound in Great Britain
by Clays Ltd, St. Ives PLC

For Maureen

The cards are dealt,
Bets placed.

The weary gambler sits back,
Smiles.
The game is up.

The moment of the winning hand
Is seized.

For Annie, For Tony

these children
beyond all dreams of children

beyond possession time place

held by luminous dancing threads
of memory and possibility

The Riddle

You never saw it used but still can hear
The sift and fall of stuff hopped on the mesh,

Clods and buds in a little dust-up,
The dribbled pile accruing under it.

Which would be better, what sticks or what falls
   through?
Or does the choice itself create the value?

Legs apart, deft-handed, start a mime
To sift the sense of things from what's imagined

And work out what was happening in that story
Of the man who carried water in a riddle.

Was it culpable ignorance, or was it rather
A *via negativa* through drops and let-downs?

Seamus Heaney
The Haw Lantern

– *Acknowledgements* –

I have received a great deal of support in the writing of this book.

I am especially grateful to Lucinda Franks, whose friendship brought me to life as a writer and moved me to go on. I must also thank Bernard MacLaverty who, in the earliest days, offered the unwavering encouragement I needed; Jon Silkin and Lorna Tracy, Editors of *Stand Magazine*, who unconditionally acknowledged and supported my beginning efforts, as they have done with so many new writers; Beryl Bainbridge and Malcolm Ross-Macdonald who believed in this book when it took its first steps as a story; and Malcolm, especially, whose unflagging conviction about my writing made publication possible. Special thanks go to my agent, Anthony Goff, and to Elspeth Sinclair, Senior Editor at Heinemann, for their total commitment to *The Sense of Things*.

Ailbhe Alvey painstakingly typed the first draft from a heap of scrawled pages; but more important to me than her time and patience are the understanding and friendship which she has given freely throughout.

The Department of Social Studies in Trinity College have been most forthcoming in accommodating my writing, in particular the past and present Heads of Department, Vivienne Darling and Noreen Kearney.

The teachers in the Primary School of Loreto College, St. Stephen's Green, Dublin, have extended to me and my family the most abundant warmth and good will imaginable as we settled into our new life in Ireland. How can I ever thank Margaret Gath, kindergarten teacher at Loreto, who has generously and lovingly cared for my daughter, and whose unquestioning support, guidance, and beloved friendship have meant more than she knows or would ever take credit for. The extraordinary sustaining spirit of the other teachers – Sr. Hildegarde, Principal, Mary O'Brien, Terese Keenan and Margaret Campbell – has given me enormous peace of mind during the writing of this book.

Several special people in America have helped me greatly: my mother and father, who have stood by me through every phase of my life and have supported my writing with confidence and encouragement; Alicia Sainer, Richard Morgan, and Carol Glassman, who read and commented open-heartedly, as usual, on the first draft of the book; and Edward Rabinowitz, Lee Crespi, Judy Levitz, Carol Edkins, and Sandra Turner, whose enduring presence spans the distance from one world to another. To my dear friends in Dublin, Ian Daly and Anne Cleary, with whom I have shared the high times and low, I express again my love and loyalty. To Maeve Dwyer, Miriam Wiley, Frances and Michael Fitzgerald, and Peter and Mary O'Sullivan, I say thank you for your affectionate support and many fine evenings which kept the writing in perspective.

To Rita: thank you.

Much of this book was written in Louisburgh, Co. Mayo, where the most generous people on earth re-united this frenetic American with the truth of her soul. In Louisburgh I discovered the extraordinary restorative power of the Irish kettle, the lounge in Durkan's Hotel, the turf fire, and rain; the healing inefficiency of a long chat. In Ireland time seems to last, does not elude, can be embraced. Ireland has taken me, like a force-ten gale overpowers Carramore Strand, shifting sands and alter-ing ports of call forever. Without Ireland there would be no book, no life of writing or reflection. My enduring gratitude to the people who showed me the way: Mary, Brid, Padraic, Mairead, and Maire O'Grady, John and Eileen Durkan, John and Bernadette Burke, Johnny and Mary Durkan; and to all the children in these families without whom life would be a dull old business indeed.

My thanks of course to Rosie, that faithful companion in good times and bad, that uncompromising, unflinch-ing Springer Spaniel who stood watch over this book and the author's dubious mental health at all hours of the night and day.

And finally: to my beloved, indefatigable writing group – Renate Ahrens-Kramer, Sheila Barrett, Catherine Phil MacCarthy, Cecilia McGovern, Joan O'Neill, and Ann O'Sullivan – whose unshakeable faith and unfailing good judgement made this book not only possible but absolutely essential, I am on my knees, my head is bowed.

Dublin, Ireland
May 1993

– chapter one –

I was a weak person last year, age twenty-eight. When I got to Louie's the day after Mother's funeral, the suitcase felt heavy and my body went limp, all muscles shrivelling in the grip of that particular person's memory. Naturally I loved her more than anything. Her distant voice cried out to my left ear, A daughter's place is with her mother. I say 'distant' because, as previously mentioned, she is dead. The voice I heard was an experience of the imagination. Rather than actual. I am deaf in the right ear.

At a time like that, which I call 'change' or 'hardship', my head tips slightly back until it locks in place. The eyelids descend. Whoever I am floats away. When I was young Mother used to say 'what lovely posture, Joanie.' Actually, it is a physiological truth that under stress blood moves from the extremities to the inner core. Therefore a person's hands and feet feel cold when he or she is afraid. This phenomenon is the body's strategy for ensuring survival of the vital organs. The relatively minor problem of cold hands and feet can be solved by, (1) a lukewarm – not hot – bath, or (2) gentle massaging, either of which can be done alone. People are often alone in times of fear.

I stood at Louie's door and rotated my head first left then right, and coughed hard twice, covering my mouth. These steps, repeated in the same sequence on each occasion, stimulate the natural flow of adrenalin which then carries me back from wherever I've been. When Mother was alive she used to say: 'Cut that out, Joan Marie Pardee, you're going to hurt yourself twisting your neck and coughing like that. Those bones are connected to the throat.'

I had taken biology in college so I tried to explain to her that circular motion of the neck *per se* does not cause coughing, and can in actual fact relax the muscles and lower blood pressure. But she thought I was trying to embarrass her because she never went to college. 'For someone who lasted ONE TERM you act mighty hoi polloi, J M Pardee. I've done my share of learning through living, which is a boast no young person can make.'

I didn't like to disagree with Mother because she was a sensitive woman who felt ashamed of herself, no reason given. For example: the first day at college they held a reception for the new students and their parents. Which I suppose was a burden for Mother because my father is dead. Well, they're both dead now, and here she was at a social function on her own even though she is not a feminist. When the Dean introduced us to my roommate and her parents I could feel my eyelids going as soon as I saw the other girl's soft white skin and high heels. I immediately turned my head around and coughed.

'Well,' said Miss Greer. 'Isn't this just lovely for the two of you. Amanda Cummings Bartlett, this is Joan Pardee and her mother, Ernestine. And Amanda's parents, John and Muffin Bartlett. Now, let me see all of you get to know each other! That's the spirit of learning!'

Afterwards my mother was angry. She said I had disgraced her in front of the Bartletts, (1) by telling them no one in our family had ever gone to college; (2) by the head-rotating and coughing business which she said made me appear snobbish; and (3) by saying my dead aunt had left money to send me to college because we do not believe in handouts from a school and because my father had no life insurance when he died. This may or may not be true. I told her I got excited meeting so many intellectuals. She didn't believe me.

'At a structured formality such as that, Joan Marie, a person wants to make a good impression so others will show respect. You smile, you talk slowly and clearly, you look confident, and above all you mention the positive – which you could easily have observed me doing as I spoke with Mr Bartlett.'

What she meant was that when Mr Bartlett told us he was leaving to return to his law practice in New York,

Mother commented that her husband was on a business trip to Florida. Mrs Bartlett looked confused and said, 'Oh, I thought Joan said he had died, I'm so sorry. What is his business?' Mother replied: 'Air conditioning, sales and service.' I was starting to feel dizzy when Mrs Bartlett turned to me and said, 'You must be very proud of him.' I dozed off and heard my voice float a reply in the direction of Mrs Bartlett's soft eyes: 'I didn't realise he was there.'

Later Mother said this comment made us appear to be a family that did not stick together on the facts. I told her politely that I did not like the lie about Daddy, but she shouted, 'It's not a lie, Joanie Smartie Pardee, it's conversation,' and slapped my face. She had hit me before but I do not believe these blows caused my deafness. Or rather, my partial deafness. In college I found out that speaking up is not one of my strong points. Professor Whitlock took me aside one day and said to relax. He told me he felt certain I had good ideas to express but that people had to be able to follow my train of thought.

A few days later I explained to Miss Greer that I believed I could formulate comments and questions more effectively in my room. Hopefully when my clarity had improved, I would be able to go to class and say something interesting. Miss Greer put her arm around me and looked as though she might cry. I do not understand why she should have been upset. As far as I could tell Miss Greer had everything. Mother explained that some people are just never satisfied, no matter how much they accomplish. Finally Miss Greer suggested that perhaps I wasn't ready for college. I came home.

Amanda Bartlett had all the best clothes from a store for ladies. Under her bed a perfect row of pretty shoes stood, so to speak, at attention, while the shiny new pens and notebooks on her side of the room pumped out rays of hope for good grades and a husband: the grades for her father, the husband for her mother.

Every night just before bed, she sat straight up in the chair at her desk in a plush flannel nightgown. She lay her hands flat out on top with the thumbs and fingers stretched apart until she bit her lip. Then she would close her eyes and pray. She went to bed early.

It was around three in the morning when she used to wet the bed. Eventually I just stayed up reading Descartes. I'd let the rush of water finish. Then get a nice fresh sheet, nightgown, and towel from the stacks in her closet. At that point she would wake up.

'I'm wet again, Joanie Marie,' she'd cry. Curled up and whimpering like an old woman in the corner of a nursing home.

'I know,' I would say.

I peeled off the wet nightgown. I towelled her down. She was shivering, so I kept the towel around her until the new nightgown had dropped all the way to her feet.

She was tall, and, well, beautiful. Then I slipped it out from under.

I tucked her into my bed with a hot water bottle until I'd re-made hers, rubber sheet wiped off first. When she got back into her own bed she said, 'I've never had a friend.' I liked Descartes and the stillness of night. On the other hand, interruptions have never bothered me.

I know I hurt Mother when I left college: the week I came home I found a letter she had written to Miss Greer, and made a copy for myself. I am aware that to do so was dishonest.

> Dear Miss Greer,
>   I am writing to apologise for my daughter's
> poor performance at your school. This
> disgrace was not caused by her upbringing.
> As the mother, I told her many times, if you
> don't do the classes you aren't doing college.
> I myself did well in school. You probably
> won't believe this because all you know of me
> is Joan, but I won the Charles Carroll No. 46
> School Reading Improvement Prize, Junior
> Category, when I was seven.
>   I was hoping Joanie would make me proud.
> Maybe there is still time, although as you
> may have noticed when you met me, I am a
> high-strung person who takes care of
> everything to the letter.
>   I have had two by-pass operations already
> and my doctor says I must try to settle
> down.
>   My husband died suddenly when Joanie
> was three. He fell eight stories from

scaffolding (construction man). I suppose you're wondering if he'd been drinking. The same thought crossed my mind.

I believe Joan Marie never got over losing her father. Somehow she took to him rather than to the mother, which I believe is abnormal psychology for a daughter, who most college people say needs the mother above all. I did sing to Joanie after he passed on and she often fell asleep in my arms.

I am sure you will understand what it means to try and get a child on the right track in life. Therefore I have taken the liberty of saying certain personal things which I would prefer you not repeat.

Respectfully yours,
Ernestine Pardee

I am not one to dwell on the past. But the statement about my father possibly drinking before he died is an example of 'faulty recollection'. To begin with, I was twelve when he died. Secondly, Mother had imperfect pitch. She often held me and rocked us after he died. However, she did not sing, so to speak, *per se*. These two points illustrate the effects of cerebral vaso-constriction on the functioning of memory for past events even while recent memory is preserved, due to the acute stress of grief.

My father's supervisor, Bob, said the accident happened this way (he came to the house late one night when Mother thought I would be asleep): Daddy ate his lunch quietly on the eighth-floor platform, sandwiches and a can of Coke. Then he carefully wiped each corner of his mouth with the paper towel my mother packed in his lunch-box. Stood up to stretch with his face to the sun. After a moment he looked at Bob and said, 'Well, Robert, looks like a great day to take it easy.' Then he jumped.

Mother told Bob that the company should be sued for not protecting its workers from high winds, but Bob just held his face in his hands and sobbed. I for one do not believe my father had been drinking and I was not in favour of mentioning to a public official like Miss Greer that my father ever did anything more than the job he was paid to do.

I can report conclusively that he never missed a day no matter what the weather. On Fridays when he got paid he brought every penny home, plus a Mars Bar for me. Which he pretended to hide in his pocket to make me think he'd forgotten, but I'd always guess which pocket and pull the bar out. Naturally when he said, 'So who's my best girl, who wants to give Dad the biggest kiss,' I would take a little jump into his arms and kiss his neck while he rested his head on my shoulder after a hard day. I am getting emotional even now.

My room had no windows. After my father died I bought a can of yellow paint and Mother and I brushed two bright squares on to the far wall. Which actually made you think you could see out. I sewed curtains for each of these from green and yellow hand towels. Mother thought I had picked the colours on purpose to remind us of sun and grass. She said cleverness like that might mean I was an artistic type of person. If so I would have to work hard at the practical side of life with little hope of praise or material gain.

Actually, those were the only towels I could find at the time. I don't know why I didn't tell her. As a result of my deception she died with a false impression of me. I believe it is important to please your mother, but not if you have to lie.

– chapter two –

After college I felt I would lose all sense of priority if I had no purpose and no identity within a human group. So I got a job at Louie's pastry shop. The day I went to see him I fixed my eyes on a pair of *cannoli* in the window and put my head around twice. Coughed, covered my mouth. In general, tried to build confidence.

'Joanie!' he cried. Italians are an emotional people. 'What are your doing home now? Now is college, right? What happened to college?'

'Hi, Louie,' I said with sincerity. 'I believe that a person with my abilities will contribute more by living and working in the real world. Some people are afraid of life and hide in college. I don't want that to happen to me.'

'Neither do I, Joanie. But college is the only way to get ahead. You're young, you need an education.'

'Actually, Louie,' I said, 'I thought I would learn more about supply and demand and worker morale by observing a real business. In college I was planning to specialise in how world socio-economic forces, interacting with biochemical destiny, affect the life of the everyday individual.'

Louie looked at me. He couldn't believe how much I had learned in only one term.

'Joanie, of course I will give you a job. You'd make a great worker and I could use the help. But what about your mother? Does she know you're here? She likes to have a say in these things I'm sure.'

I had not anticipated this question as my mother and I have separate bodies. However, the unexpected does not bother me so I answered calmly.

'She doesn't know yet,' I said. 'I am eighteen and trying to practise using my initiative, although I respect my mother's views. I was waiting to see if you had a position vacant. You didn't advertise for the job.' I was beginning to wonder why no one else had applied.

Louie laughed. 'One thing you learn about economics as you get older, Joanie: people come first. Why should I put an ad in the paper when you walk in here for nothing?'

Mother set up a diary in which she planned to keep track of my hours and my pay, to be sure Louie didn't cheat us. Then she went to the shop with me.

'Mrs Pardee,' said Louie. 'Welcome! So! Will you let your lovely girl learn about the world in my little shop?' He held out a hand to my mother but she pretended not to notice.

'I'm nobody's fool, Joanie,' she used to say, and she

wasn't. Mother read out the statement she had prepared in advance.

> Mr Fusco, this is my first point, not being rude
> of course: what will she in fact learn? Being
> the mother, I am the one who knows what
> Joan can handle. Therefore, any questions
> regarding stress and strain will be answered
> by me. I don't mind consulting. But deciding
> is another matter. Thank you for your
> cooperation.

Mother laid the piece of paper on the table. She squinted her eyes and stared hard at Louie. She knew how to make people admit what they were trying to hide. Louie had put out mugs of coffee and a plate (with paper doily) of anisette cookies. I myself did not believe he did so to take advantage of us. We all sat down. He took Mother's statement.

I could tell Louie was reading every word because he put on his glasses and followed one line after another with the index finger of his right hand. I said nothing and watched the anniversary cakes, which come frosted white with pink, blue, or yellow trim and your choice of flowers in the same colours plus green. I am an excellent judge of people and I felt that Louie would agree with Mother about who's who. I was right. However, I believe that people who brag get a terrible come-uppance.

After a moment Louie looked at Mother. He said, 'It

would be a pleasure to have Joan work for me according to your instructions, which I will put right here.'

He walked over to his little office with the glass partition and taped the sheet of paper over his desk. 'I'll need you to come in on a regular basis to let me know how you think she is doing, Mrs Pardee. I can't handle this without you.'

When we got outside Mother put her arms around me to such an extent that I could feel certain parts of her body. She said my name: 'Joan Marie.'

I let my head rest on her shoulder as she stroked my hair. My heart was pounding frantically as blood rushed through me crying Danger! Danger! I don't even know why I am saying this because of course I was in no danger.

'Joan Marie Pardee. Your own business career. Have I helped you achieve this? Have I helped you be strong?' I said yes, and I meant yes.

Mother often came in to Louie's after that to buy things we didn't need. Louie would give her a cup of coffee and any pastry she wanted (no charge) while he sat with her to review my progress. I wiped the other tables while they talked. Out of respect for the right of individuals to privacy, I concentrated on not listening. Putting a piece of cotton in my good ear helped. In my right ear, I hear only the ocean, occasionally the faint sound of two happy children playing on the beach with their mother and father.

Sometimes Louie took Mother and me to doctor appointments. Other times she told him she felt tired and he would make ravioli for us to carry home. Mother leaned against him as he walked her out of the shop after conferences. 'It's not easy, Mr Fusco,' she'd say. And he would reply, 'I know.' This type of thing went on for years.

For me, most days were the same at Louie's. First I cleaned the cases with a fresh cloth. Warm, soapy water (in a bowl), while Louie (in the kitchen), organised the fresh pastries. We don't do bread or rolls – nothing yeast-based. Then I examined whatever was left from the previous day for freshness. Checking day-old goods is an important part of the job. On the one hand, you don't want to waste saleable items, but on the other, you can't let customers buy stale goods which they take to be fresh, or they won't come back. When Louie taught me how to evaluate day-old pastries he said that the most important aspect is the crust, which is allowed to be slightly firm but not too hard. If I am not sure, he said, throw it out. There is no sense taking chances with valued customers.

Next I would open the kitchen door to let Louie out with the big trays of new items. We would discuss what to put where. Acceptable day-old pastries always went in the back of the display cases, to be sold first. Later I folded boxes from large, flat, pre-cut cardboard. These came in three sizes: six-pastry, eight-pastry, and twelve-pastry, maximum depth two layers. After a dozen you go to a second box. I also folded boxes during slow times as the day went on without compromising my primary commitment to customer service. Christmas, Easter, and Mother's Day are the heaviest sales periods.

The only day I ever felt confused at the bakery was Monday, March 28th, the year Mother died. The 28th was four days before the event itself.

I walked in as usual at 8.40. As usual Louie was sitting at the table in the back drinking coffee and reading the paper. But that day he was crying. A grown man, that is.

'Oh, Joanie,' he said. 'I can't believe it, I can't believe it. I miss her already. Why didn't you tell me?' He got up and stared at me with sadness. I asked him what was wrong.

'Joanie, look at you, standing there. It's all right to cry, Joanie. I'll help you, you'll stay with me and I'll take care of you. Everything will be all right.'

'But everything is all right. I'm fine.'

'Oh, no, no. You're still a child. You still need your mother and now she's gone.' He was sobbing.

I couldn't understand what he was saying because I knew my mother was sitting in the kitchen having her tea and making out the shopping list.

'Anyway,' he said. 'It's a beautiful statement about a wonderful person.' I picked up the newspaper.

Ernestine Pardee (age not given) passed on peacefully Saturday evening at her home. Formerly married to Hal Pardee, who died many years ago in a tragic industrial accident, Mrs Pardee is survived by a daughter, Joan Marie, aged 28, who has worked successfully in business since her graduation from college several years ago. A neighbour who rang the *Morning Press* described Mrs Pardee as a 'model parent' who made a lasting contribution to the community, despite her own suffering. Her daughter Joan expects to carry on the family tradition of service to others. Joan is quoted as saying: 'My mother was a gentle, confident person who taught me how to face life, even though she had many hard times herself. I know I will be able to manage without her, but she will be in my thoughts every day.'

Contributions may be made, in care of this newspaper, to the African Children's Famine Relief, a charity supported by Mrs Pardee for many years.

I felt dizzy as Louie put his arm around me. I rotated my head twice to work out the normal morning stiffness. Then I said, 'Excuse me. I'll be right back.' I had never taken off any time and thought that under the circumstances he probably wouldn't mind. I also thought he might like to be private while he was crying. I apologised for asking earlier what was wrong. I couldn't recall my mother ever giving to charity.

I walked calmly into the house, but Mother wasn't in the kitchen. For a moment I felt nervous, not long enough to mention. I went upstairs and knocked on her door.

There was no answer so I opened it. My mother was sitting in bed wearing her best nightgown, the one with a high lace neck and long lace sleeves. Propped up by a mountain of pillows. She looked like a tiny queen. The *Morning Press* was opened on her lap.

'What are you doing home from work at this hour?' she asked.

'Oh, I just forgot something. I'm going right back.'

She clasped her hands together on top of the newspaper and turned her head away from me. 'Although it is a sunny day, I do not feel well.'

Mother completed her food shopping on the 28th, and died on April 1st. The fact that the refrigerator was full presented Louie and me with a slight problem, as everything perishable had to be moved quickly to his house. We borrowed a trolley from the supermarket. She must have been expecting company.

Physiologic disintegration via molecular change – the essence of the death process – is, paradoxically speaking, the system's final message of hope: without breakdown there is no release from earthly suffering. Without it, the spirit remains trapped in the snare of daily realities.

I am making and decorating the anniversary cakes now; I keep a ledger of income and expenses; I clean and lock up when Louie is too tired; I order the correct amount of flour each month, and buy new racks and trays from our supplier as needed.

These are examples of the kind of change I am talking about.

– chapter three –

In other words, during the year since Mother died, things have gone along. Louie's only problem is his thirty-five-year-old daughter Angela who lives a few blocks from us and is married to a Jewish alcoholic named Benny Manini. He hits her and sleeps with other women. The mother was Jewish. Now Angela can't have children. Louie and I live above the shop in the building Louie has owned since Angela was a child.

Although approximately one in ten Americans suffers from the disease of alcoholism, it is, according to a report published last year, a recent and relatively rare phenomenon to find members of Benny's faith drinking to excess. 'Experts believe that Jewish alcoholism is the unfortunate result of assimilation with groups who have traditionally turned to alcohol for the wrong reasons: White Anglo-Saxon Protestants to free up emotion, Irish Catholics to keep it down.'

I told Louie this is exactly the problem with alcohol, it has something for everyone, and you can't blame Benny. The Jews are afraid to be themselves after what happened.

Benny runs a discount carpet warehouse. Except for drinking he is a thorough person. He likes Angela in the house by a certain time and the food cooked a certain way. Which I can understand. Precision is absolutely essential in the carpet business.

You would never know to look at Louie that this sort of thing went on. As he himself says, he doesn't deserve it. 'At my age, Joanie,' he told me, 'your children are supposed to be settled and happy, but Angela will never settle down. I ask myself, how did I get a daughter who lives with a drunk?'

Which I agree is surprising because Angela is a psychiatric social worker. She has a nice job helping people who are out of control. On Saturday mornings she gets extra training in Pathological Mother-Child Symbiosis.

Angela usually eats her Sunday dinner with us. If Benny is sober she lets him come, too. Occasionally she drops into the shop, which is how my mother knew her. When Angela was twenty, her mother (Louie's wife), who was then forty-four, died of a heart attack. Angela and Louie had a conversation about that situation one Sunday a few weeks ago.

'If you had got off your ass once in a while,' shouted Angela, 'she could have rested when she was supposed to. Pass the broccoli.'

Louie shook his head, leaned back in his chair. Reached both arms out to Angela.

'Angela, will you ever relax? Will you ever forget the past? I did what I could. Your mother was not well.'

'Any why? Why wasn't she well? Because she did everything. Kept the books, ordered supplies, baked from four in the morning, cleaned. Everything but sit around charming the customers because you had that all to yourself. Mr Nice Guy ten hours a day while she slaved away. This is delicious.'

Saltimbocca alla Romana. I folded my hands politely in my lap, closed my eyes for a moment, and rotated the head twice.

Age is apparently less important in determining high risk for coronary failure than eating habits and stress. Some doctors recommend low-fat, low-cholesterol diets and at least an hour a day with a dog or a cat. Mrs Fusco never had the proper diet or a pet so she was particularly vulnerable.

'And what's wrong with being nice?' said Louie patiently. 'Does everything have to be a fight? You didn't mind me being nice enough to put you through college and graduate school.'

'It's a fight because you say nothing. Nothing is what I get from you. This is why Mama ate too much and this is why she died.'

'She had a hormonal imbalance, Angela. That's what the doctors told us. A physical problem, a simple physical problem.'

'I work with doctors,' she said. 'They don't know what

they're talking about. They're a bunch of ignorant liars. Mama ate because of unmet dependency needs, the same reason Benny drinks. Because his mother didn't love him, because she didn't love herself as a Jew. So he has a poor self-concept and turns his anger inward in self-destructive behaviour.'

'Angela, what are you talking about, inward?' asked Louie. 'Look at your face. The man is a nasty bum.' She was wearing sunglasses, which is how Louie and I can tell when she has a black eye.

'Who are you staring at?' she yelled. 'I suppose *you* live with Queen Elizabeth.'

Wasn't that nice, I think she meant me.

'Why don't you look at *her*? She's a zombie, she's out of her mind.'

We all chewed for a moment. Then Angela said to Louie, 'Will you make the coffee or will I?'

'I will,' said Louie. He got up. 'Angela, Joanie is my friend, she's got no one else.'

'Neither have I. You just called my husband of ten years a bum. You're full of opinions when it suits you and when it doesn't, you're all sweetness and light, friend to everyone except your own family.'

'That's enough in front of Joanie. You'll hurt her feelings.'

'Feelings? What feelings? She doesn't feel, I feel. She's a block of wood, the two of you. If you really cared

– 22 –

you'd get her some help. She has a thought disorder. Is there any more milk?'

'She's a hard worker, Angela. There's nothing disorderly about her. The milk is by the window.' If anything I am probably *too* thoughtful.

My mother told me indirectly to watch out for Angela. For some reason she didn't trust her, although I am not supposed to know this. The reason I do know is that Louie showed me my mother's will even though she told him not to.

It consisted of several parts: (1) a signed, notarised statement making Louie my legal guardian: 'Although she is over twenty-one and well educated, I feel and know that my daughter Joan Marie will require adult guidance while I am away. Should Mr Fusco pre-decease her, the last place I want her to go is with Mr Fusco's daughter Angela Manini and her husband Benny. Knowing them, they will probably be divorced by then anyway. But Joan is still not to go with Angela under any circumstances. After that, I don't know what to say. There is only so much one person can do.' Signed: Ernestine Pardee; (2) a letter to Louie, containing, among other statements, instructions about me. Plus more about Angela and Benny. Something else that was in that letter, (3) I prefer not to mention at this time. There was no letter for me.

Dear Mr Fusco:

Firstly may I say how grateful I am to you for teaching Joan the ins and outs of baking. This particular combination of genetics (her intelligence, from my side of the family) and environment (the active, industrial atmosphere of your shop) worked ideally, just the way science and nature intended.

I am about to die so I am asking you to take charge of Joanie in my long absence.

A few general comments regarding her care:

1. She is a light sleeper and frequently sleepwalks. I kept a gate across my stairs. When she bumps into it she will cry out, 'Mama, help me, help me' and usually run screaming back to bed by herself. If she loses her way, just get up, hold her hand non-judgementally (even though sleepwalking is abnormal for someone her age) and guide her. Reassure her by saying, 'You've had a bad dream, Joanie, it's all right, I'm here.' Sometimes for extra impact I add 'I love you.' She does not wake up through these episodes, but even when asleep children seem to prefer a sense of security over a sense of danger.

2. For the most part you will not have to hit Joan to get her to cooperate. She is a self-starter. I usually strike her when she talks back because respect is important, but on most issues she can be reasoned with to go along with the adult point of view.

She liked to talk a lot when she was very young, but I dealt with it quickly each time, so by age five or six she had quieted down considerably and learned to read. Immediate response means a lot to children because it makes them realise they can count on you.

3. I am worried about Joan's circulation. I mean this physically, not socially. When she twists her head around like that I worry that a stroke may be coming on. Therefore I am attaching a list of doctors I have consulted, fourteen in all. None, thank goodness, have found any basis for concern. However, medical science is no substitute for a mother's knowledge of her own child, so I enclose her yearly schedule of tests and the doctor or hospital responsible. Being a child Joanie doesn't really care, of course, but I prefer the electrocardiograph, the CAT scan, and the barium enema to be repeated at least every eight to ten months. Some of the doctors do not go along with me, but it's not their child that's at stake. The lie detector tests are administered by a private consulting firm, Jimmy O'Boyle Investigative Services Ltd.

He finds Joan very truthful, a sign, he says, of superior arterial blood flow to the brain. He does not therefore believe that Joan is going to have a stroke. Mr O'Boyle is a former policeman. He gets paid cash.

4. I hope you will not take offence at my remarks in the guardianship document about Angela and Benny. Joanie cannot take stress. Her father was the same way. His side of the family were all high-strung people, unlike my family who have their feet on the ground. So I do not like Joanie exposed to liberal ideas

such as fighting within marriage. Joan has
her own mind, from me, and I'd like it to stay
that way.

It is an exaggeration to say: 'Being a child Joanie
doesn't really care.' Angela told me childhood ends at
around age ten, the beginning of the Latency Period
when sexual desires should be suppressed in preparation
for the irrational turmoil of adolescence. This is a theory.
Therefore, being twenty-nine, I am not a child.

When Angela left after dinner, Louie told me not to
take seriously all the, well, garbage that comes out of
her mouth.

'Her life is a mess,' he said, 'and she blames everyone
else.'

I'm not sure what he means because Angela has
always been nice to me, although I have a feeling she
may be jealous of the inner peace I have found since my
mother died. The loss of her own mother made Angela
angry at life. I understand what she is going through
because the hardest thing after losing a loved one is to
face reality. For example, Angela believes that dark
glasses hide her bruises, whereas actually if you wear
them (the glasses) at dinner under normal lighting conditions, people will know the truth: i.e., the glasses
will give away the very thing they are meant to con-
ceal. What I am saying proves that the main purpose
of alcohol in marriage is to alter reality in one's mind

by compromising healthy brain cells. Even while objectively, to any outside observer, things are still just as bad.

– chapter four –

Angela turned to Benny because he paid attention to her and recognised her as a woman. She says that Louie and Mrs Fusco treated her like Rapunzel: 'Locked me up and threw away the key, made me dead to my own sexuality. The mother cuts off Rapunzel's hair. Why, Joanie? Think about it, I'm serious. To deprive her of sexual feeling for the Prince! Everyone knows hair is a symbol in the primitive unconscious of sexuality, of lust. If she were a man, the mother would have cut off his balls. Benny gave me back my hair, so to speak.' I must admit I had never thought of it that way.

In other words, Angela and Benny had sex before marriage and Louie wouldn't speak to her until she apologised. She did, three and a half days later. She told me she didn't mean the apology and had said 'I'm sorry, Daddy' only because she needed money to finish graduate school. I myself think the apology was sincere and so does Louie.

When I first knew Angela we were eighteen and twenty-three respectively. She and Benny, then thirty-two, had been dating for about six months. I don't know exactly what time of day they first had sex.

As I said before, Benny's mother was Jewish. His father was Italian. Shulamith and Aldo Manini. There was another son, born without a lower jaw, who never came home from the hospital. Originally Mr Manini owned Carpets Galore and other things on the side with a partner. One day the partner died suddenly and Mr Manini made Benny President of C.G. instead of the partner's son. So then Mr Manini died suddenly and now Benny is only Vice-President. Shulamith Manini disappeared right after that and took up airport work with Jews for Jesus.

When Benny and Angela met, he was living in a back room at the carpet store with a gun under his pillow. I think it was loaded, although I can't imagine anyone trying to steal a roll of, say, Misty Pink with underlay. These rolls are not the kind of thing you could sneak out a door like jewellery. This is what I mean when I say Benny is a thorough person. He cares about his merchandise, he guards it with his life, which is a way of saying to customers: 'I appreciate you.'

When Benny is sober and allowed to Sunday dinner he and Angela come at twelve o'clock. When he is not coming she yells at him and doesn't arrive until one o'clock.

I can tell by the footsteps on the stairs (plus I look at the clock) that Benny is there. I smooth down my dress, run to the door and stand quietly with my hands behind my back, not getting excited. Benny opens the door and comes in first because when he is sober he likes to prove he is responsible. Angela lets him walk in first because she likes to prove it, too. The last time he came I hadn't seen him in fifty-seven days.

'Well. Look at Joan Marie will you. Look at her, Angela.' Hands on my shoulders, holds me away, eyes appreciate me. 'If I'm not mistaken this is a new dress. Am I right?'

'Yes.'

'I thought so. A beautiful dress, in fact.' A hug. 'It's always good to see you, Joan. I'm sorry I had to be away for a while. Are you all right?'

'Yes. What's in the bag?'

'A little something.'

'Flowers. Well. Aren't they lovely.'

'Of course they're lovely. They're for you. What do you think, I'd buy something ugly for Joan Marie?'

Louie came out of the kitchen. So far Angela hadn't said a word. She watches how Benny acts with other people so she can mention it nicely to him later.

'Benny. Good to see you looking so well.'

'Hello, Louie. It's been too long.' We all sat down.

'I told him you were working on a big contract, Benny,' said Angela. 'Why don't you tell him about it? Seven hundred square yards for a new school, Daddy.'

'Relax, Angela,' said Benny. 'He knows I wasn't working in some school for two months.'

'He was drinking,' I said.

Benny laughed and threw an arm around my shoulder.

'That's what I like about you, Joan.'

Angela rolled her eyes. 'Jesus, Daddy. Where the hell did you get her?'

'Pay attention,' Benny said to Angela. 'You might learn something.'

'And what's that supposed to mean?'

'You heard me.'

'Lovely, just lovely. I thought this was going to be a nice day.'

'It is,' said Benny. 'I'm enjoying myself immensely. What's your problem? Maybe you need a drink.'

'Very funny,' said Angela.

'That's in poor taste, Benny,' said Louie.

'I'm serious. She's not the alcoholic. Have a fucking drink if you want one, Angela.'

'Joanie,' she said politely, 'would you please get me a small glass of red wine?' I went into the kitchen.

'Very small, Joan,' called Benny. 'My sobriety depends on Angela. If she gets high I might commit suicide. Did you know I went on my last bender because she sneezed? Control yourself, I told her! Go outside to sneeze, I'm a vulnerable man! Think of my dependency needs! And do you know why I'm not drinking now, Louie?'

I brought Angela her wine in a juice glass.

'Thank you, Joanie,' she said.

'Benny. Calm down,' said Louie. 'Look what you've done now, it isn't bad enough you drink.'

Angela was holding her glass up to her mouth with both hands and sniffling loudly.

'No, really,' said Benny. 'Let me tell you. I'm not drinking now because Angela cooked pot roast last Tuesday. I love pot roast! So I stopped drinking. See? Alcoholism is simple when you understand psychology.'

'You do love pot roast!' cried Angela. 'Don't make fun of me! You have a disease. You're going to die from it and I'll be left alone after all we've worked for.'

She finished her wine and put the glass down.

'Joanie, would you mind getting me a Kleenex please.'

I got it and she blew her nose.

I said, 'I'll throw it away for you.'

'Thank you, Joanie,' she replied. 'I don't know what we would do without you.'

'Which reminds me, Benny,' said Louie. 'Joan and I have been talking about re-modelling the shop.'

'The floors only,' I said.

'Right,' said Louie. 'Just the floors for now until we figure out our financial position.'

'For God's sake, Louie,' said Benny, 'you've got plenty of cash coming in, the place is full of customers.'

'Benny, some weeks are better than others, you know the situation out there yourself.'

'But are you keeping track like I told you?'

'Mama kept track, Benny,' said Angela. 'Mama ran the business.'

'Well,' said Louie, 'Joanie does a ledger.'

'Is that from the register?' asked Benny. 'Or does she count what you keep in your pocket, too?'

'That's for household expenses, Benny, the money I hold aside. And for Joanie's future.'

'Future?' Angela howled with laughter. 'Future?? Your mind is playing tricks in your old age, Daddy.'

My dictionary defines the future as: 'The time yet to come; undetermined events that will occur in that time.' How it happened before the dictionary, no one knows.

'Angela, stop. You've got Joanie closing her eyes over there with talk like that. She can't take it.'

'She can't take it? What about me? Nobody's saving for my so-called future, for Christ's sake.'

I opened my eyes.

'Benny,' I said. 'Just to let you know. I count the money in the register every day. I write down the amount and then I give it all to Louie in an envelope marked "For Louie". When I order supplies I tell him how much each item costs, he gives me exact change, I pay the supplier, and then of course I write it down. There's no waste. I'm very careful about what I order.'

'I have no doubt about that, Joan.' He put his arm around me again. 'But what exactly do you write down?'

'Louie said to subtract the expenses from the earnings,

and if we're making money then throw the figures away. So I write the same thing every day: "Today we took in more than we paid out." '

'That's it?' screamed Angela. 'That's what you write down? I don't believe I'm hearing this conversation! There must be something wrong with my fucking ears!' She jumped up and went out to the kitchen. In a moment she came back with the bottle of wine.

'Angela,' said Louie, 'what's the difference? We always have more than enough, there's always extra. You don't have to worry.'

'Worry doesn't come close to describing what I feel right now, Daddy.' She poured another glass of wine and took a long sip. 'Maybe I need another ten years of psychoanalysis. You're all crazy. But do I go anywhere else? No. Do I do anything about it? No. I need my head examined.'

'I think you're fine the way you are,' I said.

Angela burst out laughing. 'You would! That's what you'd say to Hitler! "Oh, Joanie," he moans, "I feel so bad about killing all those Jews. Maybe there's something wrong with me." "Oh no, Adolf," says Joanie, "I think you're fine the way you are." '

She couldn't stop laughing. Tears were streaming down her cheeks.

' "I think you're fine the way you are!" ' she roared, and doubled over, slopping her wine on the carpet. (Autumn Radiance.)

'Angela,' said Louie. 'What you're saying is in very bad taste.' Poor Benny, to hear her talk that way about the Jews.

'Thank God no one here is Jewish,' said Benny, 'or they might take offence at the crude nature of your remarks, you bitch.' I closed my eyes, but he didn't hit her.

'I'm sorry, Benny,' said Louie. 'I honestly don't know how she turned out this way.'

'It's either your fault or mine, Louie. It's never hers.'

After that Angela fell asleep. Louie and Benny and I had a lovely dinner. We decided to go ahead with the floors. Benny thinks we have enough money. Anyway, being Vice-President, he can arrange a discount.

– *chapter five* –

Just before Benny was ready to leave at seven o'clock, he sat on the couch beside Angela and tried to wake her. He stroked her hair and kissed her forehead. She groaned and tried to shake him off by rustling her body and turning away. He didn't move. Instead, he gently touched a shoulder. Louie was downstairs in the shop getting things ready for the morning.

'Ange, wake up. It's time to go.'

She rolled over.

'Benny,' she said groggily, her eyes still closed.

'It's okay, babe, I'm right here.'

'I'm sorry I said all that about the Jews. It was completely uncalled for.'

'Don't worry. Hitler came out looking a lot worse.'

'It was the only thing I didn't resolve in my analysis. I hate the Jews for not fighting back. I know they couldn't. I know oppressors are always stronger. But still I wish they would have told that bastard Hitler where to go. That way I'd feel less impotent in my own struggle to achieve autonomy in the face of this overwhelming pull of primitive regressive urges. Sometimes I just want to give up and let someone else take over.'

'Who doesn't, Ange? Nobody's in charge of their own life, you know that.'

'Benny. Just promise me you won't drink again, that's all I ask. Is that so much? It's our only hope. We both love work, we make good money, we're great in bed. We've got it all. Alcohol is the one problem. I'll forgive everything if you stop drinking.' They kissed. I looked away as quickly as I could.

'Two points on that, Angela.' said Benny. 'One, I am stopped. Two, I hear you and I promise. You know I mean it this time. I'm sorry for what I've put you through, honestly.'

'I mean it this time, too, Benny. I'll leave you, believe me I will. It's no life, wondering how you're going to act. We could have had a beautiful day today, for example.'

She sat up slowly.

'Are they going to do the floors?'

'Absolutely. Right, Joan?'

'Yes,' I replied.

'Joan is going to come into work one day and pick what she likes, and I'll have the boys out right away.'

'You're so good, Benny,' said Angela. 'And there I go yelling at you again. Take me home, will you, my head is killing me.'

She got up and walked slowly over to me. My hands neatly folded in my lap. I looked up. It's her eyes. Deep black ponds, moist in apology, swimming above my self.

'Joanie,' she said, 'I'm sorry. Sometimes I say the nastiest things. Please believe me, sweetheart, I don't ever mean them the way they sound.'

'I know.'

'The last thing I want to do is hurt you.'

'But you don't hurt me.'

'Poor Joanie! You just think I don't because of your defences. Somewhere in there you're hurt. You're hurt very bad and you protect yourself by denying reality, by disconnecting from your emotions. I understand that, but I don't want to be part of any more pain or sorrow for you. It's just that sometimes I can't keep my big mouth shut.'

'Amen,' said Benny. 'Let's go.'

'One of my clients even said it to me the other day,' Angela continued. ' "Be quiet for a minute so I can think", she said. I'm working on it, Joanie. Believe me, no one works on themselves like I do. I'll probably even go back to my analyst. I just want you to understand that change on the level I am talking about takes years, it's very deep, very profound, not a matter of one-two-three, bingo, you're there. Nothing happens without insight, Joanie, nothing. I am where I am today because of insight. And until I figure out this one last thing – why I am in such a rage – I'll keep right on yelling. I'm just asking for patience from everyone until I assess what's going on, and it may take a while because most likely it's at a pre-oedipal level, oral aggression, etc., the usual.'

'I can wait,' I said.

She yawned.

'Jesus! Is that the time? I've got a staff meeting at eight in the fucking morning. Sorry about the language, Joanie. There I go again.'

She leans down to kiss my cheek good-bye. Her hair strokes like silken fingers of ballerinas pulling invisible taffy towards their lips. Reaching out, drawing in, floating up and floating down. These mystery fingers, caressing tiny mounds of slippery air, elusive shapes in the abyss. Will Benny kiss me, too?

'Enjoy the flowers, Joan,' he says, and smiles. 'Just call me when you're ready to come out to the office. We'll look at samples and I'll take you to lunch.'

Then they were gone. I alone went into the kitchen to do the dishes. The baking pan, puckered up with grease, took 'forever'.

– chapter six –

I heard Louie come up from the shop around nine. The dishes were done, his coffee organised for the morning. I came out of the kitchen.

Louie gets up at four to bake. I awaken at 6.30, and at seven, when he comes back, I make him breakfast and more coffee. He watches the morning news. He is tired. I drink tea with lots of milk and sugar which my mother used to call cambric tea when we had tea parties in my room age four to twenty-seven. A few months out while I was in college.

They went like this: a little card table, red top and white enamel legs, comes out from my closet left of the bed. I wipe off the dust with the edge of my little pink skirt. Mommy slaps me and says: Stop that this instant young lady, get a cloth. I give her the teapot from the tea-party shelf, so carefully clutched and handed down as if an ancient chalice that we bow our head and put a prayer on it. This exact teapot is all mine from Santa and Mrs Claus who knew what I wanted. And Rudolf who drove the sleigh in bitter cold.

Then Mommy scurries like the good fun she is down

to the kitchen to make the tea, the special one and only cambric tea.

> I'll be right back Miss Pardee
> Miss Pardee you rhyme with tea!
>
> Set the places for the guests
> and I'll take care of all the rest!

There were four chairs to match the table. Folding chairs, white enamel with red backs, so I always set four places. One each for Mother and me, and one each for Mr and Mrs Frot-Pot. Their table manners were very bad, which is why we never went out for our tea. Mother and I spent the first ten minutes of every party correcting them and the last ten cleaning up their messes and threatening never to invite them back. They ignored what we said and came to us for years, which is the part I liked best about them.

Now it is p.m., night-time, another era.

Louie lowered himself slowly into his favourite chair, the ample one with huge arms. A hippopotamus of a chair we always say, because we believe a hippo to be relaxed and friendly, besides gigantic.

'It's only nine o'clock and I'm exhausted,' said Louie.

I got him his slippers and a cup of coffee. As usual I sat on the floor against the side of the chair and tipped my head back.

'You tired, too?' he asked.

'Yes,' I answered.

'Angela is enough to wear anybody out. Did Benny promise to stop drinking again?'

'Yes.'

'Naturally. I need to ask? She gives him whatever he wants, no questions, as long as he says what she likes to hear. I gave the girl a good education but she's got no brains when it comes to Benny.'

'They love each other,' I said.

'Love?' He sighed. 'Who knows. I rely on your judgement in these things, Joanie. What do I know about people? I should give up.'

'Maybe we ought to get an accountant,' I said.

'What do we need an accountant for?'

'Benny didn't like how I keep the ledger.'

'No, Joanie. He never said that. Besides, it's not Benny's ledger, is it. It's our ledger, Pardee and Fusco, big-time operators. We'll keep it any way we like. And don't even ask what goes on with his own books, by the way. He's a fine one to talk.'

'There was an ad in the paper today.'

'An ad for what?'

'A jargon-free book for non-accountants. Construction of accounts, content of accounts, analysis of accounts. Long-term strategic planning, profitability, liquidity.'

'All we've *got* is liquidity, Joanie! Don't give us more liquidity, whatever you do!' He laughed.

' "Speak the same language as your bank manager and frighten your competitors." '

'Joanie. Listen to me: we don't even use a bank, never mind a manager. And there isn't another shop with quality like this for a hundred miles! Nobody can touch us when it comes to pastry. Thanks to you we don't need to change a thing. Do you see what I'm saying?'

'Well, I was just thinking.' I closed my eyes.

Louie reached over the arm of the chair and put his hand on my shoulder. 'Why so quiet?' he asked. 'What is it? You think I'm laughing at you?'

We sat.

'Let me guess,' he said.

He paused. Then he leaned forward, picked up his glasses from the coffee table. Settled carefully back into the chair. Louie likes the glasses on and his fingers working his chin when he is facing a problem.

'You think Benny is disappointed in you. You think he doesn't respect you.'

My eyes kept on being closed, although I had had plenty of sleep the night before.

'Now we're getting somewhere,' he said. 'And if I recall correctly, partner – even a man my age has a few grey cells left – something like this happened the last time he came to Sunday dinner.'

'I don't remember,' I lied.

'I do.' He paused. 'Angela whined on and on about the new dress she was wearing. "Look at what Benny bought me, Daddy, look what Benny bought me," till I wanted to commit murder. Stole is more like it, he never paid for anything with his own money. Anyway, you put your coat on after she mentioned that.'

'It was very cold that night.'

'I agree, Joanie. It was very cold.'

His hand, still resting on my shoulder, rubbed it gently, no talk. Sitting on the floor next to this chair isn't the best thing for my back but that's where I seem to end up every night around nine.

In a moment Louie spoke again.

'Are you ready for the hot chocolate?' he said.

'Yes,' I replied, as he got up to go into the kitchen. 'I'll shuffle the cards.'

'Good,' he answered. 'And no cheating. I'm going to keep my eye on you tonight, Pardee. You've won the last two times and it's not fair.'

The way we do this is, either two-out-of-three or three-out-of-five hands wins (five-card poker). Which it will be is decided by whoever picks the seven cards with the highest sum total. Aces, while high in the poker game, count for only one point in this tally. Kings are eleven, Queens nine-and-a-half, Jacks six-and-three-quarters.

The winner gets to pick the book we read that night and may choose (a) to read, (b) to listen to the other person read, or (c) a little of both. The winner may change his or her mind in the middle; the winner may loan his or her choice or choices to the loser. On the question of how long to read, we usually stop when the time comes.

'Now for hot chocolate and a little gambling,' sings Louie.

Big steaming mugs come out on the tray with *frollini con latte e miele*. Yum. The rule is I deal.

'Okay, Jesse James, just try to rob this one from me,' he says as he looks at his seven cards.

He wins: thirty-nine-and-a-half to twenty eight. He picks two-out-of-three hands for book choice plus reader, and wins that! Two pairs to my one pair, three kings to my nothing.

'Ha! What did I tell you,' he says. He opens the ledger. 'I loan book choice plus reader.' The book choice part is difficult because I am enjoying two books at the moment: Descartes, of course, and an anthropological study called *Patterns of Love Among Two Tribes in East Borneo*. When Angela saw this book she said something I cannot repeat and suggested I give up diffuse models of identity. She told me to study something one of her professors wrote called *The Creative Development of the Full Potential of the Normal Human Ego in the Context of Authentic Commitment to the Bonds of Mature Heterosexual Love: Separation, Individuation, Autonomy, and Reality vs. The Regressive Power of Dependence, Submission, and the Idealisation of Primitive Authorities (Womb and Breast)*.

It was all right. A little boring. For some reason there were no people in it.

Suddenly I heard the two happy children in my right ear.

'Junie,' said the little boy, 'read me a story, read me *Little Red Riding Hid*. But don't say about the woof eat her up.'

So that's the book I picked, with myself as reader, even though Louie has heard it a 'million' times. Later, Edward John said 'Thank you, Junie Marie,' because I always leave out the parts that make him nervous.

– chapter seven –

Myself, I am a morning person. Although I do not neces-
sarily go to bed early. It depends on whether I am figur-
ing things out about Mrs Cunningham-Freeman.

She comes into the shop every day, a.m. She returns
either in the afternoon, or at ten p.m. If it is night-time
she presses the bell over and over demanding service.

'I'm a customer!' she screams. Louie opens the window upstairs and shouts back, 'Yeah? Well, I'm Grace
Kelly.' He slams the window. 'Tell her majesty I'm
moving to Siberia, tell her we put cow dung in the flour.'
Being an accommodating type of person I am pleased
with whatever Louie or the customers say. I do not repeat
insults from either side which are shouted at me in
confidence.

The reason Mrs Cunningham-Freeman has to come
back is because she was in a rush in the morning. She
gets a hairdo every day before teaching yoga to autistic
children, and yet a woman needs her sleep. So most of
the time she forgets about the *torta di mandorle* for her
Wednesday meeting of Free The Hostages, the *coppa de
crema zabaione alla parmagiana* for her Thursday meeting

of Socialites Against Deforestation, or the anisette biscuits for Mr Cunningham-Freeman. He is away Monday through Friday negotiating major government contracts and likes something with a little zip in it for Saturday morning.

My problem with Mrs Cunningham-Freeman is that I am supposed to remember when Mr Cunningham-Freeman changes his schedule, which days are therefore switched, and how she wants to adjust her order. If different people attend hostage night and deforestation, she wants to get additional items preferred by particular people as a gesture of her sensitivity to others. She doesn't let me know until the last minute. Which is fine with me. She also wants to take whole-wheat treats to Total Self-Respect which meets every Sunday night at the Country Club. Louie says whole-wheat goes against everything about pastry but she insists. 'She wants me to make junk,' says Louie, 'I'll make junk. This is what it's come to, Joanie. I'm a whore, nothing but a whore. To think a woman like that gets me to bake whole-wheat. Charge her double. Let her think I'm a charity.'

Last week she rushed in with one of her lists.

'Hello Joanie, I hope you don't mind but I'm in a hurry today,' she shouted as she banged open the door. Mrs Ferrara and Mrs Constanza were already waiting. However, Mrs Cunningham-Freeman prefers to go ahead of everyone. Which is understandable in a petite person, 4'11", who had no brothers or sisters. She told me her parents were always losing her at the race track when she was a child because they couldn't make her out in a crowd. Angela believes that the experience of not being seen by her parents, both of whom, to make matters worse, wore glasses, has led Mrs Cunningham-Freeman to feel she will be ignored in shops.

'Don't worry,' I replied. 'I'm not busy.' When Mrs Cunningham-Freeman arrives the other customers know to sit down, stay calm, and help themselves to free coffee while she goes first. Before the free coffee I was losing customers. I can't concentrate on anything when I see Mrs Cunningham-Freeman come through the door. She was wearing a bright red jogging suit, blue bandanna, pearls, diamond earrings, and cowboy boots with three-inch heels and leather fringe.

'I thought you gave up jogging,' I said. She likes to talk before discussing her purchases. She laid her list for the week on the counter.

'Oh, I did, Joanie,' she sighed. 'My joints were in terrible shape. I thought I had rheumatoid arthritis. Would you say I looked sick before?'

'No,' I said.

'I felt sick. I'm so afraid of dying. It's my biggest fear. That cured me of running.'

She looked down. I realised she had started to cry. I handed her a box of tissues I keep for customers. Mrs Ferrara, aged seventy-two with a cane, wobbled over.

She put her shawl around Mrs Cunningham-Freeman's shoulders.

'That's right, get it out,' she said. 'My husband used to travel a lot, too. At least yours is rich. I got so sick of his lies and excuses I pretended to go deaf, the no-good cheating bastard. I'd smile sweetly, then he'd smile back. He thought I was a fool, believing every word he said, and did I believe any of it? No! Ha!'

She laughed and slapped Mrs Cunningham-Freeman's back.

'May I take your order?' I said.

'I'll wait,' she replied. 'This is getting interesting.'

She sat down. Mrs Constanza got her another cup of coffee. 'Put out some of those nice *savoiardi*, Joanie honey.'

'Look at me,' said Mrs Cunningham-Freeman, dabbing her eyes, when I got back behind the counter. 'I'm making a spectacle of myself.'

'Why are you crying?' I asked.

'I wish I were more dynamic.'

'Well,' I said, 'the red is nice.'

'I know, but it's not enough. I need goals, I need direction.'

'You want substance and meaning in the context of mundane reality.'

'That's it,' she said. 'Substance: I want to be a person.'

My father, on the other hand, was thirty-nine when he died. The best part about that day, April the 10th, which was overall not a good day, was the Mars Bar under my pillow, and of course the valentine. They are both still under my pillow although now it is a different day. Finding these items that night surprised me at first. You don't expect the dead to be in a position to follow through. I am no longer surprised, however, because on the 21st May at 10.42 p.m. after I had read E.J. *Snow White* 12.7 times for good luck, I heard my father mention that he bought the card on February 14th, the Mars Bar April 9th. Suddenly everything made sense, even the message in the card. When we talk about 'substance' this is the kind of experience we are referring to. Sometimes I even read *Snow White* to Louie so the luck won't run out.

'I don't know what she's talking about, "person" ', Mrs Constanza, aged sixty-seven, said to Mrs Ferrara. 'What more does she want? Look at that outfit. The women today, I'm telling you.'

Mrs Cunningham-Freeman turned to Mrs Ferrara and said, 'Was he with someone else when he died?'

'What do you think?' shouted Mrs Ferrara. 'He wasn't with *me!* You think I'd be caught dead on a waterbed at the Dew Drop Inn? Ha!' She brought her cane down with a bang.

'That's funny,' said Mrs Constanza. ' "Caught dead." I get it.'

'Well,' said Mrs Cunningham-Freeman, 'I just meant was he alone.'

'Alone?' replied Mrs Ferrara. ' "Fifteen people at my meeting in Albuquerque, Irma," he whined. When they found him he was tied up to his secretary. "Great meeting, Irma, can't get away." You're not kidding.'

'I wonder what they call that,' asked Mrs Constanza.

'May I take your order?' I said.

'Well, that's the difference right there,' said Mrs Cunningham-Freeman, poking the counter five times with her finger. 'My husband is involved in big government contracts. That's actually a difference in my mind.'

'What you want to watch out for in differences are the similarities,' I said. Although I have no idea whether he even has a secretary let alone gets tied up in meetings with her.

'Listen to our girl there,' said Mrs Constanza. 'No wonder she got into college. What subject was that, Joanie honey?'

'All the subjects would be related, Mrs Constanza. I took an integrated curriculum with special emphasis on interactional forces, interconnecting dynamics, that kind of thing.'

She stared at me. 'Your poor mother, God forgive me.'

'That's all right,' I said. 'She didn't mind.'

'If I had a child like you I'd shoot myself.'

'Thank you,' I replied.

Mrs Ferrara likes to pursue a subject. She said to Mrs Cunningham-Freeman, 'You actually believe he's negotiating contracts five days a week fifty-two weeks a year? You know how many contracts that is?'

Mrs Cunningham-Freeman started to cry again.

'The government is a big place,' she said.

'Nobody can negotiate contracts five days a week fifty-two weeks a year. Don't be stupid. Maybe he has another family somewhere. Boeing and Lockheed don't even have that many contracts.'

'You don't have to shout at me!' wept Mrs Cunningham-Freeman.

'You're being too hard on her,' said Mrs Constanza to Mrs Ferrara. 'She's not that bright.'

'I don't mind if you want to give me your orders now,' I said.

'Oh, be quiet!' snapped Mrs Ferrara. 'Can't you see we're busy?'

The telephone rang.

'Louie's and Joanie's,' I answered. 'How may I be of service? Oh, hello, Mrs Wilson. Yes, it is a lovely day. Certainly. How nice. Congratulations. Yes. I am writing it all down just the way you like me to, one word at a time, each word complete before I go on to the next.'

'Congratulations for what?' whispered Mrs Constanza.

'How the hell would I know?' the old woman screamed. 'You could at least wait until the poor child hangs up. She's got a shop to run here.'

By now Mrs Cunningham-Freeman was sobbing. 'He *told* me it was government contracts.'

'You fool! You fool!' There went the cane again. I could hardly hear Mrs Wilson, and her husband president of the bank.

'So I believe him,' said Mrs Cunningham-Freeman. 'I just do. It isn't right the way you talk. Just because *your* husband cheated on *you*. I'd like to know what he wasn't getting at home.'

'You believe whatever you want, honey,' said Mrs Constanza. 'It's a free country.'

'Certainly I'm listening, Mrs Wilson,' I said. 'It is easy for me to concentrate on numerous demands at one time. That is my job, losing my mind in the service of others. I thrive on hard work.'

'Do you think that girl is going to faint?' said Mrs Constanza. 'Look at her move her head like that.'

'Can't you ever mind your own business?' snorted Mrs Ferrara.

Mrs Constanza waved her hand to me and whispered loudly, 'More *savoiardi* when you get a chance.'

'Thank you,' I said to Mrs Wilson. 'I'm feeling fine. I'll read it back. "Congratulations My Beloved Bertie Comma Third Quarter Profits Up TEN Million Exclamation Point Good Boy Exclamation Point." '

'You hear Mrs Big Wheel Monica Wilson on the telephone?' banged Mrs Ferrara. '*That's* what mine wasn't getting at home: horse turds.'

'*Ten million!*' whispered Mrs Constanza. 'I wonder how much he takes out of that.'

'As much as his grubby fists can stuff into his drooling maw,' replied Mrs Ferrara. She opened her mouth as far as it would go and bared her false teeth. Sometimes I wonder if I am up to running my own business.

'I am concentrating, Mrs Wilson, thank you,' I said, although in fact I was trying to sort out the trouble with Mr Cunningham-Freeman's government contracts. Mrs Cunningham-Freeman is my friend and she has no life without the government.

'Yes, Mrs Wilson, I agree it is a lovely message. What would I add?'

'Why are her eyes closed?' asked Mrs Constanza.

'She's sick of looking at you,' roared Mrs Ferrara.

'I just wondered,' said Mrs Constanza.

'Well, Mrs Wilson, we recommend that customers express themselves in their own way. Cakes are a personal vehicle for emotional contact. I *am* thinking, Mrs Wilson. Perhaps you could mention "Hope To See You Soon comma The Children Are Fine." You're welcome.'

'Isn't she something,' said Mrs Constanza, 'the way she can think of the right thing on short notice.'

Mrs Cunningham-Freeman looked at me. 'Do you think Bruce works for the government?'

'What she means, Joanie honey,' said Mrs Constanza, 'is do you think he's lying. Myself, I would go easy on her.'

'Tell her!' Mrs Ferrara shouted at me. By now the cane sounds like a machine-gun on our old floor. Mrs Ferrara's wrists are limber and the cane shoots up and down rat-a-tat-tat. My head is pounding, my heart is racing.

To make matters worse, Mrs Ferrara thinks she is the devil so I have to watch what I say to her. She might turn out to be an important customer. Mr Ferrara agreed that she was the devil. However, having this belief in common was not enough to make the marriage work. He took her to a mobile psychiatrist who tied her to a chair in his van and asked her to touch two fingers in front of her face with both eyes closed for $150. Even though diagnosis is essential to any treatment of pseud-onymity, she refused to close her left eye, shouting, 'Give the devil her due,' and spitting at the doctor. Nothing was ever proven.

'We have a special today,' I said. 'A pound of Sienese almond cookies at a dollar off.'

Mrs Cunningham-Freeman took up my hand and kissed it. Petals of a rose could not be a gentler/Than your lips upon my pleading skin/They soothe and heal the injured tissue/That cries and bleeds within.

Her hand was trembling. 'It's fine with me whatever you say, Joanie. I just want the honest truth.'

She entwined her fingers with my own fingers. She brought her face close to my own face across the counter. My own face might slip off from the heat. Another person's eyes on top of my own eyes.

'Tell her!' shouted Mrs Ferrara.

'Go easy, Joanie honey,' said Mrs Constanza.

'Tell her!' Rat-a-tat-tat.

'Spare her, Joanie honey.'

'I want the honest truth, Joanie,' said Mrs Cunningham-Freeman.

'The phone is ringing, Joanie honey, answer the phone. Don't keep customers waiting.'

'Speak of the devil!' cackled Mrs Ferrara.

'I bet it's Mrs Wilson again,' said Mrs Constanza. 'She wants to change her order. You better answer that. Joanie honey, are you all right?'

'She's thinking, she's thinking!' shouted Mrs Cunningham-Freeman. 'Can't you people be quiet long enough to let the girl think?'

'Tell her! Give the devil the hindmost!'

'Under contractual government obligations,' I said, 'which bind a person insofar as the commitment to completion is not abrogated prior to the factually documented rather than verbally concurred objective basis for compliance, that person would be simultaneous. This condition is dictated by a system of well-established links to the government's external accountability audit division. That's how I would see it.'

'Good girl,' screamed Mrs Ferrara. 'I knew it! He's a no-good cheating bastard!' She whacked her cane full force against the table-leg.

'You did the right thing, Joanie honey,' said Mrs Constanza. 'She couldn't take it.'

Mrs Cunningham-Freeman squeezed my hand to her

face and wept. 'Oh thank you, Joanie, thank you. I'm so relieved.' Suddenly she flung my hand down on the counter. 'See?' she shouted at Mrs Ferrara. 'You and your dirty mind! Take your shawl. No wonder Arnold left you.'

'Well, he didn't exactly leave,' said Mrs Constanza. 'You should at least be fair.'

Mrs Cunningham-Freeman flung the shawl to the floor. She unperched herself from my stool and tottered in her cowboy boots to the door. Which she banged open.

'You people make me sick,' she said. 'You're just jealous of my Bruce, the way he adores me. Joanie, everything's there on the list. Have it ready early tomorrow, I'm not sure what I have to do first.'

The only problem was that the list she left on the counter was 'Nine Pathways to Inner Freedom.' When she came back the next day she accused me of distracting her.

I've got to work on achieving a more thorough concentration.

– chapter eight –

Benny decided we should have breakfast together at six in the morning before I looked at samples. An all-night waitress he knows at The Paradise Lounge goes off-duty early. He likes to say hello before she leaves. Benny is a night person, too, so besides the American way of life he and this woman, Candi Jones, have a lot in common. Her parents come from a different country. She is therefore not who she is, which is what I mean by American.

As a result, when I met Candi for the first time that morning, it would not have occurred to me to say 'Your wig is stunning, I have never seen such a blonde wig.' Or, 'Benny tells me your parents can't read or write English even though they have a book about the Kennedys on their coffee table. And gave a salesman from Atlas Back-to-Nature Lawn Care Products $5,000 down on the Encyclopedia Brittanica.' These things you would not mention in a free country where people had to change their names to get in. Unfortunately the Joneses live in a slum and do not have a garden. I suppose the salesman forgot to look out the back window.

Even a morning person would find six o'clock early for breakfast. But Benny said it is another world at that hour, unspoiled and promising. '*Tabula rasa*, Joanie,' he said. 'Write your own history.' He thought I didn't know my Latin: Nothing Yet Is Lost.

I saw his black Cadillac, like a Roman temple with its majestic curved wings, floating down the street towards the shop. I was standing in front, 5.30. Molecules of the freshest air had been rolling at my face, little taps. I put my head back to devour with my own eyes the purity of this endless sky without light waiting for someone to draw themselves on it. I felt that Louie's barber was patting aftershave on my cheeks and yet I am not a man. Some people realise they are alive as they happen. Others believe it even when they are not moving. As to early mornings, Benny knows what he is talking about.

The Cadillac has electric windows, all bright silver glass that keeps people from seeing in. Then there are the black leather seats, the mahogany steering wheel and dashboard, as well as matching panels on the inside of the doors. It also has a radio, tapedeck, and special frequency police monitor for listening in on law enforcement vs. the criminal element. He has converted the glove compartment into a bar in case he gets thirsty in the front seat. Luckily for Benny someone who used to work with him died suddenly and no longer needed the car. It is a great help to Benny's tax position.

When I got in the car that morning, Benny said, 'Hello,

Joan. Prepare for take-off.' One at a time, I pushed each little sliding lever on the control panel until all the windows were down. Then he said, 'Doors to manual.' I locked the doors by pressing *one* button. 'Whap, they're locked,' said Benny. Then he put his glass of Scotch into the special rack on the door. Resting his arm behind me on top of the long front seat he said: 'Into your spot.' I slide in next to him, his arm but not his hand unavoidably against and therefore touching my back. My side touching his side. Bucket seats have ruined all this, which is why Benny prefers an older vehicle.

Benny says, 'You didn't have to wear your uniform.'

'I like to look nice,' I reply, 'especially when I am in an official capacity.'

Benny smiles. 'And you do look nice. White is good any time.'

He turns on the ignition. 'How about that? Just back from the shop, in A–1 condition.' He revs the engine, vroom vroom. 'You hear it?' he shouts.

'Yes,' I say over the noise. I have strained my vocal chords. I lift my chin and massage them slowly.

'Fuel injection,' says Benny, lifting his Scotch gently from the rack. He takes a long sip and replaces the glass. 'Now,' he says. 'Pilot to co-pilot, are you ready?'

Benny keeps his foot on the brake. The gear shift, on the steering column, I push carefully up until it slips nicely into the notch. We're about to start. I close my eyes and put both hands on the wheel.

'Open your eyes, for God's sake!' laughs Benny. 'I don't need another ticket!' Angela handles his traffic difficulties and told him enough is enough. Mind you, she thinks all the summonses are because of the men who drive the installation vans.

I opened my eyes. My hands gripped the wheel. Benny was about to let up the brake and accelerate. Right now it is obvious that he is teaching me to drive. No one, not even Benny and me, knows this for sure. Besides, I am only up to steering which is less than the total experience.

Suddenly the car lurches forward. 'They don't make them like this any more,' he shouts. Wind is whipping in and out the windows like a clutch of hockey players. I have pinned my cap on to my head so it won't fly off. No one else is on the road.

'Stay to the right!' screams Benny. 'Rules of the road, kiddo!' The main thing about steering is: you can't turn the wheel too quickly. Small corrections do the job. Unless avoiding an accident. By now we are approaching thirty. I ever so slightly adjust us and we slide over. I arch my neck to see the white line.

'It's there,' calls Benny. 'Keep your eye on the road!'

My awareness moves carefully on to Benny's arm, off my back. I cannot mention other aspects.

'Now for the real fun,' chortles Benny, as we head for the four-lane highway which will shoot us to The Paradise Lounge, one block from Carpets Galore, in 'no' time.

I see the sign, 'Next Left For E-W Expwy'. This is not a difficult manoeuvre for me as there is no on-coming traffic. Also the arm/back awareness stirs up a whirl of daring which wrestles free of the underlying suction.

I have to be careful about my steering technique. I tend to hold or turn the wheel thus: I grip tightly, full hands. Then I lift them suddenly with a quick twitch probably less than one cm off the wheel as if they are Tinkerbell. Then I hold on again. This happens constantly for no known reason, to which Benny now and then replies, pretending to be impatient, 'Oh, sweet Jesus, hold the wheel.' I am puzzled because I do not feel I have let go.

We are on E-W Expwy. Gradually Benny accelerates. We are doing forty. Forty-five. Fifty. FIFTY-FIVE. SIXTY-FIVE.

'Benny!' I scream. Oh my voice!

'Don't bounce on the seat, Joan,' says Benny, above the roar of the crowd. 'It'll throw off your concentration.'

Was I bouncing? This time I myself see that we are drifting and ease us slowly back with a subtle turn-lift-turn of the wheel. We are flying. We are on air. Yet we are bound to earth. Where air and earth meet: another locus of awareness. No wonder you pay more for a Cadillac.

The Paradise Lounge is a busy place at any hour. A sign on the front door says: 'In Paradise There Is No

Such Thing As Time.' The fluorescent pink glow inside helps you forget (a) daylight, (b) darkness. There are no actual windows. If you insist on seeing out, someone has painted lovely murals behind the bar. A golden sunset, a golden sunrise, a golden beach, a bright blue sky, a family of doves.

There are four actual waterfalls with pink water, each with its own pool and rock garden. The pools are full of goldfish and coins. Tables and chairs surround each waterfall. Candi and the other waitresses wear extra short bathrobes, slippers, and Hawaiian leis. They serve drinks called Sweet Nothings, a blend of rums. Upstairs are private rooms for business consultation. The place is packed.

Candi smiles when she sees us. This is how I know it is Candi.

'Hello, Benny,' she says, both arms out to him. He takes her hands. He looks at her. She looks back. They have never been more sure of anything in their lives.

'So,' says Candi. 'This is your Joan.' Still holding one of Benny's hands she takes one of mine and rolls her eyes. 'You never said she looked like *this*.'

'I can't tell you everything,' laughs Benny.

'Come on you two and sit down. My favourite table.' She says to the bartender, 'I'll be in the back, Gino.'

'So who's your friend, Benny?' says Gino.

'Joan Pardee, meet Gino Stromboli,' answers Benny.

'Watch out for him. He's the type that respects his mother.'

'Ah, enough with you , Manini. You're going to give me a reputation around here. Nice to meet you, Miss Pardee. If you ever wise up to this guy, I'm available.'

'Thank you,' I said. Wasn't that nice.

'Miss Joan Pardee is too good for you, Manini,' calls Gino as we walk away.

When we sit down Candi says to me, 'I didn't realise you were a nurse. Benny told me you worked with his father-in-law.'

'A lot of people make that mistake,' I replied. 'One, flour doesn't show up on white. Two, I like a trim, professional appearance.'

I took off my cap and name-badge to indicate that I was relaxing.

'Oh, I agree,' said Candi. 'You look a lot sharper than I do in *this* get up.' She laughed. 'At least you don't embarrass our Mr Manini. At least he takes you out.' She winks at Benny. He winks back.

'I don't need to take you out,' he says quietly. 'I could go out with anyone. With you I like to stay in.'

There is a pot of tea and a large mug waiting on Candi's table. She pours, generously. She adds sugar and milk. She holds the mug close to her lips with both hands and blows.

'I need this,' she says.

Then she put on my cap.

'How about this?' she said to Benny. 'Would you respect me more if I wore a little hat for you?'

Benny said, 'No, nothing would help. You're too far gone.'

To me she said, 'Does a hairdresser fix your hair like that, sweetheart?'

'No,' I replied. 'I manage it myself.'

'Good for you,' said Candi. 'I'm hopeless at hair, look at this limp rag.' She scrunched it up with her hands. 'I dyed it blonde so I'd look like I went to finishing school. Guess what? It didn't work. I'm still a dumb Polack.'

I knew it was one of those countries. And it isn't a wig after all.

'Benny tells me you went to college,' she says to me. 'Lucky you.'

'Candi,' said Benny. 'You've got more brains than ninety per cent of Harvard.'

'It doesn't teach you as much as people think,' I said.

'No?' she said. 'Only people who had a chance to go would say that.'

'I hardly learned anything.'

She looked at me. 'Benny told me you got through more books by the time you were ten than most people read in a lifetime. That's not nothing. You want to know what I'm good at?' asked Candi.

'Yes,' I said.

'Candi,' said Benny.

'I mean it, Benny,' she said. 'This is a serious

conversation. I'll tell you what I'm good at, Joan: up-keep. My parents live in a small apartment. They're very old. I can fix anything.'

'Mechanical proclivity,' I commented.

'You see? That's what I mean,' said Candi. 'It would never occur to me to say it like that. Whereas right away you've got the proper word.'

'I can't help it. Whereas a skill is something you're in charge of.'

Candi looked at Benny. 'You're right about her.'

To me she said: 'Guess who does the plumbing and electrical work around here? Guess who fixes the sprays in the fountains when they get clogged?'

'Who?' I said, already sensing the answer.

'Me,' she replied. 'You think any of these macho men could figure out how to come in from the rain? God love you.' She reached over and pinched Benny's cheek.

'A person doesn't need as much proneness for college as she would for plumbing,' I said.

'Thank you,' said Candi. 'Finally someone under-stands me.' She was starting to look nice in my cap.

'You may keep my hat if you like,' I said. 'I have plenty.' This is true.

She stared at me. I was afraid I had hurt her feelings. Maybe she secretly wanted to be a nurse all along.

'Let me tell you something, Joan Marie Pardee: that is the best offer I've had all night.'

I got up and went over to her. The cap is a miniature

version in white of the black hat worn by George Washington in 'Washington Crossing The Delaware', oil on canvas 1851 by Emanuel Leutze, American (1816–1868). This is a coincidence. The weather that day was fierce, the river treacherous. The cap stands tall. High, flat front, arching backward at the top. Puffed out behind the head. Gently upturned flaps, back and front, extending slightly on either side.

'Before you reach your final decision,' said Benny, 'you should be aware that this hat has two purposes: number one, it catches rain, and number two it is cheaper than air fare if you lower the flaps.'

Candi had the cap at an angle. George Washington wore it straight. I made the adjustment and sat down. The flat front makes you stand firm against overwhelming odds, but not if it's tipped to the side.

– chapter nine –

For a moment all I can see is George Washington. There are approximately six boats in all. The river is frozen. Chunks of ice must be forced aside with heavy poles in order for the boats to pass. A few men descend into the water, on to ice, and heave themselves against the reluctant vessels. Others struggle with frantic horses through whose veins the peril has begun to course. I cannot reassure anyone.

What a fierce and howling wind tears at my scarf, jeopardising even the hat. The men are so cold, some wounded. All we know at this moment is the goal. General Washington stands. His eyes are fixed on a point in the future that none of us in the boats can fathom. He keeps track of what lies ahead; I get on with the struggle. The men believe they will succeed. Most know they will succeed and die. This is not a contradiction. Therefore no conversation is necessary. In other paintings the people call out to me and I answer.

Finally Candi asks, 'How about that breakfast you came for?'

This is my chance, without appearing eager, to say something that has been on my mind.

'I would like three scrambled eggs, three slices of white toast with butter and raspberry jam, a side order of four sausages, and a large glass of orange juice. No tea or coffee. I need the toilet quickly. Please, thank you.'

They both laugh.

'How does she stay so thin?' says Candi. 'And polite at the same time?' Perhaps they have never met someone who is indifferent to food.

'The bathroom is back and to the left,' says Candi. 'And I'll get the breakfast right away, you poor starving thing. How about you, Benny?'

For a moment he says nothing. Then: 'I suppose I could use a nice breakfast, too.' Pause.

He doesn't seem right. In fact, his hands are shaking. Slightly, that is. Not enough to notice.

'And no booze. I've been drinking too much.'

So I decided to remain seated for now.

'How much?' says Candi.

This question does not help Benny relax.

'What's that supposed to mean?' he asks.

'Nothing. You just seem worried.'

'Obviously I'm worried. I've got to cut back, for Christ's sake.'

'Okay,' says Candi.

'Why are you looking at me?' he asks. 'What's bothering you?'

'Don't fight with me, honey. Your drinking bothers *you*. And p.s., you know I don't like it. We've been through this before.'

'Maybe if I take the bottles out of the car.'

'Benny. I never want to lose you. It's simple. I don't know what else to say.'

'Well, there's no reason I have to drink while I'm goddamn driving. I'll eliminate the booze in the car.'

'Okay,' says Candi.

'In the meantime I'll just have a small one now, nothing more until lunch, and I'll go easy tonight.' He took a deep breath. 'I'll take the old bull by the horns.'

'Good idea,' I replied.

'Benny,' said Candi, 'do you hear yourself? You just said you're not having any this morning.'

'Well, I figure if I take the bottles out of the car.'

'You figure if you take the bottles out of the car what?'

'Then that's a start.'

'You can't start in two places at once?'

'Candi. Take it easy. I'm upset.'

'I know, angel pie, but you're the one who mentioned it.'

'All right, all right, I'm sorry.' He is rubbing his forehead now.

'What am I supposed to do, Benny? You say, "I'm worried." You want me to tell you "No problem, go ahead and kill yourself, fine with me?" You want that?'

'Candi, enough. For Christ's sake. I know what's going on.'

'Do you? I'm not sure. Sometimes I can't figure you out.'

He put his head in his hands. She ran her fingers through his hair.

'So what the hell am I supposed to do about it?' he asked. 'You seem to have all the answers.'

'Why is it on your mind?' replied Candi. 'The last time was four months ago after you hit Jesus Perez for mixing up an order.'

'Four months ago I didn't sleep next to a bottle. Candi, I'm scared. I can't get out of bed in the morning without a drink. If I do my hands shake so much I can't shave.'

'You can see the little nicks on his face,' I said.

'Those? They're from something else,' said Benny.

'I don't think so,' said Candi. 'It looks like you've got the shakes, babe. This isn't fun and games anymore.'

'Who said it was?' he cried. 'Do you see me laughing? I'm asking for help.'

Candi looked at him for a 'long' time. If I get up to go to the bathroom now, Candi might forget what she is about to say and then Benny will keep drinking. I grip the sides of my chair, sit up straight, and close my eyes.

'Maybe you are,' replied Candi. 'I can't decide. I keep turning it over in my mind and I just can't decide.'

'Jesus, Candi. What does it take? You don't have to sound so superior. Do I look like a happy man?'

'Oh, honey, I know you're worried. I can see that. And I love you no matter what. But the thing I don't know is whether you're ready to change.'

'I'm *ready*, Candi. For Christ's sake. What do I have to do to make you believe me? I need your support.'

Candi shook her head. 'Benny, I have to be honest with you. I just don't think you want to stop drinking. I feel it in my bones, don't ask me why.'

'I *do* want to stop, goddamn you!'

'Sweetheart,' she said. 'I'm no expert, but you aren't making sense at all, saying one thing and in the next breath saying something completely different. It won't work. That's obvious.' She took a deep breath. 'Look, maybe what I need to do is not let you drink when you come in here. I can't sit by doing nothing.'

'Who the hell do you think you are?' he shouted. Banging the table with his fist.

I open my eyes. I feel I cannot hold it much longer.

'Gino will serve you,' I said.

'No, he won't, Joan,' said Candi. 'He'll do what I tell him. Anyway, you don't believe your Benny either. He's only fooling himself.'

By now Benny is on his feet. His hands are really trembling.

'You fucking whore,' he snarls. 'Of all people.'

'That's right,' she says. 'Of all your so-called friends I am the only one who will tell you.'

'Come on, Joan,' he says. 'We're getting out of this dump.' He looks at Candi. 'The hat ought to do wonders for your sex life, you ugly bitch.'

And she looks so smart in my hat. Even with the tears in her eyes.

'Come back when you can, Benny. But not drunk, not dead. Okay, pal? A small favour for an old friend.'

'Go fuck yourself,' he replies, and walks toward the door. He turns to see where I am. As I stand, it runs down my legs.

'Jesus Christ!' he shouts. 'Did you wet your pants again? You're not sitting on my leather seats, I can tell you that, you big fucking baby!'

He storms out the door and slams it behind him.

I agree with Candi that small talk is no substitute for the real thing. For example: (1) a teacher once said to Mother: 'The problem is Joan Marie misses her little brother, she needs to talk about him'; (2) Angela said to Louie, 'She suffers from one of the most profound cases of incomplete mourning I've ever seen, she needs to grieve'; (3) Mother said to the teacher, 'There is no brother'; and (4) Louie said to Angela, 'What do you mean "incomplete", she's lost everything.'

These comments, like Angela calling Benny an alcoholic, or Benny calling me a big fucking baby, would be known as 'your' opinion. The real thing, well, only the people themselves may know. In any case, I weighed 5 lbs. 14 oz. at birth and was probably conceived the same way as the next person.

Candi brought me a pink towel. When I got outside, Benny was waiting for me. He didn't mean what he said because I always put a towel.

He smashed two new bottles of Chivas Regal on to the pavement. He gulped down what was left of the third and smashed that, too.

It didn't matter about the breakfast.

– chapter ten –

'This is Jesus Perez,' said Benny, leading me into the office. 'I'm going out. Jesus, show Miss Pardee whatever she wants.' He went out the door for thirty-eight days. Mr Perez was sitting behind the desk, aged twenty-seven. This I knew already.

'Hello, Miss Pardee. Mr Manini mentioned that you would be coming. How may I be of service?'

I don't remember the name of the aforementioned teacher, but she thought I wasn't talking up enough in class. I sat still each day, age nine. This was nice. Yet not participatory to the required level. As previously mentioned I did college in the same easy-going style.

In my case the teacher asked the parents to come in for a conference. My mother asked my father would he attend even though she knew he did not go along with the whole idea of group discussion. Mother thought a change of personality would improve his outlook. He went to work instead.

Oh. Now I remember. It was Mrs Rita Crocker. She asked was the father living at home. Being a private person, my mother said it was none of her business.

I am quite sure, Mrs Crocker, that you are not paid to meddle in taxpayers' intimate affairs.

I am concerned about Joan, Mrs Pardee. She needs to talk to someone.

Anything she needs to talk about she can tell *me*. Do you have children, Mrs Crocker? A mother is not 'someone'. My daughter talks to *me*. Go ahead, Joan Marie: talk. What is it you want to discuss? Nothing? See? She's fine. You say her reading is at an adult level. What more do you want? Believe me, I won't tolerate any pressure on my child. I'll take you to the education authorities. *Now* look what you've done! Wake up, Joan Marie! We're talking to you!

Mrs Pardee, I cannot allow you to do that to Joan in my classroom. You're hurting her.

Wake up, Joan Marie Pardee! Your teacher is talking to you! This is a school!

You've got to stop, Mrs Pardee. I'm going to have to call the Principal.

There. No thanks to you.

Joan, it's Mrs Crocker. Are you all right?

Of course she's all right. She has to learn respect. Talk to your teacher, Joanie Marie. Tell her you are going to participate.

Mrs Pardee. Please try to understand. I am not criticising Joan. She is a sensitive, intelligent child. But she is unable to follow what goes on and cannot relate to the other children. She needs help.

Half the class is niggers! And let me tell you, Mrs Teacher, if you let any of *those* near her, that's the end of your so-called career!

Mrs Pardee, I believe that Joan is upset about losing her brother. I am worried.

What brother? There *is* no brother, Mrs Crocker. This is false information being used against me. I know my rights. You could lose your license for passing on false information!

Please believe me. I am trying to offer support. I just don't have the time with forty-six other children. In order to arrange an appointment with the school psychologist I must have your written permission. That is all I am asking of you, Mrs Pardee.

Therefore, the conference officially ended.

After that I began to raise my hand. *Very* good, Joan! That is the correct answer! Sometimes Mrs Crocker would pull a chair up beside my desk no matter what the other children said about me: 'They're not important, Joan.' And we would read or draw together. It is hard to believe she used to put her arm around me. Edward John had been dead almost a year. I liked Jesus Perez right away. Thank goodness I had another cap and a fresh towel with me.

The warehouse is full of gigantic carpet rolls and vinyl sheeting. These are organised one on top of another. Each on its own mount so a particular sample can be unrolled to whatever length and examined. Stacks of flat samples litter the floor, 'books' of colourful squares everywhere. In a democracy there is no excuse for not knowing what you want. People died so you could choose from a range of suitable options.

'I am interested in purchasing a new ceramic tile floor for my pastry shop. I would enjoy plain white.' I sat in the chair next to the desk and folded my hands. Being a customer is not difficult if you take it one step at a time.

'We don't usually recommend ceramic tiles for a pastry shop,' replied Mr Perez. 'They're too slippery considering the flour. However, white is a lovely colour. What is on the floor at present?'

Biceps are stretching the cut-off sleeves of a black T-shirt. I am not looking at his new jeans which are also stretched, in this case by the size of his thigh muscles. I have found that once you decide not to notice something, the rest falls into place.

'At present,' I said, 'the floor consists of old wooden boards dating back to the early 1900s. This would have been prior to the development of synthetic materials.'

'We'll need to put hardboard over it first. What is the approximate size of the area you wish to cover?'

'The main room with the tables and display cases and counter is, well, large. Louie's kitchen is also large but a different shape.'

'We'll measure those for you.' He wrote something on a piece of paper.

'A person walking at a normal pace could cross each room fairly quickly.'

'The speed would probably be the same on wood or tiles,' said Mr Perez. 'But as I said, we really wouldn't want you to purchase the tiles. I wouldn't feel right knowing you were walking around on a slippery floor, even with those rubber-soled shoes.' He glanced down at my feet but I didn't notice.

'I'll be careful,' I said.

'Well, I imagine it's hard to slow down when the place is full of hungry customers.'

'I thrive on pressure.'

'Actually, I would recommend the non-slip vinyl in your case.'

'I'll take it,' I replied.

'The vinyl comes in either sheet or tile form.'

Believe me, I am not looking at Mr Perez' thick wavy black hair which is pulled back into a pony tail. Oh, my. I just realised: he is a hippie.

'Both involve the same type of floor preparation,' he continued. 'Both come in two thicknesses, 2.5 or 3.2 mm. Obviously the 3.2 is a better quality, more durable, long-er-lasting.'

'Could you please elaborate on the other advantages and disadvantages of each?'

'Installation is slightly easier with the sheeting and therefore cuts down on your labour costs. We would unroll it and cut as we go, from the wall out. However, with a sheet you are stuck with the one colour or print except for the borders which you can be a little creative with, if you like. I mean, with which.' He coughed.

'With the tiles you can make any design you want, provided of course that you choose the same thickness throughout, naturally. The other thing about tiles, which is why they work well in shops that get a lot of wear and tear, is if one gets damaged you can easily replace it. With sheeting you'd have to replace the whole thing.'

'I'll take the tiles.' Now *I'm* nervous. He's actually getting *me* nervous.

'That would be my recommendation,' he said.

'Will stains come out? I provide free coffee.'

'The tiles are tough, non-porous, non-absorbent vinyl. You just wipe up any spills with hot water and detergent.'

'I myself would never have spills. It would be the customers.'

'I know what you mean about dealing with the public. The general public, that is.' He coughed again. 'I like to advise customers that the replacement tiles will always be slightly different in shade than – I mean from, sorry – the original because of wear and tear. Also, later on different batches of the same tile may vary slightly in colour. If you see what I mean. Or it may be out of stock. Stock changes occur approximately every two to three years. I therefore recommend to customers that they purchase extra tiles from the one batch at the time of installation to ensure availability and for the best possible match of replacement tiles in the future.'

He took a deep breath. 'I imagine you prefer the non-shine, matt finish?'

'I'll take two rooms in the non-slip, non-shine, non-porous, non-absorbent vinyl tiles, 3.2 mm thickness, plain white.'

'At the moment Armstrong is a world leader. American, of course.'

'I like Armstrong but I am a budget-conscious consumer.'

'You won't find better quality or value for the money. The tiles are $5 per box, ten tiles per box, two boxes per square yard. A full role of sheet vinyl is 90 feet long, and six and one half, ten, or thirteen feet wide. $6.99 a square yard cut, or $4.99 per square yard if you buy a whole roll.'

'I'll take the tiles.'

'Oh, yes. You wanted the tiles. My apologies.' He wrote again. I opened my handbag.

'Would you like a deposit on that?'

'A deposit will not be necessary. Thank you anyway.' He opened a drawer and took out a fat book. 'You need to select a colour.'

'I'd like white, please.'

'These days there are about a dozen different shades

of white. He laid the book out on the desk and leafed through it until he came to 'Whiter Shades of Pale'.

'I'll take number 101swb5, "Plain White." '

'A lovely choice.' He wrote.

I don't want any special favours because of my uniform, so I decide to take the envelope out of my handbag.

'Here is $1,000 down. The balance upon satisfactory completion of the work, which I will personally supervise.'

'Mr Manini won't be too happy if I let you give this to me.'

'All right,' I said. I took the money back. So far we have an excellent working 'relationship', the cornerstone of quality.

'Now there is the matter of installation,' said Mr Perez.

'Right away, thank you.'

'There will be some disruption to normal business if we do it during the week. The first part is putting down the hardboard.'

'We are open seven days a week, at your service. Sunday is very busy, after eight, nine, ten, and eleven o'clock mass at St. Teresa's. However, I treat religious customers the same as anyone. We close at one on Sundays. Of course we have slack periods, too.'

'How about two o'clock?'

'We go upstairs for our dinner at two.'

'I'm afraid you'll have to move everything.'

'We can't.'

'Fine.' He wrote.

All of a sudden it occurs to me that Mr Perez might be wondering how I manage to get out to church myself. Perhaps he is a member of St. Teresa's.

'Actually,' I said, 'I do not go to church.'

'That's all right,' he replied. 'We install each job objectively, regardless of the customer's background.'

What a relief.

'I don't either, by the way.' Now he is not only making me nervous but confused. *Me*!

'I mean, I do not attend church.' He coughed. 'There is, therefore, no problem with a Sunday installation from a religious point of view. Of course, I would have to measure first, but that can be done any time.'

'Today at one o'clock, thank you.'

'Was Mr Manini going to drive you back?'

'He is unavailable.'

'I'll take you and I can measure then. Do you have any preference as to which room I should install first? I recommend the kitchen area.'

'I'll take the kitchen area.'

'Fine.' More writing.

'I don't drive except for steering. I hope soon however, to encompass the entire spectrum.' Just so he knows I'm not asking him to do everything, measure, install, *and* drive.

Why is he looking at me like that? Maybe he feels I

am criticising his driving by drawing attention to my own abilities.

'It's no problem for me to steer on the way over,' he replied.

I was right: he thinks I thought he can't steer.

'Luckily I am not good at steering,' I said. 'I do it, of course, because like so many things it has to be done. But I have shallow depth perception as well as poorly timed hand-eye coordination, located mostly in the eyes.'

At this moment I did not notice Mr Perez glance at himself in the old mirror opposite the desk, on the wall behind me, next to the door of the office.

It is all right with me if people want to be alone, so I looked down at my good white shoes and socks which were still slightly damp from my appointment with Candi. They do not smell because I carry spray deodorant with me just in case.

So I did not see Mr Perez carefully but quickly smooth his hands over the top of his head. Now I understand what is going on: he believes his hair is too thick. He pulls it back to keep it tight and therefore flat. Still, he is not sure he has done it well enough today. He did not expect to meet someone like me. You'd be amazed the fantasies people have about women in business until they meet one head-on. It is the same thing as my surprise when I discovered a hippie doing carpets. As if they just sit around between wars.

'In case you were wondering,' said Mr Perez, 'you will be able to use your new floor almost right away. The adhesive we use takes about an hour to dry. So we'll give you a nice, solid result in next to no time, with minimum disruption to customer's peace of mind and year-end receipts. I just need to know which room to do first.'

'The kitchen would be my preference.'

He looked at his paper. 'You said that before. My apologies.' There is that cough again.

I take a packet of Throtz antiseptic-anaesthetic lozenges out of my handbag and place it unobtrusively on the desk so each person can make his or her own decision. However, someone has to take the lead in a situation. I pull the packet towards me. I take out one of the small square sheets of tablets and push the one in the upper right-hand corner out through its foil backing into my hand. I replace the square and close the packet. I open my mouth and arrange the lozenge onto the tip of my tongue. I close my mouth and hold the thick, smooth disc up against the roof of my mouth. I edge the packet closer to Mr Perez.

'Changeable weather we're having lately,' I say, faking a cough to help him feel at ease. Which under the circumstances is not the same as a lie.

'Yes,' he said. He picked the packet up between his thumb and forefinger, turned slightly around, and slipped it into the breast pocket of the army jacket hanging on the back of his chair.

'Will we get going? My van is parked outside.'

He stood up.

My goodness.

A man who is shorter than a woman.

– chapter eleven –

'This is a lovely van,' I said. Bright blue like a summer's sky. 'Carpets Galore – Why Pay More.' A sensitive way to advertise. Yellow lettering makes an impression.

HE TAKES MY ARM and escorts me to the passenger side. Perhaps, after all, he is not a Communist. It will be necessary to step up. In fact, it will be necessary to lift my uniform over my knee. I may have to apologise to Mr Perez and take the bus. Everyone has things they are not exactly proud of.

'Can you manage this?' he asks. 'I don't get many ladies riding to jobs. Except for her.' He opens the door.

'Oh, Mr Perez!' My voice has been giving me problems all day and no wonder. This time there is an extensive black dog with a jumbo head spread over the entire length of the front seat. It opens its eyes slowly and for goodness sake smiles at me. Then it groans contentedly, all set to go back to sleep. And us needing this van for legitimate business purposes!

'It's all right,' said Mr Perez. 'Let me assure you she

is not aggressive or vindictive.' He looked at the dog. 'Come on now, Miss Forth. We've got to sit here, too.'

Don't ask me how. She is wearing a yellow ribbon and bow around her neck.

'Do you like dogs?' he asked.

'Just recently,' I replied.

The dog rolls over on her back. Her paws dangle in mid-air.

'Miss Forth, cut it out. I'm so sorry, Miss Pardee. This is not proper procedure at all.' He reaches in and tries to push her up. I reach in and tap her tummy twice.

'Now she'll never move,' he says. 'Not with treatment like that.'

'I'm sorry for interfering,' I say.

'Oh, I'm only making a joke,' he says. 'It would appear that you are a natural with animals. Maybe it would help if I got in the driver's side. Then she'll think I'm going on a job. Well, I *am* going on a job.'

The lozenges haven't helped his cough. Then again, they are still in his pocket. And the jacket is still on the back of his chair in the office. Look at me. I don't know what I am saying.

Mr Perez goes around the van to the other side and opens the door. The dog, whose head is at my end, arches her neck and looks at me upside down.

'I think she wants me to pet her again,' I say.

'Let me try to move her,' says Mr Perez. He shoves her rump. '*Sit up*, Miss Forth! This lady is a customer!'

She refuses.

'Really, I am so sorry. Normally she is very obedient. She's not used to someone else in the van.'

No doubt he is afraid of losing my business. Perhaps he thinks I think he is not reliable if he cannot make his dog sit up. I do not think this. Dog training and laying vinyl tiles are two different and unrelated skills. Or perhaps not. Thus, he is worrying for no reason. But the worried person himself does not know this so you should never say, 'There is no reason to worry like that.'

'There is no reason to worry like that,' I say. 'No matter what happens I plan to purchase my floor covering from you.'

All of a sudden I realised something else.

'And I will not tell Mr Manini that you took Miss Forth with us in the van. Nor will I tell him she disobeyed.'

He took a deep breath. 'He's warned me about her sleeping in the van, getting hair on the samples. But she doesn't sleep in the back at all, just in front.'

'I believe you,' I said.

'I don't want her to get cold sleeping on the pavement outdoors. And no one else will take care of her when I'm out on a job. This is the whole problem.'

'She certainly should not be left alone.'

'At the same time I don't like to go against Mr Manini's orders.'

'My view of the situation would be that he will not find out.'

He looked at me.

'My apologies for delaying you.'

'When you get back to the office,' I said, 'take one lozenge. Dissolve slowly in mouth and repeat every three hours, not to exceed eight in twenty-four hours.'

I rubbed Miss Forth's neck which was still arched in my direction.

'It's time to sit, Miss Forth,' I said.

She rolled on to her stomach, pushed herself up with the two front legs. She sat in the middle of the seat. Her thick head touching the roof of the van. Her eyes looked eagerly ahead. It is clear to me at this moment that General Washington will succeed.

There is just enough room for Mr Perez on one side of the dog, me on the other. I pull my skirt up with none of the anticipated difficulty and climb in.

Mr Perez is the shortest. He sits on an extra cushion. I did not take my towel out of my handbag because if I put it down he will feel that I feel dog hairs are disgusting. Which I have discovered they are not, despite everything. Miss Forth turns to me and tries to take my hat.

'She is utterly impossible today,' says Mr Perez.

'I have plenty,' I say. I tip my head in the dog's direction. Miss Forth takes the hat in her teeth. She holds it proud as can be. Mr Perez starts the van and eases us on to the road.

'She's a Labrador,' he says. 'She believes she has just retrieved a duck.'

'Belief is nice,' I reply.

'She comes from a long line of champions,' he says.

'Large champions in particular, I would imagine.'

We are now having a 'conversation'.

'Yes. She is large. Would you like the radio on?'

He is afraid I think he is boring. If I say 'yes' to the radio, he will feel humiliated. On the other hand, perhaps he thinks I think it is up to me to keep our relationship interesting because of the fact that women are more emotional than men. It is quite possible that he is trying simply to ease my sense of responsibility. Therefore, if I say 'no' to the radio he will feel unappreciated. He may even go so far as to believe that I believe that women know more than men about social custom.

I regret to say there are a third and fourth possibility. (3) He thinks I think he knows nothing about contemporary music and current events. He wants the radio on to demonstrate that he is up-to-date. If I say 'no' to the radio, he will feel that I feel life has passed him by. (4) He thinks I think he does not take care of material possessions, i.e., the radio will have a poor quality of sound because he forgot to retract the antenna in the car wash. So if I say 'no' to the radio he will feel shabby.

However, to think that someone thinks you are boring is worse.

'No, thank you,' I reply. 'This is such a fascinating conversation that I would prefer not to be distracted.'

'Well then,' he continues, 'as I was saying about Miss Forth, you were no doubt wondering where she got such an unusual name.'

'Several possibilities came to my mind immediately: forthright, forthcoming, forthwith.'

'Yes. Her mother's name was Forthright Meringue. Her father was Come Hither Forthwith. You know your pedigrees. Not that it is easy to get a short name out of big words. So they called the mother Miss Right, which the father agreed was perfect.'

He looks at me. He has made a joke and now wonders: does she think I am funny?

'Ha, ha,' I laugh.

He appears relieved but does not smile. He is embarrassed to admit he needed that. I hesitate to realise another possibility (a) as to why he looked at me and (b) as to why he did not smile. All I will say is that after he made the point 'agreed was perfect', he took one hand off the steering wheel. He smoothed his hand over the top of his head, front to back, and then snuck a glance in the rear view mirror.

'So Miss Forth's real name,' he continued, 'is Miss Sally Forth As In Fear Not. Sometimes my grandmother calls her Sally.' Cough. 'I live with my grandmother because she needs me, not because I like it.'

'Either way is morally sustainable.'

'Mr Manini says I should live on my own. He says I need some fun in my life. I thought he might have mentioned something. Not that I care. My grandmother had a lovely farm in Pennsylvania where she used to breed black Labradors. That was a long time ago, before I was born, I think. But I've grown up loving animals. Even in a city.'

'No one should have fun unless they enjoy it.'

'I've been trying to find my own place,' he said. 'It's very difficult. Some landlords are so careless. They don't take care of their buildings and yet they expect two months' rent in advance and one months' deposit against damages. I can't see paying all that money when I'm trying to plan for my future.'

He is slowing down to stop at a light. He puts the automatic shift into park.

Cars are beginning to honk.

'The light is green now,' I say.

He engages the gear too quickly and the van stalls. Horns are blaring. He turns the ignition key and pumps the accelerator.

'I don't believe this,' he says. 'It won't start.'

I open my door and jump down onto the road. Miss Forth, still clutching my hat, turns placidly towards me to evaluate the situation. Behind us six cars are stopped.

I call to the man directly behind, 'It could happen to

anyone.' I can tell by his wife's hairdo that she is saying, 'Fuck you.'

I climb back into the van and slam the door. Some people.

Mr Perez turns the key again and the van finally starts. He is sweating.

'Take your time,' I said. 'We're in no rush.'

'This is all I need today. I can't understand the problem, this van never stalls. I am so sorry for delaying you.'

The vehicle begins to move.

'Don't go,' I say. 'The light is red again.'

Mr Perez jams on the brakes. Miss Forth drops my hat and licks Mr Perez on his glistening face.

'Thank you, Miss Forth,' he sighs.

The light is finally green. The van jerks forward. Mr Perez quickly reaches over and turns on the radio.

'What a lovely, clear sound,' I remark. 'You must be one of those people who never forgets to retract his antenna in the car wash.'

'Well, if I do say so myself it is one of my strong points.'

Not only that. I can hardly believe my ear. He is tuned to 'Music From A Simpler Time', 10 a.m.–2 p.m., seven days a week, 104.6 on your FM dial.

My favourite programme.

– chapter twelve –

Just before we arrive at the shop, I reach down and pick up my hat for Miss Forth. I feel she may want something to chew on while Mr Perez is measuring.

We arrive. The only thing I had not counted on was Angela getting a day off. I take my name-badge out of my handbag and pin it on my lapel. Mr Perez goes to the back of the van for his toolbox. I am in a professional situation now so I ease myself down from the seat without excitement.

As we walk towards the shop, he says: 'May I ask what those numbers on your badge mean?'

He is referring to the '6–12–41' beneath 'J.M. Pardee, Associate Director'.

'The day Pearl Harbour was bombed by the Japanese,' I reply.

'I was afraid I might have been prying,' he said.

'It's all right,' I said. 'It wasn't my fault.'

He opens the door and I do not hesitate to walk through first.

Louie is boxing rum baba for one customer and has four others waiting. I do not interrupt the speeding train of thought now pulling him quickly into the kitchen, back to the counter, to the boxes, to the ball of string, to the cash register, to the 'thank you very much'. And in only a month we put out the ices again. After lunch I will take over and Louie will go upstairs for his nap.

Angela is sitting at the table in the back just beyond the counter. This is the table where Louis and I take our breaks. She is smoking furiously and drinking black coffee. The ashtray is full of butts.

'Hello, Mrs Manini,' says Mr Perez.

'Where is he?' says Angela.

'Excuse me?' replies Mr Perez.

'Don't act smart, Jesus Fucking Perez. Where is my husband?'

Except that now she is looking at me. In a moment Louie will not be happy about this entire situation.

'That's right, Associate Director,' she says. 'He was supposed to be back here four hours ago. With you.'

'Perhaps he had an appointment,' I suggest.

'The only appointment I knew about is the one he had with you for breakfast at some diner and then to pick out a goddamn floor. It is now almost two o'clock.'

'He only had time for the breakfast,' I said. 'I picked the floor myself.'

'Oh, yeah?' she said. 'Well, let me tell you something. For the next four days I have cancelled appointments with eight obsessive-compulsives, five manics, and six-teen catatonics. I have postponed the presentation of my paper on "Aspects of Anal Retention in the Pre-Psychotic Development of Oral Expulsion." I have pre-paid my analyst for three sessions I was going to miss, despite my being at the most critical point in our transference.'

'You never said he was sending you to someone else,' I replied. What a blow to her narcissistic progress.

'Oh, God, Joanie. Haven't I been able to teach you anything? I finally feel he listens to me. That's what I'm talking about.'

'I thought you told me he'd been sleeping.'

'He stopped that. Now I feel he is a real person with whom I can develop a true cathexis.'

'That's a big improvement,' I said. Angela always feels better when she thinks Dr Plotz is awake.

'What are you looking at, Perez?' she shouts. 'You never heard of cathexis? Well, buddy, you could use one, let me tell you. You guys are all alike.' She squashed her cigarette in the ashtray.

'And why do you think I've changed my whole life around for the next four days?' she asks us. Louie has started to give Angela a certain look in the middle of rushing. Two customers are left. Sometimes Louie and I bow our heads and say to each other, 'Pray that door doesn't open again.' This would not be out of unkindness to innocent customers, only exhaustion. Right now it is due to Angela.

'I wouldn't have any idea, Mrs Manini,' replies Mr Perez nervously.

'I'll tell you, Perez, because you're a doormat just like me and he steps on you the same way: Benny and I were supposed to fly down to Disneyworld at twelve o'clock for our anniversary. Eleven years of marital bliss.'

'Congratulations,' I said.

'We had a condo booked and everything. We agreed to take stock and renew our vows.'

'Congratulations,' said Mr Perez.

Finally Louie is done with the customers. He storms over to the door, pulls down the long shade which on the outside says 'Closed For Lunch' and storms back to the table. He throws his hands into the air.

'You want my customers to hear all about your Dr Plotz? You want them to hear all about your Benny Manini? Is that what you want, to put your own father on welfare? That's what you're going to do to me, Angela. Why don't you buy a bullhorn and stand in the street? "My analyst doesn't love me, my husband doesn't love me, my father drove my mother to her grave." Tell them everything, Angela. Show them my prostate X-rays, go ahead.'

'Daddy, calm down,' says Angela.

'Hello, Jesus,' says Louie. 'Welcome to the insane asylum.' They shake hands.

'Thank you,' says Mr Perez.

To Angela Louie says, '*You* fell in love with him. You *married* him. You were the one who said to me, "Oh,

Daddy, he's so good to me," Oh yeah? Well, I must have missed this little feature of his personality.'

'Come on, Daddy,' says Angela. 'This is just one incident. We still love each other.'

Louie looks at me, looks at Mr Perez, and back and forth again. He holds out his hands, shrugs his shoulders.

'What do you kids think? Huh? Have I lost my mind or is this guy a complete bum? And then I'll make us a little lasagna.' He pulled up a chair and sat down.

'Honestly, sir, I really don't know,' says Mr Perez.

'Sorry, Jesus,' says Louie. 'I shouldn't put you in that position. Joanie will tell you – I'm not too good in the sensitivity department, but I mean well.'

'Obviously,' says Angela, 'something has come up and he couldn't get to a phone. He bought the tickets.'

'How do you know he bought tickets, Angela?' said Louie. 'Did you *see* tickets?'

'I didn't need to. He said he bought them last week. He knows how much Disneyworld means to me.'

'Jesus, don't ever fall in love,' said Louie, shaking his head. 'Take it from me.'

'Thank you, sir. I'll remember that.'

Angela turned to me.

'Joanie,' she said, 'you still haven't said where Benny went. It's all right. I can take it.'

'But he didn't tell me.'

'Where did you go for breakfast? Maybe he told someone there.'

'It was just a diner. It didn't have a special name.'

'So what kind of name then?'

'Imparticular, difficult to specify.'

'Good Lord, Angela,' said Louie. 'You're making her
nervous. Let's just stop, okay? Peace. How about it?'

Angela took her hand from Louie. Suddenly began
drumming her fingers on the table.

'Just take your time, sweetheart,' she said to me. 'You'll
remember. That's my girl.'

'I don't remember.'

'You'll remember.'

'Angela, please,' said Louie. 'Enough. Relax. I'll help
you. Leave Joanie out of it.'

'I'm sure he wouldn't have told anyone there,' I said.

'He might have. Keep thinking. Open your eyes,
sweetheart. That's it.'

'Just stop, Angela!' said Louie. 'Lay off the poor child!
You're making me lose patience! You think it's her fault
some drunken bastard didn't take you to Disneyworld?
How many times in eleven years did he show up anywhere he's supposed to?'

'Daddy, this is no time for jokes.'

'Am I being funny? How many times? You think I'm
laughing at a daughter that's going to end up in the
street with nothing? You think Dr Plotz will remember
you then? No. *I'll* have to take you in, that's who. Your

father. So don't go blaming our Joanie. You'll give her stress.'

'*Our* Joanie? You're the one who should calm down! Speak for yourself! She's not mine. You take *her* in but not your own flesh and blood? Is that what you're telling me? You're telling me you don't want me back? I'm the one with the goddamn stress! She's in Never-Never land! My husband can't make one lousy phone call on my anniversary and you'd take *her* over *me*?'

'Angela, stop it. I'm not saying that. You're my daughter, I love you completely, always. You know that.'

'Oh, yeah?' Angela's eyes flashed at me.

'You'll tell me this instant, Joan Pardee, where my husband was this morning and where he has gone or we'll see who's on the street. My mother left *me* exactly half – her half – of this house. You get my drift? You can fake mental illness all you want, but it won't protect you if I exercise my rights.'

'Angela,' said Louie. 'You didn't have to tell her that. What good does it do? You just make the poor girl nervous.' He put his head in his hands.

This was something I did not know.

'Well, the *poor* girl better jog her memory. She lives here because *I* let her, no one else. Do you hear that, Miss Pardee? You tell me what time my husband took you to that whorehouse this morning, and where he went with one of them on my anniversary, or you don't have a home.'

And now I have slipped from a slab of ice into the water. I try to grasp the gunwhales of the boat, but my fingers are frozen twigs. The backs of my hands turn blue, casting an eerie light on the unforgiving river. As I go down, the water, cold as a steel clamp, grips my body. If only I had a blanket, a pillow. My lungs are being crushed. Soon my blood will come to a halt and all will be forgiven.

The other soldiers look away. General Washington gave an order based on the common good. If he turns back for only me, the dream will die. What is one individual in the forward march of thousands?

'Open your eyes and breath properly,' says Angela. 'No one is fooled.'

Louie jumps up from his chair.

'She's having a heart attack! She can't get air!'

Louie pounds my back. 'Open your eyes, Joanie! Please, Joanie, open your eyes!'

The first thing I saw was Mr Perez.

'Are you all right?' he enquired.

'Yes,' I replied.

Louie collapsed into his chair.

'Thank God,' he said.

'I'm sorry, Daddy,' said Angela.

'Now are you satisfied?' screamed Louie. 'You nearly killed her! Do that again and you'll never set foot in this house as long as I live! Do you understand me? You're a disgrace to your dead mother!' He was breathing heavily himself.

He took my hand.

'Listen to me, Joanie. Listen carefully. You will never have to leave here, never. Do you hear me? Tell me you hear me, Joan Marie. It's Louie.'

'I hear you, Louie. It's Joan Marie.'

'Ignore this woman,' he said. 'She is poison. She has no say over you.'

'Oh, Daddy,' said Angela, 'just stop it. You're being melodramatic. She was having an hysterical reaction. It's the only way she gets attention.'

'Actually,' said Mr Perez, 'I don't know where all the confusion came from.' He coughed politely. 'When Mr Manini dropped Miss Pardee off at the warehouse this morning he mentioned that they had McDonald's in the car for breakfast. He said he decided not to go out at all because he and Mrs Manini were going down to Florida after his appointment with Jay-Mac. They're one of our big suppliers. My understanding was he went directly to Jay-Mac. I'd be happy to phone over there and check for you if that would ease your concern.'

Angela smiled.

'That won't be necessary, Perez. My father often gets upset over nothing. I could have told him myself there was a simple explanation.'

'Well,' Mr Perez continued, 'I think Miss Pardee has gotten herself a bit mixed up as to details in the

excitement of making her first purchase of vinyl flooring.
I've seen that happen before.'

He looked at me. I looked at him.

All of a sudden I was starving.

To say nothing of cold.

– *chapter thirteen* –

Which is a noticeable thing: what you feel in one situation – such as hunger – was felt before. Such as freezing cold. In my case, the time would have been much previous.

The book Edward John liked most was *Wobble Dee and Squabble Dee, Friendly Creatures from Outer Space*. This was in addition to *Little Red Riding Hood* ('Once upon a time there was a little girl who was loved by everyone who knew her.') and *Snow White and the Seven Dwarfs* ('She took the rosy apple and bit into it. No sooner had she done so than she fell down dead.') Both these books were cited formerly in a different yet similar context.

I now mention (a) the freezing cold, because I used to tuck E. J. into his crib and then, aged two-and-a-half, into his bed before reading; and (b) hunger, because while reading we enjoyed a cup of tapioca, two spoons.

'Chew quietly, E. J.,' I whispered.

For food was not allowed in our room due to children being filthy and acting too full of themselves to clean up like normal human beings. The refrigerator and cupboards are locked. There are ways, however.

Each child is allowed only one blanket because of being greedy and not learning to go without. There is also no speaking after lights out. So Edward John simply does patty-cake when he starts to shiver. This is the signal.

As there is no walking after lights out, I crawl with my own blanket over to his crib or his bed, depending on what age I am referring to, stand without adjusting my feet, and cover him carefully. His little hands reach up in the dark and pull my face down to his face. He loves to kiss my nose. 'Junie nose,' he says. That's that.

In the early morning while he is still sleeping comfortably I crawl back for my blanket and cover myself as if nothing unruly has occurred. Thank goodness we don't have to go through this any more: E. J. and I have seven blankets apiece on our beds at Louie's! Can you imagine.

Some nights during books at Louie's Edward John eats *eight* little tubs of tapioca. Louie says give him milk and animal cookies, too, if he is still hungry. He is. I run in and out of the kitchen as much as I want. 'You Pardee kids are going to eat me out of house and home,' says Louie from behind his newspaper. He should talk.

E.J's three books are on a shelf next to his bed that Louie put up specially. Inside each book the little boy has written his name. Not to brag, but I taught him. 'Mye bok. Ebwarb John Parbee. Aged 4.' I am convinced that if he hadn't drowned that year he would have figured out his b's and d's.

Oh, my. E.J. is asking me right now for *Wobble Dee and Squabble Dee, Friendly Creatures From Outer Space*. I knew I heard something. The two happy children live with Louie Fusco.

' "Have you ever heard of Wobble Dee and Squabble Dee, friendly creatures from outer space?" ' I read. For this we both sit up in his bed, mashed together. I tuck him under my arm.

'No,' replies Edward John, shaking his head gravely. 'They are not allowed in my house.'

'That's right, E. J. No monsters in *our* house.'

I continue.

' "Wobble Dee and Squabble Dee come down from outer space each evening to visit Earth children and make lots of good trouble. Would you like them to visit *you*?" '

'Yes!' screams Edward John.

'Good boy, Edward John,' I say. 'That's what they like to hear.'

'Keep it down in there, you two,' calls Louie. 'Think of my poor suffering ears.' He is making a big old joke, which goes on every night during books. E. J. and I are used to it. Louie likes to join in, and why not.

I read on.

' "Wobble Dee and Squabble Dee are *so* happy you want to meet them! Now: count to five *very* slowly. Then turn the page *very* carefully to let Wobble Dee and Squabble Dee into your home." '

Edward John takes a deep breath and begins.

'One. Two. Three.' Pause. 'Four.' Pause.

'Five!' he screams, flinging the page over. Up pop Wobble and Squabble, right into our own home. Just as the book predicted. Although tattered from so many visits, their feet are still glued to the page and they still stand. We do not experience 'cardboard characters' the way one might think. Wobble Dee dangles to the side. His eight arms and three antennae are too much for him, even being bright pink. He has two big blue eyes which cross over into each other. He is often confused. Squabble is the same as Wobble only purple with clear, red eyes which do not cross. Both smile, no teeth. The other difference is that Squabble stands up perfectly straight and has little fists at the ends of his eight arms: he defends Wobble against invading alien forces from Earth known as 'Parents'.

'Hello, Wobbadee and Squabbadee!' squeals E. J.

' "Hello, boys and girls. My name is Wobble Dee. My name is Squabble Dee." '

E. J. snuggles closer to me. All of a sudden he is shy.

' "Hello, Edward John" ', I read.

I put this part in on my own initiative.

Each time I say this sentence, E. J. lifts his face and says, 'Junie Marie, tell me again how does Squabbadee know my name.'

'He knows the names of all the best boys and girls on the Earth, E. J. Therefore, he knows your name.'

'I like Squabbadee,' replies Edward John. He settles into my shoulder. Then he is asleep.

I like Mr Perez.

I put the book away, pull the seven blankets up snug as a bug to his chin, and turn on the extra lamps. Louie says electricity doesn't cost that much. So if E. J. needs light, turn them on.

– chapter fourteen –

'So how about that lasagna?' asked Louie, getting up.

'I'm starving,' I said.

'McDonald's wasn't enough for you,' said Mr Perez.

'I think I'll run upstairs and place a few business calls,' said Angela cheerfully. It is time to look for Benny again. She left.

'I've got to get down to business myself,' commented Mr Perez. 'But Miss Forth needs some fresh air.'

Louie came back to the table as Mr Perez got up.

'Sit down, sit down,' ordered Louie. 'You've got to eat.' Both of them sat down.

'I was just saying to Miss Pardee that it is time to walk my dog. She is in the van but nowhere near any samples. She is very patient and well-disciplined.' Cough.

'You've got a dog?' Louie actually loves animals. I know this because he talks like Mr Ed when he has to visit the bank. 'Benny never mentioned.'

'Sir, Mr Manini doesn't agree with her being around during the day. She doesn't distract me but he is afraid she will. He is afraid the customers will not get top-class service and attention. But I would never let her interfere with business, I can assure you. It's just that my grandmother went to the doctor today. Then for a walk with some of her friends. So I took the dog with me, naturally. Not that I want to be insubordinate.'

'Let me give you some free advice,' said Louie, leaning confidentially toward Mr Perez. 'Ignore Benny Manini. Look the other way when you see him coming. Put plugs in your ears. Pull a hat down over your face. Run. The same with my daughter, God forgive me. You hear what I'm saying?'

'Yes, sir: live my life to the fullest, be my own man.'

Louie slapped the table. 'Exactly. Now, how is your lovely grandmother?'

'She is very well, sir. Sometimes she gets Meals-on-Wheels for lunch, a hot lunch, that is. And she visits her friends at the Martin Luther King Senior Citizens' Centre three times a week.'

Oh. So the grandmother is a militant and passed it down.

'She still manages to get around on the bus. And cooks dinner for me every night.'

Louie shook his head. 'Amazing. I hope I'm like that at eighty-four. Right, Joanie?'

'I hope so,' I replied.

'And she's a real beauty, Jesus. They don't make them like that anymore.'

'Thank you, sir.'

'Well, our lasagna should be ready by now. You never ate my lasagna, did you, Jesus?'

'No, I don't believe so.'

'Well, you're in for an experience. Go get your dog, Miss What's-Her-Name.' Louie stood up.

'Miss Sally Forth As In Fear Not,' I replied.

'That's a name?' Louie's hands are in the air. 'Don't tell me: she's a debutante from Atlanta.'

'That's a funny joke, Mr Fusco,' said Mr Perez.

'I may not look like much, Jesus,' said Louie. 'But I've been around and I know when I am in the presence of a lady.'

He winked at me. I flicked my hand at him. Oh stop that. Isn't he something.

'Well, as I say, she is very polite,' commented Mr Perez.

'So get her. Let her do her business, then bring her in.'

'Pardon me?'

'Invite her to lunch, Jesus. You don't keep a lady waiting out front! Where are your manners?' Into the kitchen he goes, this bundle, this Louie of mine.

Mr Perez looked at me.

'Are you all right now?'

'Yes.'

'What happened?'

'I got a severe chill. Skeleto-muscular.'

'Would you like me to get my jacket for you? It's in the van.'

'Your jacket is back at the warehouse.'

– 113 –

'Oh. So it is. Thank you for reminding me.'

'You're welcome.'

'I see what you mean about these floors.'

'Wear and tear.'

'There's nothing like good vinyl,' he said. 'You'll be amazed at the difference.'

'I'm beginning to agree,' I said.

'I guess I'll go out and get Miss Forth.'

'I'll wait here and think.'

'It's been a long day for you.'

'I thrive on pressure.'

'Me too.'

He went out.

The difference is that my mother could not afford what we needed even though my father earned plenty of money. Therefore, discipline was absolutely essential. Louie is able to pay our electric bill. Thus, when he sees me with a light on in my room he is not compelled, for example, to rip the cord from the wall and smash the lamp on the floor leaving E. J. sobbing and shaking because he might be next. People with enough money do not need a display such as this to concoct thrifty children. My mother was simply making the point that we all had to try. Otherwise the family will be jeered at by immigrants. Do you want that, Joan Marie Pardee? Do you want the scum of the earth spitting on this family?

They're up there in bed, Hal. She's been reading to

him again after hours. With a light on! I said lights off! Well, it's off now I can tell you. I won't have it, Hal. I won't have contradictions. Go up there and see for yourself how they behaved towards me! Go up there and be a team!

Ernestine, it's only six o'clock. They need to get up, they need to play. How can I see them if they're in bed at six o'clock?

Play? *Play*? Is that what you think of your responsibilities. Is that what you call teamwork?

Ernestine. They just need a little time in the evenings. An hour. *I* need it. I want to see them.

You go right ahead! Look at them all you want, buster. You can *have* them as far as I'm concerned. And don't come running to me when they get their own ideas! It's easy for you to say!

A door slams. Another.

My father's weary footsteps on the stairs. He knocks on our door.

'Are you there, Princess?'

'Yes, Daddy,' I reply.

'Are *you* in there, Inter-Galactic Warrior?'

'Glaktik waiting for you, Hal,' sniffles E. J.

'May I come in?'

'Yes,' we say.

He kneels by E. J.'s bed first and gives him a kiss on his head. We are both flat on our backs. 'I'm glad to see you,' says Hal. Then he eases himself down on to the floor, on his stomach. He reaches under the bed and unfastens the strap. He pushes himself out and stands up.

'Come here to me, Edward John,' he says, removing the strap from atop the blanket and untucking the little boy. He takes E. J. in his arms. Who by now, face buried in Daddy's shoulder, is, as previously alluded to, sobbing and shaking. He will quiver the rest of the night. I, at my age, am over that part. You can't be constantly dwelling on things you have forgotten about.

'I was a very bad boy this afternoon, Hal,' says E. J.

'No, you weren't, E. J. You are never a bad boy. You are the best boy.'

'I be good tomorrow.'

He looked up. Wiped his eye with a fist.

'We got to get Junie now, Hal.' They love to chat man-to-man, especially when it's about me.

My strap is tighter than E. J.'s because I am older and could have stopped us before we got out of hand. Therefore it is more difficult to undo. My father struggles, half under the bed, for sixty-three seconds. I count to myself while Edward John sits on top of me patting my head. He also smacks dainty kisses, where else, on my nose. My arms, stiff next to my body, have gone numb. This is a relief. When you feel them you know what has happened. As I have pointed out you cannot get on with a happy life if you make too much of things that are over with.

– 116 –

'Almost,' calls my father.

'Almost,' calls E. J.

'Here it comes,' calls my father.

'Here it comes,' calls E.J.

My father emerges. 'There we are.' He hoists E.J. off me and pushes the strap aside.

'Joan,' He leans over me. He is breathing quickly. I forgot: I can stop counting. I open my eyes. He is smiling.

'Hello, Princess.'

'Hello, Daddy. We were reading with a light on after lights out no reading.'

'I know. Come over here, E.J. They both sat on the edge of my bed. Daddy reached into his back pocket and took out a small brown paper bag.

'Goody,' says Edward John.

'I'm sorry, Daddy,' I said. 'It was my fault. And now I got you into trouble.'

'It wasn't your fault. And don't worry about me.'

The bag crinkled as he reached into it. Two Mars Bars. This experience is known as synthesis: here I was again, just slightly wanting something to eat, not enough to mention. A week later E.J. fell in the sea so that was the end of tying him down.

Mr Perez came in the door with Miss Forth. He has straightened her bow for the occasion.

'Say hello.' He gives her a tap. Waving from side to side she glides toward me. Look how proud.

She sits next to me. 'Shake,' says Mr Perez. She delicately lifts a Brobdingnagian paw up to my lap and flops it down.

Louie comes in with the lasagna.

'This is a *dog*?' he bellows. 'This is not a dog, Jesus. This is a bear!!' Louie is full of mischief whenever he is about to eat a good meal.

'Hello, Miss Sally Ann Worthington Sweetwater The Third,' he says.

'Louie,' I said. 'Debutantes are people, too.' You have to take a stand somewhere.

'I'm sorry, Miss Sweetwater,' he said to Miss Forth. 'I forgot you are a person.'

When someone misses the point so completely, you might as well give up.

– chapter fifteen –

Angela came back as we were finishing. She was surprised to see Miss Forth sitting up at the table eating
lasagna.

'Christ Almighty,' she said.

'Hello, Mrs Manini,' said Jesus.

Miss Forth leaned down to her plate and picked up
another piece of garlic bread.

'You've lost your fucking mind, Daddy,' said Angela.

'Yes,' he replied. 'I believe you've mentioned that
before. Now sit down and stop using foul language in
front of these children or I'm donating my half of this
house to lobotomy research. See how *they* treat you.' He
stabbed a wad of lasagna with his fork and plowed it
into his mouth.

'I'm sorry, Daddy,' said Angela. She sat.

'This is truly delicious,' said Jesus.

'I said I'm sorry,' repeated Angela.

Louie lifted his face to the ceiling and pointed his knife
and fork upwards.

'Dear Lord, bathe me in eternal gratitude for the
crumbs which my humble daughter is now stuffing

down my throat. I'm sorry, too, Angela. The good Lord has made it so you're still my daughter, no matter what.'

'Isn't he something?' said Angela to Miss Forth.

Miss Forth turned to Angela and yawned. There is nothing like a nice meal.

'Joanie,' said Angela, 'what I said to you before was absolutely despicable.'

'I know,' I replied.

'Good,' she said. 'Because I would never ask you to leave unless I really had to. It's just that I cannot anticipate year to year what Mr Manini's professional commitments may be, the possibility of relocating, and so on. There may be a chance we would need – to help us successfully enter the next phase of our relationship – to develop a more flexible arrangement, such as the Commuter Approach which has been in the news lately. Two people simply cannot control each other. This is what most couples never understand, which is why the divorce rate is so high. What with people living together, day in and day out, year after year. This is the traditional marriage which is obviously not working. It leads to all kinds of problems. The main one, as I say, being divorce, along with child abuse, extra-marital affairs, embezzlement, that sort of thing.'

By now Louie's chin is propped up in the heel of his right hand. His eyes are wide with disbelief, although Angela sincerely means everything she says.

'Unfortunately I am not familiar with the latest in social developments,' said Jesus.

'You wouldn't be, of course,' said Angela. 'The Commuter Approach is a term coined by a team of psychiatrists in Washington who have been studying the low divorce rate among couples who live apart. What I am saying is that I think Benny and I may have matured to the point where, like these couples, we are ready for this type of more demanding arrangement.'

'I think I read about one couple out West who are into that,' cough, said Jesus.

'Perez,' said Angela, 'Commuter Marriage is not something one is "into". We are talking here about new social arrangements as a response to present-day realities. Commuter Marriage is the equivalent of radical self development. Society has just begun to evolve to this level.'

'These certainly are exciting times,' said Mr Perez.

'This is what has always made America great, Perez: new definitions.' She banged the table with her fist. 'If we don't like something, call it by another name, *innovate*. Instead of couples saying: "We have failed each other, we must get a divorce," Commuter Marriage allows them to say: "We have progressed to a more highly developed plane, let's live apart." '

Angela sighed contentedly.

'So where do they commute to?' I asked.

'I'll tell you where,' said Louie. He is still staring at

Angela. 'McDonalds. They go straight to McDonalds, isn't that right, Angela? All these couples meet in McDonalds to talk over old times, slap each other on the back. Really, Ange, you test my love.'

'So that would be the actual location of the marriage?' asked Mr Perez.

'Daddy,' said Angela, 'you may find modern, creative solutions to chronic dsyfunction a laughing matter. But millions of Americans racked with self-doubt do not.'

'Who's laughing?' said Louie. 'I feel like crying. And let me tell you the only people not crying are the ones who take their commitments seriously. Benny spits on your marriage vows. You know it, I know it. But I want you to keep your mouth shut about the details in front of these kids in *my* house.'

'They could meet in different places,' I said to Mr Perez.

'Well, a restaurant is probably the best,' he replied. 'They can eat and talk at the same time. And it's fun for the children, the different give-aways.'

'If any children survive,' said Louie.

'Angela wants to meet here,' I said. 'She is thinking of relocating the marriage here.'

'I doubt that will be necessary, Joanie,' she said. 'I am just trying to be flexible.'

'In which case,' Louie said to me, 'you and I get on the next plane to Sicily. I can't wait.'

'I wouldn't mind a change myself,' said Mr Perez.

'Daddy, don't be ridiculous,' said Angela. 'Benny isn't capable of the type of independence I am talking about. Both partners have to develop inner strength for Commuter Marriage to work. Benny isn't there. It is a matter of my being patient while he grows.'

'In any case,' said Mr Perez, 'Miss Pardee could always move in with my grandmother and me. That wouldn't be any trouble at all.' Which was a nice thing to say, even if he doesn't mean it.

Angela glared at Mr Perez.

'Didn't you come here to measure the goddamn floor, Perez?'

'Angela,' said Louie, 'the man is eating his dinner. He is a guest in this house. Sit right where you are, Jesus.'

Mr Perez was struggling to get up quickly and obey Angela. Consequently he bumped the table and spilled his glass of water. Miss Forth jumped down from her chair and began licking at the pool forming on the floor.

'Pardon me, pardon me,' cried Mr Perez.

'When we want your ideas, Perez,' said Angela, 'you can be sure we will ask for them.'

'My sincere apologies,' he cried. 'I'll clean up, I'll measure.'

'You'll do no such thing,' said Louie calmly. He stood up, put his hands on Mr Perez' shoulders and steered him back into his chair. 'You're having coffee, you're having *zabaigone*. You know how many years this floor has been here, Jesus? You know how long my wife may she rest in peace and I commuted back and forth across this floor to each other? Don't ask. And has the floor fallen in? No. The floor knows how to wait. Has the Pope changed his mind about the Virgin Birth? Of course not. Some things will never happen. Why, even Angela,' he went on, 'after changing so much, after giving Dr Plotz enough money to build his house in the country, even Angela is still the same.'

We are all back in our places. Miss Forth has finished with the floor. I reach down and remove her bib. She pads over to the corner and flops down. She is asleep.

'Does Miss Sweetwater take coffee?' said Louie.

'No, sir,' said Mr Perez, panting.

'Stop breathing so hard, Jesus,' says Louie. 'Or Angela will think she is in charge, and if there is one thing we don't want, it is Angela in charge.'

'Yes, sir. I can picture it.'

'So you see what I am saying.'

'Yes, sir. Complete loss of backbone.'

'That's it, Jesus. That's the boy. You're catching on.'

'Wow. We're in the presence of two real men here, Joanie. I tell you, I'm tingling all over,' said Angela. 'Anyway, Perez, you were right about Mr Manini. He did go to Jay-Mac just as you suggested. They've sent him to Puerto Rico for an emergency conference on rubber-backed indoor-outdoor carpeting.'

'I thought it must be something along those lines,' said Mr Perez.

'He just couldn't get to a phone and sent apologies through them. There has been a hurricane in Puerto Rico and all the phone lines are down.'

'And if you believe this,' whispered Louie loudly to Mr Perez, 'you believe he sells that junk at cost.'

'What was the emergency?' I asked.

'The sharp increase in rubber prices,' replied Angela.

'I guess Benny was pretty upset,' I said.

'Of course he was, sweetheart,' said Angela. 'He works hard and a downturn in the economy affects his mood.'

Louie looked at his watch.

'I never thought I'd see the day,' he said, 'when it's a relief to get back to customers.' He stood. All of a sudden he looks tired even though lunch is the only thing that has happened. One by one Louie pulled our empty plates in front of him and made a neat stack.

'Good lasagna, right, Jesus?' said Louie.

'The best,' replied Mr Perez.

'Are you trying to imply something with that last remark?' Angela asked Louie. 'If so, leave me the hell out of it. I've met some of the nutcases that come in here. You two draw them like a magnet. If you're under pressure, Daddy, it's your own goddamn fault. This is probably hard for you to believe, but once in a great while something is not *my* fault. However, I realise that such an advanced concept of personal responsibility is new to you.'

She licked the tip of her left index finger and pressed it hard across one eyebrow and then the other. She closes her eyes when she does this.

Angela has plucked the eyebrows. Therefore her face takes up a lot of room. Especially when, as now, her bulky hair has been grabbed at the back of her head and yanked it into a tight, massive pony tail. I say 'yanked' because I have seen her do this and it sears my scalp. She seems to be forcing herself against a determined gale which tries to whip her back.

The result of this struggle is that the eyebrows edge up at the ends, and the skin of her cheeks and forehead is stretched off the bones. Or so it seems. Or so I fear. And one knows this can actually happen because one has seen scientists on television testing people in a wind tunnel. To say nothing of what the Indians did to White settlers.

On the other hand, I appreciate that Angela cares about her appearance. She calls it 'heightened self-awareness'. The eyebrows are two black threads. She believes that what she calls their 'delicate' look coordinates with her sharp nose. 'While at the same time offsets my big sad-sack eyes and fat sloppy fucking lips.' I am only repeating what she said.

'You see these plates, Angela?' said Louie. He held them up like an offering, but without hope. 'I am now

– 126 –

going to take these plates out to the kitchen. I am going to put them in the sink, wash my hands, and get ready to earn my retirement if I live long enough. I am going to close my eyes just like you, Angela, and imagine I lead a normal life. I am going to believe that we had a lovely meal together. That I have a sweet, happy daughter who returns the love I feel for her, who is married to a devoted husband with normal impulses. Why should I spend the rest of my life facing reality? Who wants to be alone? I should learn from you, Angela: *pretend*. That's what I need to do. *Lie. Deny. Smile.* Why have I been wasting my time when the answer to all my problems was right in front of me?' He walks away from the table.

'You'll get no sympathy from me, buddy boy,' snarled Angela, tossing her hands at him. 'You don't listen, you don't pay attention, you never did. The only thing you care about is playing it safe for yourself. You want me to be sweet? I'll be sweet. Anything you say, Daddy.'

She picked up the bowl of sugar and poured it over her head.

'There. See? Now you have a sweet child.'

The sugar cascaded down Angela's hair on to her anniversary dress, her chair, the floor. A small patch of white granules clung to the top of her head. She grinned, arched her back, and flicked her head. Sprinkling the pony tail with white specks.

'God, that was good,' she said. 'I am a new woman.'

She slid down in her seat and sighed. 'To tell you the truth, I could almost come.'

Louie kept walking. Went slowly through the doors to his kitchen.

'Now, Perez honey,' Angela said demurely, blowing him a kiss, 'measure the fucking floor like a good boy.'

– chapter sixteen –

Another part of my life is tenements. Brown plus odours. Rasping jeering voices. All of which push against me like a crowd. Shoving is an urban experience unknown in agrarian societies.

There are Asians, Negroes, Spanish people. The Spanish ones knifed the Asians for selling fruit to homosexuals, so now most of the Asians have gone back. The Italians don't mind coloured people killing each other, or homosexuals shopping in coloured shops. It keeps them away from our neighbourhood. Which none of them come near. Italian young people hit outsiders with lead pipes because some groups arrived before others.

This is how it is: Unionville, where I live, was once a town full of regular White people. Before that were the Indians, different shades. For a brief time the two types were peaceable neighbours. Eventually all of it became New Jersey. Many French settled in Unionville, hence the 'ville' aspect. Which was retained over the years as a reminder of our forefathers' cultured Norman heritage.

In the early days, of course, all the land was farms.

This is where I come into the picture: I fully believe that the house I grew up in was once upon a time a farmhouse belonging to early American settlers. This potential fact means that for all intents and purposes I am a direct descendant on my father's side of five generations of pioneers originally related to French nobility. My great-great-great-great grandfather probably was Mayor of Unionville in 1830.

In the old days they farmed mostly pigs and chickens. Sloping down to the Hudson River were green fields. Fields of wheat and corn, meticulous rows of vegetables. Across the river, settlers saw more land. No skyscrapers, no heliport, no weather forecasts. Just the outdoors itself. Weathermen came later, after the Industrial Revolution. When people started pinning things down.

'The vastness of the sky, the clarity of the river, the comfort of the lush harvest, swelled the pioneers with gratitude.'

Now the banks of the Hudson River opposite Manhattan have condominiums stuck in them. Water's Edge, Manhattan View, River View, River Run, Edge View.

When I was younger, the first condominium was built. Everyone was glad because old shipping warehouses were torn down. The area around the condominium was paved over and named, 'Water's Edge, New Jersey.' Gradually condominium towns jostled in against each other. Residents knew for sure where they lived by reading signs placed at regular intervals along the road: 'You Are Entering Edge View', 'You are Leaving Edge View'; 'You are Entering River Run', 'You are Leaving River Run'; 'You Are Entering River View', 'You Are Leaving River View.'

Last year they tore down the Water's Edge and built a twenty-four-hour drive-in fortune teller with quick window service. Therefore I am not certain whether Water's Edge, New Jersey, is still a place. The Post Office probably has regulations to cover the setting up and taking down of locations. New warehouses replaced the old ones on whatever scrap of land. Now these too are abandoned, awaiting demolition.

Just beyond the condominium road which winds its way along the river is a steep, rocky hill, which to the eye of a child appears to shoot up to the sky with menacing force. If you stand on the road you cannot, of course, see what is on the other side of the hill. All that would be visible is a rusty chainlink fence on top, overgrown with grass and weeds. The fence is supposed to keep children from falling down the hill. There used to be two signs on the fence: 'Danger' and 'No Dumping'. These have been stolen or removed. Each possibility has its own implications. From there, at the top, you can look down and see the condominiums. The dumping is done after dark.

Anyone can see why, as a child, I thought I lived in 'Union-The-Hill'. I have since heard that someone before

– 131 –

the French actually named the town Union Hill. This I believe because it makes sense.

Our house was located on the corner of Sycamore Avenue and South Main Street. Number 11 Sycamore, next to the Cardozos and across from the Motleys.

I say 'was' because my mother failed to file her will with the County. After she died I suppose the County did not know where I was. After Louie and I had moved the food, my clothes, and E.J.'s three books over to his house, I forgot about Sycamore Avenue. Angela took the furniture she needed. She told me I would have no use for it, being incapable of living my own life. In particular she took two matching dining-room chairs. The two which remained of the four. Mother, Father, Boy, Girl.

Angela felt the chairs had been damaged. She has since had them refinished. After E.J. died, Mother threw his chair down the hill. After my father died she threw his chair down. Angela may have taken other things. Either she didn't say or I don't remember. I think I would remember.

I doubt she took any of the actual wood. What I mean is that our house, like most in the Sycamore-South Main area, was a wooden frame house with a front porch running across the front of the house. These were massive, lumpy places. My father called it 'The Barge', and put a sign over the door to that effect. Even though we were not near the Erie Canal.

The whole thing got to be a bit lopsided after he died

because he was the handy one. The porch tilted to the right as you faced it, and slightly forward. The basement filled up four inches when it rained; brown water came out of the taps. The three wooden steps up to the porch rotted and had to be covered with old planks from the hill. Unfortunately these were warped. Nails wouldn't hold them down and they banged like a gun when you walked up. The porch itself was not high so we stopped using the steps. Gradually I suppose you would have to say the porch rotted, too. Grass grew out of the roof, the gutters, and cracks in the front path. Our lawn kept getting higher because the Scalia twins wanted fifty cents to cut it. Also their father was a social worker who found homes for illegitimate babies and we didn't associate with people like that. The doors and windows all shut, thank God, and could be locked.

The old wallpaper in all the rooms inside was to have been steamed off, and the walls re-painted. I guess my father was busy before he killed himself. He didn't get around to finishing the less important details.

After he had gone for good, some of the paper curled partway down from the moulding near the ceiling of each room. Strips in the living room split, cracked, and fell down. These could be snapped into tiny pieces. In other places the paper had wide gashes across it where my father had thrown himself at the wall with a scraper. He sobbed. This would have been their bedroom.

'I can't get it right, I just can't get it right.'

He rested his forehead against the wall. I sat on the edge of the bed with my hands folded nicely in my lap. He had promised me an old piece of wallpaper for my dolls-house.

I mentioned the wood itself because from the time I moved to Louie's until the house was bulldozed by County officials to make way for a car wash, the Negroes and Spanish fought over the wood. They also fought over the appliances, the doors, the bathroom fixtures, the carpets, the lamps, and the roof.

Mr and Mrs Motley boarded up their house and moved to a retirement village in Florida. The Cardozos bought a shotgun. The other eight houses on the street were abandoned. A few were sold at very reasonable prices to the new element, who up to then had been confined to North Main and Canal Street.

Their school was by the railroad yards. Whereas Sycamore and South Main were near the hill overlooking the river, buxom trees and the nice school. Porches for sitting.

A ten-year-old Puerto Rican girl with braids was raped and strangled on our porch by squatters. She was trying to run out the front door with the large spaghetti pot. As I understand it, Negroes got most of the long pieces of wood from the outer structure of the house. And from the roof. Spanish people got floorboards and kitchen linoleum.

It never occurred to me to give my new address to the County.

– chapter seventeen –

Louie's is on North Main Street, where the Italians are pressed on one side by Negroes. On another by Haitians. I am not sure of all the various types. I believe they overlap. The same families never stay long enough. The Irish are gone.

Angela and Benny do not live in Unionville. They live in a $400,000 white colonial with Grecian pillars modelled after those favoured by Thomas Jefferson. The first time Louie went he called it a mausoleum and has not been asked back. It has five bedrooms, six bathrooms, two kitchens, two living rooms, two garages, a swimming pool, sauna, musak, and computerised robot called James. He answers the door, takes telephone messages, cooks meals in the microwave, and laughs if you tell a joke. I have not been invited. I don't remember the name of the town. The driveway is 700 feet long and 200 feet wide in case Benny buys a Cabin Cruiser.

In other words, before I moved in with Louie it was a long walk from Sycamore and South Main to his shop and house at the far end of North Main. Number 147. At least a mile. My school was only two streets away from Sycamore. Two blocks North on Main, turn left, four buildings in. Hillcrest Avenue. The Hillcrest School.

For many years Louie's was the only pastry shop in town. Even after Cake Time opened on the South Side Mother and I continued to go to Louie's. Nothing could compare.

Cake Time was part of a chain and eventually moved to the shopping mall in Paramus. Most of the stores up and down Main did this. The rest went out of business. No one shopped locally any more. They loved the malls, they loved their cars. They did not like to walk near certain people or buy from the same shops as those certain people.

The shops and houses which were not sold were mostly boarded up. Some remained. The last real estate agent left a long time ago, although For Sale signs are still up. Most are rusty. Riddled with bullet holes.

Many of the people who moved out still come back to shop at Louie's. Mrs Cunningham-Freeman, for example. She has a new house in the same town as Angela, if only I could think of the name. Mrs Cunningham-Freeman is a direct descendant of a General who fought the British in the Battle of Saratoga.

In earlier times the walk from my house to Louie's was lovely. There were coffee shops. My favourite was Bazini's: thickest butterscotch sundaes, strongest coffee for my mother. Drug stores. Favourite, Gilmore's: best selection of penny candies, two for a penny; friendly to my mother re emergency prescriptions over the phone. Groceries/Delicatessens. Favourite, Gagliardi's, because it is still there and Mrs G. is a friend of mine. Freshest *prosciutto*, leanest corned beef. Widest selection of cereals, breads, cheeses, and pet food. Never rude. Let my mother come behind the counter and weigh portions herself.

The library. Closed and then re-opened as the Martin Luther King Senior Citizens Centre, previously mentioned. Largest selection of eighteenth-century sociology. Softest chairs, dusted shelves. Pictures of George Washington, Thomas Jefferson, Abraham Lincoln. Most patient, most knowledgeable librarian in the world, Mrs Dayton.

I overhear her say to my mother: 'No, Mrs Pardee, she hasn't been in to us in a long time. We agree she shouldn't be sitting around all day doing nothing.' Then Mrs Dayton walks back to 'World War II' and gives me the thumbs up. If I leave in five minutes I will be able to get to where I am supposed to meet my mother, on time, by going quickly past the places she had gone in to look for me. I just realised Mrs Dayton and I never spoke to each other. She retired. She died. I suppose we didn't need to.

And then finally I am at Louie's. Nearly at the end of Main Street going north. Sycamore is nearly at the end going south. Who would have thought.

There are two doors: the one on the left, glass, has a

bell that clangs as you open it. It opens into the shop, 'Louie's 147'. The one on the right, marked '147a', leads to a flight of stairs going up to the house. Really a sprawling high-ceilinged apartment, vastness taken up with low-lying stuffed chairs, sofas, mountainous tables, oak book cases with glass fronts, lamps, radios, and a thirty-two inch television. Long, thick curtains block out most of the light. There are vases of all shapes and designs, antique china plates, bowls, laundry, and mail. I left out the beds because those doors can be shut. And the kitchen because it is immaculate and has no door.

I have a bedroom off the hall past the kitchen, which is off the living room. Angela's old room also opens on to the living room. Louie has taken the door off this room, widened the opening and put in another television, a few tables and lamps, newspapers, and magazines. When I first saw Louie's house I thought he had a furniture business on the side. Such is not the case. He and his wife just loved life and couldn't get enough of it.

The actual building, the house itself, is a high, wide, wooden structure with a flat roof. The colour is robin's egg blue, white trim. There is a small parking lot to the left which Louie owns. Here he keeps the garbage cans near the side door.

In the display window to the left of the door he puts a tray of assorted pastries tilted up and carefully labelled. Beside this tray is a small cooler for the ices. There are three burnt-out buildings to the right, others along the way. A delicatessen, chicken take-away, and two hi-fi stores across the street. A doughnut shop, a pizza shop, a discount furniture store, and a branch of the Hollywood Beauty School are all further south. There are grocery stores on both sides up and down, a couple of fruit stands.

In many of the buildings people actually live. These are apartment houses now. We get the exterminator every month because of the rats. Louie let me take two fat tomcats from the animal home to pounce around out back in the vacant lot. These are Fudge and Jolly even though I never see them.

Dominick Puzzi is the landlord for most of the ten-ements. They are in violation of building codes, health codes, and fire codes. He laughs after he collects the rents. Then he forces his Chicago White Sox cap on to his bulging head and wedges himself behind the wheel of a white BMW. He is, well, fat. People on the street shout at him in Spanish about his weight and body parts. 'Fuck you, you dumb dingoes,' he calls. 'You don't like my rents? Go to Salamanca. I got plenty of takers for a nice home like this in sunny suburban New Jersey.' He speeds off.

In summer, in the heat, his tenants sit on orange crates drinking beer or wine. Blaring radios. Betting, buying, or selling. The girls dance in halter tops and short-shorts in front of their boyfriends who tie ropes around their waists.

The only time they come into us is in the summer when we have air conditioning and put out the ices. We used to sell them year-round. Now it's only June through August and we give them away for nothing. Local residents only, limit three per day per customer, 9.30–4.30. Louie says the ices cost him nothing and keep the kids from shooting us in our sleep.

– chapter eighteen –

I have never been much of a dancer. The Negro and Spanish kids are always trying to teach me. There is one routine which for some reason is known as The Hot Pussy. At least this is what the boys and girls called out to me one day as I passed by to do the shopping. Just after I had gone to live at Louie's.

I reply, 'Not right now, thank you.' The boys say, 'Maybe later, Joanie Maria, we got big ones.' The girls say, 'Hey, white girl, you ever do it?' They sidle up to me and feel the sleeves of my uniform.

'You a nurse or what?' asks one named Brenda.

'No,' I say, 'I am Mr Fusco's assistant and I prefer white because of the flour.' I have told her that before. I say it again (1) slowly, in case she did not understand me the other time; and (2) politely, to show that I respect her and her friends.

But Brenda appears not to have heard me.

'Hey,' she says to her friends, 'she a nurse, ever'body, a real live nurse!' Someone turns up the music and Brenda dances against me, knocking my hip with her hip. She starts to unbutton her blouse.

'I'm serious, Maria,' she says to me. 'If you a nurse, feel my heartbeat. It's real nice. You wouldn't want me to get an attack, would you? Go on, I could be sick. Stick your hand in there.'

'But I'm not a nurse,' I say.

'Sho you are!' says the girl. 'Don' lie to us, baby. You *look* like a nurse. Don' she girls? Don' she look just like a nurse?'

'She a nurse, Brenda, she definitely a nurse,' calls out one of her friends. 'And I want her to check me out, too.'

'You know somethin', honey?' says Brenda, stroking my cheek. 'You look like Tricia Nixon.'

'Your heart may be in need of professional attention, Brenda,' I say. 'I am not medical personnel. As I explained previously, I wear white because of the flour from the bakery, and of course, because of the nice, clean appearance of white.'

'Oh my. You don' like black girls, honey? That what you tryin' to say? White nurses only like to touch white girls? That don' seem right, do it? That don' seem right to me at all.'

'No, that ain' right, Brenda,' shout her friends. 'Sick people is sick people, ever'body got a right to medical type attention.'

'Maybe she like nice Spanish dicks,' says one of the boys, dancing up to me. 'You like Spanish dicks, Maria, that it? Don' mind these girls. They don' know what's good for you. A nurse got to experience life.'

'I like the Spanish as well as the Negroes,' I reply. 'I never had any Spanish dicks, however.'

The group explodes into thunderous cheering, clapping, and screaming laughter. Rapid-fire Spanish laces the air. The music goes louder. The group jumps and dances and slaps each other's palms.

'Maria,' said Brenda, 'you one sick white girl. How you ever get to be a nurse?'

'But I'm not a nurse. It's not even a hobby. I'm just going shopping.'

'She ain' goin' nowhere, Brenda,' said the other girl. 'I think she gonna fall over. Why she puttin' her head back like that?'

'Open yo' eyes, Maria,' said Brenda.

'She makin' fun of us, Brenda. She actin' superior.'

'Nobody makin' fun of me, Shirley,' said Brenda. 'No way this chick gon' laugh at *me*. Open yo' eyes, white nurse,' she shouted. 'Do like I say!'

'Maybe she tryin' to dance or somethin,' said Shirley. 'That a white dance, Brenda?'

'You wanna dance, Maria?' shouted Brenda.

I opened my eyes. 'No thank you. My name is Joan. I have to go shopping. Please. I'll be late with the shopping. Now I don't even know what to buy.'

'Your white flour too good for us niggers, is that it, Maria? Come on, ever'body, let's show Maria how to dance. She dyin' to dance.'

They are a brown sea of faces. They surround me,

bobbing, floating, grinning. Hands wash over and under me, pulling and pushing. What is that happening to my face? Some of the heads go side to side keeping time to the radio. How could it be dark already? I told Louie I would shop at two. Why can't I see? My feet are no use.

'Come on, honey,' says Brenda. 'Move yo' body.'

She puts her hands on my hips and rotates me. More cheering, clapping, screaming.

'That's it, bitch! You catchin' on real good!'

Suddenly many hands are at me. Where are my feet? I have no feet! But I have hands! I spread them out before me as I float down. I am safe on the ground. The right side of my face is cold against the pavement. My arms are stretched out in front of me.

'Now you go do that shopping, Maria,' says Brenda, 'and buy a few nice dicks in hot sauce for yo' dinner.'

'She knocked out, Brenda?' asks Shirley.

'She fakin',' says another voice.

'I'm fine, thank you,' I said.

'Why don' you get up then?' said Brenda. 'Why you staring at the ground sideways like that?'

'I can't remember if Louie said two quarts of milk or two pounds of hamburger. I know it was two of something.' I spread my fingers out slowly on the pavement. The touch of it was a lovely rough sensation, as anyone could imagine.

'I think she got a mental breakdown, Brenda,' said Shirley. 'She not right in her head. I'm gettin' out of here before the cops come. Maybe she got herself a brain tumour when we pushed her down.'

'She fell down runnin' away, Shirley, you get that straight. Did you see anybody push anybody here? I didn't. Ain' no way they gonna pin brain damage on you and me.'

By now everyone else has disappeared.

Shirley knelt down beside me.

'Maria,' she said, 'you okay? You got yourself a brain haemorrhage or anything?'

'I should have made a list but it didn't seem like a lot to remember,' I said. 'It could be he wanted both and what's confusing me is that we need two items, rather than two of one item.'

'Brenda, I'm telling you,' said Shirley, 'this is serious. We got a case of amnesia here. They goin' to get us for attempted murder.'

Brenda knelt down, too.

'Hey, Maria, you need a doctor?' she shouted.

'No, thank you.'

'You fell running to do yo' shoppin, on time.'

'You pushed me.'

Brenda jumped up and smacked Shirley on the side of the head.

'There ain' no amnesia here, you dumb nigger,' she said. 'This bitch tryin' to trick us. Listen, Maria, you fell flat on yo' own face. That's our story.' Brenda kicked my side.

'You pushed me,' I said.

'And don' let me see you 'round here again.'

'I think it was two items: two quarts and two pounds. That's where the confusion came in.'

'I'm telling you, Brenda,' said Shirley, getting up. 'We could be in big trouble.'

'And don't forget to come for the free ices,' I said. 'Louie will be putting them out next week.'

'She gives me the creeps, Brenda,' said Shirley.

Brenda kicked me again.

'You don't fool me, Maria.'

They left.

I turned my head and put the other side of my face on the pavement. I could feel the grit on my cheeks and hands. Otherwise felt light. You would think a fall like that could hurt.

I rolled over on my back, lifted my head, and sat up. By then I was certain Louie had said two quarts *and* two pounds. There was no question in my mind.

I walked the rest of the way to Gagliardi's. Mrs G. has known me a long time. She manages everything very well since Mr G. died. Mrs Constanza happened to be shopping there at the same time, what a coincidence.

'Well, aren't you a sight,' she said as I walked in.

'Fine, thank you,' I replied.

Mrs G. came out from behind the counter. She took my head in her hands. She looked stunned.

'What has happened to you, Joan? Tell me. Tell me who did this.'

'I fell.'

'It doesn't look like you fell.'

'I guess I was running. I couldn't quite recall what Louie wanted.'

'Never mind, it doesn't matter. Good day, Mrs Constanza, I'm closed.'

'That's a fine way to treat a regular customer. You haven't finished my order.'

'I'll finish it and deliver it myself by suppertime. Good day.'

'I know she's not quite right in the head,' said Mrs Constanza, 'but *dog do*? Even a mentally ill person ought to be above smearing excrement on their own face. I've never seen anything so disgusting in my life. And look at the rips in her uniform. I hope she wasn't planning to wait on customers like that.'

'I am closed, Mrs Constanza. Please leave.'

'I'm going, believe me. This is the last place I should be.'

Mrs G. closed and locked her door. She walked me to the back of the shop and pushed aside the curtain leading into her kitchenette. She has a sofa there.

'Lie here, Joan.' She eased me down. She put a pillow under my head. Covered me with the blanket that drapes over the back of the sofa.

'Don't move.'

She filled a small pan at the sink. She brought it over to me with a small towel. She pulled a stool up to the sofa, dipped the cloth in the pan on her lap, and smoothed it across my forehead.

'Does that hurt?' she asked.

'No,' I said.

'You've got a bad scrape.'

'No doubt from falling,' I replied.

She dipped the towel and squeezed it out. She wiped each cheek in a confident, circular motion of her hand. She rinsed the towel and repeated herself. The sound and touch of warm water are well known to be soothing.

'There is an odour,' I said.

'The pavement where you fell must have been dirty,' said Mrs G. 'I'm almost finished. Does your face sting?'

'No. It seems to be in the normal state of condition.'

'Good. I'm done there. May I look at your legs, Joan?'

'They're fine, thank you.'

She lifted the blanket.

'They're bruised.'

'That's unusual.'

'Don't worry. Just rest here, Joan.'

I closed my eyes.

Mrs G. dialled the phone.

'Louie, it's Geraldine. Not so good. Joan is here. I think they beat her up. I don't know. Just come down. It's hard to say. She's shaking all over. Cut and bruised, scratches. Who knows what else. I'm afraid she's in shock. Come

– 148 –

down and we'll see about a doctor. Stop shouting. You're not going to kill anyone. Stop crying. Just come down.'

She hung up.

She sat on the edge of the sofa. I opened my eyes.

'I'm very cold,' I said.

'You've been injured, Joan,' she said. She pulled the blanket up to my chin.

'When?'

'Today. You had a bad accident today.'

'Oh. That explains it. I couldn't remember whether it was two quarts of milk or two pounds of hamburger or both. I couldn't work it out. Maybe if you phone Louie he will remember. I need to talk to him. There are things I have to ask him.'

'I did phone Louie, Joan. He is coming. Right now you need to rest.'

– chapter nineteen –

Jesus measured the floors, Louie let the shade up on the door, and Angela went out to Paramus to buy dish-towels.

Before she left, however, Jesus asked me to go to the movies with him. This delayed Angela's departure.

'I would like to ask you to go to the movies with me,' he said.

'Which movie?' asked Angela. 'When?'

'Shut up, Angela,' said Louie.

'I don't know yet,' he replied. 'I have to look them up. Would you like to go?' he asked me again.

'Where?' said Angela. 'Paramus? Trenton? How far are you taking her? What time? You mean you're asking her but you don't have a plan?'

'I was planning to develop a plan,' he said.

'What would the exact plan be?' I asked.

'Can you get time off work?' Angela asked. 'You could take her to a matinee.'

'I prefer evening,' I said.

'Me too,' said Jesus.

'There's nothing wrong with a matinee, for Christ

sake,' said Angela. 'Lots of people go to the movies in the afternoon.'

'Angela,' said Louie. 'You know who watches movies in the afternoon: old fogeys like me. People with nowhere to go. I told you to shut up about it.'

Louie is rearranging things in the cases, straightening up the money.

'Jesus,' said Angela, 'do you have any idea what a movie costs these days? It's almost as much as a Broadway show. Matinee prices are cheaper, and you wouldn't have to buy her a meal. There's a theatre near my house. I could run her over and back for you.'

'She could eat with my grandmother and me,' replied Mr Perez.

'Good God,' said Angela. 'Daddy, would you kindly say something here? Don't leave me all alone with this.'

'What do you want me to say, Angela? A young man can't ask a girl to a movie? In my day that's what we did: hello, how are you, how about a movie. I realise you travel with a fast crowd – Disneyworld, social work – but some of us like to take our time. Right, Jesus?'

'Yes, sir. I was thinking of tomorrow night at six. Dinner, as I say, at my grandmother's. Then a movie.'

'I don't think you realise the seriousness of what we're dealing with here, Daddy,' said Angela.

'Good boy, Jesus,' said Louie. 'Saturday night. Now you're talking.'

'As it happens, I am free tomorrow night,' I said.

'I'll pick you up and bring you home,' said Jesus. 'And maybe you'd like to meet some friends of mine for a drink after the movie if it isn't too late.'

'A *drink*!' shouted Angela. 'Now I've heard everything! Just where do you get the idea, Perez, that Miss Pardee is a drinker? Do you hear this, Daddy? Are you listening to this bozo?'

'He sounds good to me,' said Louie.

'Perez,' said Angela, 'you may not be aware of this, but Miss Pardee's parents were both mentally ill. *She* is mentally ill. You don't need professional training at the level I have achieved to figure out that this is an individual at risk for drug abuse.'

She suddenly turned to me.

'Did my husband ever force alcohol on you, Joanie? Tell the truth, the stinking bastard.'

'No,' I replied.

'You see what I mean, Perez? You see how susceptible she is to his lies?'

'No,' he said.

'Perez, there is an unfortunate problem with alcohol in my immediate family, someone suffering from the insidious disease of alcoholism. This disease affects all family members, in particular the weak ones such as Joanie here. It's just that I wouldn't want you to be in a position to have that burden. It's different for me, I accepted oversight as part of my responsibility when Joanie came to live with my father. What's his is mine.

And, Perez: I really don't need your help looking after her.'

'Angela,' said Louie. 'The man wants to take her to a movie. That's all he wants to do.'

'Daddy, he wants to take her to his grandmother's, to a public place. Then he wants her to drink and meet people. Now I ask you.'

'Friends,' I said.

'Angela, what the hell are you getting at? It's none of your business. Didn't I tell you she's poison, Jesus?'

'Yes, sir,' he said.

'Daddy,' said Angela, 'I am talking about the fact that Joanie is not ready for this. You and I are responsible for what happens to her. Am I right? Huh? You tell me. Who is going to give her guidance? Do I have to spell it out? Let me ask you something, Perez. What are your intentions?'

'Intentions, Mrs Manini?'

'That's right, Perez. You understand English.'

'Well, I thought we would have dinner with my grand-mother, then a movie, then a drink with – '

'Perez, don't try to make an ass of me.'

'If the shoe fits, Angela. She's almost thirty years old! You want to keep her in a cage?' yelled Louie. 'She's a beautiful young woman! She's a person! He's a nice boy. You want to know what I think?'

'Tell me,' said Angela. 'I can hardly wait.'

'I think you're jealous,' said Louie. 'You're jealous of our Joanie.'

'*I'm* jealous of *her*?' roared Angela. 'You have never stooped this low, Daddy. This is incredible. Here I am trying to think of the best interests of a child and you knock me down as low as a person could get.'

She started to cry.

'I still respect you,' I said.

'Thank you, Joanie. You understand what I am trying to say, don't you?'

'Yes,' I replied.

'Listen to me, Perez,' she sniffled. 'If you touch her, if you come within ten feet of this girl, my husband and I will cut off your balls. You get what I'm saying?'

'Don't worry, Jesus,' said Louie. 'They wouldn't know where to find them.'

'That's a funny joke, Mr Fusco.'

'Sometimes in life, Jesus, the only thing left to do is laugh.'

'Six o'clock is a good time for me,' I said.

'Fine,' said Jesus. 'I'll be here at six. Do you like rice?'

'No,' I said.

'I can't stand it,' he said. 'I'll be here at six.'

'Daddy,' said Angela, 'I really think we should continue this conversation in private. You are obviously not picking up on the importance of certain things I am trying to communicate to you, and the situation is getting out of control.'

'Jesus seems to have things well in hand, Angela,' said Louie. 'Relax, please. I used to let *you* go out, didn't I? Didn't I, Ange? Come on now. I respected you, now you have to respect Joanie. Young people need a life.'

'What *kind* of life, Daddy, is my question,' replied Angela. 'Joanie is vulnerable to outside influence. She has no judgement.'

Louie threw up his hands.

'And how's she supposed to get judgement if you lock her up? Think how you used to feel, Ange, if anyone told you what to do.'

'It's not the same and you know it. I'm not mentally ill.'

She turned to Mr Perez.

'So if you are about finished here, Perez,' she said, 'you may be going. Joanie has to get back to work.'

'See you tomorrow,' he said. He slapped his leg once and Miss Forth yawned, stretched, and rose up. She followed him out the door.

Angela phoned Paramus to make sure they had the towels in green with the white stripe at the top, not along the side. They did.

'I'll be back at 6.30 for supper, Daddy,' she said. 'I'm really not kidding about this business. We've got some decisions to make.'

'Mine are all made,' said Louie.

She left.

At 6.30 Louie and I were ready for her. We had been upstairs since 5.30. Louie was in his room resting.

'Did you get the towels?' I asked.

'You'd think I was the Pentagon ordering fucking missiles. What size, Miss? Washable? Plush or flat? Forest green or lime? Wide stripe or narrow stripe? Christ!'

She threw an overstuffed paper bag on the chair.

'That is freedom of choice,' I said.

'But really,' said Angela. 'How free can you be with all that to think about?' She flopped down into a deep chair. Well, they are all deep.

'Where's Daddy?'

'Lying down until you arrive.'

'I've arrived. What's for supper?'

'Omelettes and tomato salad.'

'What kind of omelette?'

'Mushroom.'

'Good. I was afraid you were going to say cheese.'

'You don't like cheese omelettes.'

'That's what I mean.'

'You like mushrooms.'

'My mother liked mushrooms.'

'I didn't know that.'

She rubbed her forehead.

'I'm tired for some reason,' she said.

'It's your anniversary,' I said.

'Yeah. Some party, huh?' She sighed. 'I just don't know,

Joanie. Sometimes I wonder how much more I can take from him.'

'It's hard to tell.'

'The question is what I want for myself. What do I actually deserve. A woman who respected herself wouldn't end up with a guy like Benny. Am I right?'

'That's only one reason.'

'Not respecting myself?'

'Yes. I mean you could have picked him because you do respect yourself. He is handsome and intelligent. He cares about you.'

'But look what he does to me. Look how he turned out. If I thought I was worth anything I should leave him. For Christ's sake, Joanie. He's a fucking alcoholic. What am I doing married to a fucking alcoholic? I can't believe it.'

'Did your mother always like mushrooms or was it more towards the end of her life?'

'Oh, let's see.' She sighed again. 'More towards the end, I'd say. Depending on what you mean by end. A couple of years.'

'What brought it on?'

'The doctor told her to eat a lot of raw vegetables.'

'For her heart.'

'Right. And let's face it, she was overweight. She was a fat pig. God forgive me. Even the mushrooms. If she ate one she ate a hundred. I've often thought I wouldn't have fallen for Benny if she'd lived longer.'

'How long?'

'Just until I had myself figured out. Is that too much for a young girl to ask? She used to tell me, "Don't rush, Angie, don't rush so much. Marriage is for life. Once you're in you never get out." So what did I do? I rushed. I didn't think.'

'What made her say that?'

'Everybody I ever went out with, "He's wonderful, Mama, he loves me, Mama, I want to marry him, Mama." And you know what she'd say? "Angie, use your eyes and look at that boy, I'm telling you. He'll amount to nothing, he's a loser. He only wants to poke your breasts." Is that any way to talk to an eighteen-year-old girl? I didn't get a fair chance. I miss her.'

'But you told me you didn't date at all after she died.'

'I studied. That's it. That's all I did. I finished college, I got into graduate school. This was my tribute to my mother: I died. And then Benny came along. I thought a nuclear bomb had gone off. Fancy cars, roses, the best booze. And kneeling over me with that big cock dangling in my face, suck me, baby, suck me. It was enough to make a person forget social work.' She laughed. Then she lifted her face to the ceiling. 'I'm sorry, Mama.'

'So I guess the vegetable diet didn't work.'

'No. She couldn't control herself.' She looked at me. Put her hand on my knee.

'Listen, Joanie. Do you see now why I'm worried about you and Perez? You have no experience. You're the mental age of a child. I can promise you he wants only one thing.'

'But he already knows I'm buying the floors from him.'

'Joanie, he wants your *body*, he wants to *fuck* you. Get it? He wants to jam his little Puerto Rican prick into you. This is what worries me, honey. You don't know what you're talking about. He'll take advantage of you.'

She sat forward in her chair and put her hands over my breasts.

'You see what could happen?' she said.

I looked down at her hands.

'We have to talk woman to woman, Joanie,' she continued. 'In case he tries anything. First of all, sex is a beautiful experience, but only between two people who love each other. Do you love Perez?'

'No,' I said.

'Good. That's a start anyway.'

She moved her hands to my thighs. She rubbed them up and down, squeezing the flesh gently.

'This is the other thing,' she said. 'You have a beautiful figure, incredible legs. What I am doing right now, that is the last thing you want him to do.'

'I don't think anyone should unless they are asked,' I said.

'*Exactly*, sweetheart. That's what I am trying to tell you.' She held my face in her hands and drew me towards her.

'Joanie,' she said quietly, 'if you just remember that

one point you'll be fine. No one should do anything to you unless you give them permission.'

Louie came down the hall.

'Why didn't you tell me you were here?' He still sounded sleepy.

He looked at me.

'What's the matter with Joan? She looks like she's been hit by lightning.' He moved his hand back and forth in front of my eyes. 'Earth to Mars, Earth to Mars,' he said, smiling. I stared at him.

'You don't have to sit up so straight,' he laughed. 'I'm not your mother.'

'I've been trying to explain the facts of life, Daddy. I don't think you realise what you're getting her into, letting her date Perez.'

'And what, pray tell, are you thinking of, Angela? As if I didn't know.'

'Don't be an ass, Daddy. S-e-x, of course.'

'Good Lord, Angela, the child can spell.'

'That's my point, right there is my whole point: she is a *child*. What are you going to do about it?'

'I am going to do exactly one thing, Angela: nothing. You know why? Because the only place s-e-x occurs around this house is in your filthy mind. And that is where it should stay. You can't find two nicer kids than Jesus Perez and Joan Pardee. They have my blessing. Let's eat.'

'I'm telling you, she's emotionally retarded. You should be protecting her.'

'Right,' said Louie. 'Which is why I am letting her go out with the handsome young Mr Perez: to get away from you for five minutes. Every time Benny takes off on one of his toots you come over here and stir things up. Go live your life, leave us alone. I hate to think what you told her. She looks like she saw a ghost.'

'You don't teach her anything,' said Angela.

'Could we eat?' he said. 'Could we please just eat?'

He reached down and pulled me out of the chair.

'Relax,' said Louie. 'Jesus Perez is a nice boy. Nobody's going to hurt you.'

'Mushroom omelettes and tomato salad,' I said.

– chapter twenty –

Come in, Joan Marie. And Mrs Pardee. Said Mrs Johnson. My kindergarten teacher. Join our circle. We are happy to see you, aren't we boys and girls.

Yes, Mrs Johnson!

We missed Joan this morning, didn't we.

Yes, Mrs Johnson.

Sit down in that circle, Joanie: You heard the teacher.

Boys and girls, say good afternoon to Joan's mother, Mrs Pardee.

Good afternoon, Mrs Pardee.

Sit *down*, Joanie!

That's it, Joan Marie. Choose any place you like. Jeremy, will you kindly go to the snack shelf and bring Joan Marie a cookie. Good boy. We've already had ours, haven't we.

Yes!

Say thank you, Joan Marie Pardee. Take that cookie out of your mouth this instant and say thank you the way I've taught you. Show that teacher this family has *manners!*

Thank you, Mrs Johnson.

You're welcome, Joan Marie. I know you appreciate it. Would you like to stay for story-time, Mrs Pardee? Please come and join us.

I just want to hear what the story is, Mrs Johnson. I have rights as a parent. You think I have nothing better to do with my time than stand here?

Oh, yes, and I think the boys and girls would like to know the name of today's story, too. Wouldn't you?

Yes!

Mrs Johnson is in a little chair made of wood. It is a chair for a child. Therefore she sits with her knees way up, knocked together at an angle. Her feet point in at each other. While someone else might be uncomfortable, Mrs Johnson is not. 'What a pleasure it is to come to work and see all of my children.'

The children sit on the floor, legs crossed and hands neatly folded in laps. I am near the back of the semi-circle between my best friend, Margaret, and my other best friend, Jeanette. We are holding hands. Robert, Jeremy, and Paul sit behind us. They do everything together. However, they do not hold hands. There are twenty-seven children in all.

Mrs Johnson has a bright red spiral notebook on her lap. In this notebook is a list of our names. Plus other notes she might feel like writing down while we are having rest-time on our mats. After story-time. She opens the notebook.

Who will choose the book for me today? Who needs a turn today?

Me!

Me!

Me, Mrs Johnson!

She consults her list.

I suddenly realise my vaccination is sore. I rub it. Jeanette whispers: Why are you rubbing your boompy?

I whisper: I got an abaxination today. That's why I came late. That's why my mother is here. To bring me back.

Jeanette says to Margaret: Joan got an abaxination today.

They huddle in to me.

Paul has overheard.

In your rear? he enquires in a low voice.

Yes, I reply.

He taps Jeremy on the shoulder.

Joan got a big needle right in her rear today.

Jeremy closes his eyes and covers his mouth.

Pay attention, Joan Marie Pardee! Stop that talking! Do you see what's going on over there, Mrs Johnson? Those children are talking!

Yes, now, let's all be very quiet so you can hear who will pick the book. It looks as though Suzanne hasn't been my helper in a long time. Will you choose our book today, Suzanne?

Suzanne jumps up.

My vaccination is now very sore. And it itches. I am rubbing it again. I lift myself slightly up, pushing the floor with one hand. To reach properly with the other hand.

Now, go to Book Corner and pick a nice story for us, Suzanne.

Mrs Johnson places her red notebook on the floor next to her little chair and waits patiently for Suzanne. Mrs Johnson smiles.

You may talk quietly if you like, until Suzanne returns. Says Mrs Johnson to all the sweet and eager children. Who begin to poke and chatter.

Suzanne can never decide which book. Mrs Johnson has explained that each child is different, all are good. Sometimes Suzanne runs over to Mrs Johnson with a stack of books. But Mrs Johnson will not choose for her.

Take your time, Suzanne. Think about which book you like best for today, and save the others for later.

If there are too many books in Suzanne's stack, Mrs Johnson takes some of them away and leaves three. These Suzanne lays out on the floor in a line. She kneels down and shuffles the books around. I have seen this take place. But no one can say whether it will occur in the same way today.

I don't have all day, Mrs Johnson. What's taking that girl so long?

Are you almost ready, Suzanne?

My vaccination is now throbbing. I tip my little self to the left, thinking it will help if I don't sit on the right.

What does it look like? whispers Margaret.

Our heads are practically touching.

I reply: I don't know.

Jeremy says: I think it is like a chigginposk.

Let's look! says Jeanette.

I don't think I could, says Margaret. But I want to.

It will be red, says Paul. Mine got red. Come on, Jeremy. Want to see Joan's abaxination?

Jeremy's eyes are wide. He nods his head slowly.

Robert inches his way closer to Paul.

What are you doing?

We're going to look at my abaxination, I reply.

Wow.

They settle in around me. I have friends.

I did not actually realise that Suzanne had handed a book to Mrs Johnson.

Good girl, Suzanne.

I lifted my dress by rolling slightly to the left. I stretched out the elastic band of my underpants and pulled them down in the back. I felt for the spot with my finger but couldn't quite see it myself. Even when turning my head way round. Paul found it. He touched it lightly with his finger.

There it is, he said. Only a little bit of red so far. But it could get very red. I know that for sure.

The others leaned forward and peered solemnly into my underpants.

I can't see anything, said Margaret.

Yes, you can, said Paul. I did.

It really hurt when I got the needle.

That was me speaking.

I see it! Jeanette reached down and rubbed the spot with her finger. I thought it would be bigger, she said. But still, it is big.

Get Out of My Way! Get Out of My Way!

Children are tipping over, children are stepped on.

What are you doing?? Filth! Filth! Take your hands off her! Disgusting pigs!

I am gagging.

Mrs Johnson is prying my mother's fingers from Joan Marie's tiny throat. Mrs Johnson is strong. Soon, however, I am under my mother's right arm. A sack of flour. Gripped in the middle. Insides coming to the top, threatening to pour out. We are barging toward the door.

So this is what the education system in America has come to!

During my three weeks at home the vaccination healed nicely. When I returned to school, Mrs Johnson actually held me on her lap.

You've been away from us three whole weeks, Joan.

Yes, replied Joan.

We missed her very much, didn't we, boys and girls?

– chapter twenty-one –

My goodness. Jesus lives near Sycamore and South Main.

'This looks familiar,' I remark. He coaxes his van up the gentle hill which carries Unionville towards the Hudson River away from itself. We make a right on to Poplar. Then left into a driveway, fourth house. Apparently he and his grandmother live in number sixteen. Poplar was always one of the nicer streets.

'It's not a big house,' says Mr Perez. 'My mother bought it about a year before she died and I guess it was all we could afford. My father had gone back to Puerto Rico.' He looked at me gravely. 'I'm Puerto Rican.' He kept looking.

'That must be why you were worried about whether I like rice,' I said.

'I was six when my father left. My grandmother came to live with us then.'

'Twenty years ago,' I said.

'Yes. She was only sixty-four. My mother had a few problems the following year and died. She was thirty.'

'Your grandmother was thirty-four when she had your

mother, and your mother was twenty-three when she had you. Times had changed since 1890 when your grandmother was born.'

'My grandmother married late for her generation,' said Mr Perez.

'Of course,' I said.

'She was a suffragette,' he said.

'So a lot of the men wouldn't have her.'

'Later she worked for the repeal of prohibition. I hope you don't mind.'

'Your grandmother was a witness to history,' I said.

Mr Perez came around the van to my side and opened the door. He held out his hand.

'It is quite a drop from there to here,' he said.

I swung both my legs around at once. The skirt of my uniform rode up. My knees were showing. I looked at them. 'Excuse me,' said Mr Perez. He went to the back of the van. I heard him open and then close the doors. He came back with a faded towel. He laid this over my lap, covering my knees. I eased one leg down, and then the other, holding the towel against my thighs. Firmly on the ground I handed it back to Mr Perez.

'You never know when you'll need something like this,' he said. He held the towel as we walked to the house.

There is a gravel path to the front door. On either side is a small lawn of neatly trimmed grass, very green. Despite the heat, there has also been a lot of rain this summer. The path is neat, too, defined on either side by a row of carefully placed stones of different shades and shapes. There is one tree in the yard, an elm, and a modest flowerbed to the right of the door. Under what turns out to be the living-room window. Our feet crunch on the gravel. This sound does not in any way make me self-conscious for it is in the nature of gravel. I have done nothing wrong.

'My grandmother and I take care of the garden ourselves,' said Jesus.

The house is one storey, in the style known as Cape Cod: grey shingles, white trim. Bright, clear glass beams out from windows. I am surprised, believing that the family came originally from Pennsylvania. One might think they would prefer something Dutch. But then, this style of house is attractive in whatever part of the country to precise people. People who respect the type of logic our Protestant ancestors stood for.

In Salem, Massachusetts, for example, they burned witches. First they tried to drown the witch by dunking her in a lake in a specially designed bucket attached to a long pole. If the woman failed to drown like a normal person, this proved she was a witch. Therefore, she was burned at the stake. If she drowned, she was shown to be human and thus exonerated of the charge of being a witch. Not that I am against Protestants. It's just that my heart goes out to any witch who is in a no-win situation.

I adjust the flower which Jesus has brought for me. He takes a key from his pocket and unlocks the door.

'We're here!' he calls out.

Wood floors glow. One room stretches out in all directions. A small antique pine table by the door shines. Small rugs of multi-colours greet me, rejoice in my arrival. Where are the walls? What kind of music is that? A concert? Summer light pours into this house, this house is a magnet drawing light.

Here comes Miss Forth, loping across this room, two barks. She has come from a swinging door at the far end, right side.

'She likes you,' says Jesus.

She collapses at my feet and rolls over. I kneel down.

'Hello, Miss Forth.'

Today she is wearing a red ribbon.

I say: 'Today she is wearing a red ribbon.'

'Her favourite colour,' says Mr Perez.

I stand up. The swinging door opens again.

A woman is moving slowly towards me. As if in a dream. Slightly bent, she walks carefully. Placing a rubber-tipped mahogany cane firmly ahead of her right foot while the left glides to a rest beside it. She is taking each step this way: right foot, cane, left foot, rest. Right foot, cane, left foot, rest. What must be long hair, perfectly straight, auburn with highlights of blonde, is piled on her head and neatly pinned. She wears thick glasses with sturdy gold rims. Cloudy lenses. Her eyes are

perfectly blue, but look giant behind the glasses. She
has had cataracts. Miss Forth rolls back on her tummy,
sits up, and holds out a paw for this woman.

'She's had cataracts,' Jesus whispers to me.

'But my ears are perfectly fine,' she laughs. 'You don't
have to give the poor girl my medical history.'

She is thin and firm, not bony. Tall. In a young woman
who moves well this type is called 'lanky'. Svelte.

She halts just in front of me. The cane is securely
fixed to the floor. Lifting her face almost imperceptibly
towards mine, she soaks me into the blue pools behind
the glasses. She has radiant, supple skin which has
defied the allotted time. She is wearing a creamy silk
blouse with pearl buttons down the front and on the
sleeves. Also a long skirt into which the blouse is loosely
tucked. Black and burgundy print from India. Sandals.

I reach over and between my thumb and fingers gently
rub a piece of her sleeve. It has no edges, no surface. I
remember a tiny hand wandering in a canister of flour. A
cool powder lacking resistance. I have touched nothing, I
have touched the entirety.

The woman holds out her hand. By now mine are
behind my back.

'I am Lydia Enwright,' she says, smiling.

'I am Joan Marie Pardee,' I reply. This would be the
usual thing to say.

Finally she took her hand away.

'Come in,' she said, with a wave of her cane. A plush

sofa of creamy tweed awaits. 'We are so glad you could come.'

'I can't stay long,' I replied. 'In fact, I just remembered it is time for me to go.'

'Did I say something wrong, Gram?' Jesus was wringing his hands and looked as though he might cry.

'No, darling,' she said, 'you did everything just right. Joan doesn't know us yet. She wants to take her time, don't you?'

'Well,' I said.

'I knew it,' said the woman. She held her cane aloft for a moment and then brought it down slowly. She leaned forward. 'Because I am the same way.'

'Me, too,' said Jesus, letting out a groan.

'I believe the three of us have a lot in common,' said the woman. She took my arm. 'Come inside and sit down for a moment. Then if you need to leave, Jesus will take you home.'

Miss Forth padded in front of us as we walked in. Jesus ran out of the room through the swinging door.

'Do you like sherry, Joan?' the woman asked. 'I find it cures most social difficulties.'

She progressed ahead of me to a low cabinet. She bent down and opened the door.

'Perhaps you prefer something stronger. I don't know what young people drink these days. Scotch? Bourbon?'

'I'll have the one for social problems, please.'

'Ah, sherry. You have fine taste. Meaning my own, of course. I like anyone who agrees with me.'

She stood up.

'Come and take the glasses, would you?'

This is the signal to walk over to the cabinet. Hopefully I will find out when to sit down.

The glasses sparkle. A crystal eggcup atop a delicate stem. She carries the bottle, which is covered in burlap. I carry the glasses, one in each hand, pinched at the stem between thumb and forefinger. If I drop these glasses I will disappear. Thus, I take one small step and stop. Another, stop. And so on. Each time I begin with the right foot, of course. It is twelve steps to the couch where the woman is already sitting.

'Put them here,' she points. Two dark green coasters, embossed with gold lettering: L. E. 'I'm a snob when it comes to my Spanish sherry,' she says. Pouring.

'I feel the same way,' I say.

'Good,' she smiles. 'Something else in common.'

She replaces the bottle.

'Now. All you need to do is sit down. Jesus will get the dinner on for us.'

Should I go left around the coffee table, or right? The matching chair, the loveseat, or the sofa? She is on the sofa. I will go for the chair, which is to her left. Therefore I bear right, edging around the front of the coffee table, and back myself into the chair.

'Oh!' I am falling.

'Everyone gets a shock when they sit in that chair. I am so sorry. Have you landed safely?'

'Oh!'

'It really is quite comfortable when you get over that first jolt. Do you like it?'

'Yes,' I reply. I have stopped sinking. But my skirt is way above my knees. How will I lean forward to get the drink? All of a sudden she is reaching over with it.

'Here, Joan. You'll never be able to get this yourself. Anyway, it's good for me to stretch once in a while. Are you sure you're all right?'

Again I take the glass between my thumb and fore-finger. In it a rich gold liquid sways.

'Yes,' I reply.

She lifts her glass. 'I am glad to meet you, Joan. Cheers.'

I lift my glass.

'I am glad to meet you, Joan. Cheers.'

I was beginning to get the idea.

She took a delicate sip. I watched. Then I put my lips to the rim of the glass and tilted it daintily to my mouth. The sherry touched my lips and washed over my tongue. I swallowed. Streams of tingling heat caroused down my legs and out my arms. My eyes feel soft even now. The memory.

'There must be alcohol in this,' I said.

She laughed and took another, more definitive, sip.

'Indeed. I wouldn't touch it otherwise. It is a mystery

to me why young people today need all those fancy concoctions. The finest drug known to mankind is right here. Cheap and legal.' She held her glass up to the light.

'Is that the orchid Jesus gave you? I can't quite tell.'

I felt for it. My head.

'Yes.'

'In my day we wore them on the dress. Have you finished? May I offer you more?'

'I wonder what has happened to Mr Perez.'

'We all do,' said Mrs Enwright. 'We assume he went back to Puerto Rico. That may or may not be the case.'

I looked at the swinging door. Puerto Rico?

I touched the glass to my lips again. A drop of sherry swirled around my tongue and burned a path down my throat. I smiled at Mrs Enwright.

'I am glad to meet you, Mrs Enwright. Cheers.'

I lift my glass. My eyelids feel soggy.

'This is a real pleasure for me,' she said. Miss Forth wandered over to the couch and sat on Mrs Enwright's foot. Mrs Enwright dipped a finger into her sherry and stuck it out to Miss Forth.

'Do you like dogs?' she asked. 'Sally is one of the best I've ever had. She probably matters far too much but I can't stop myself.'

Miss Forth is slobbering on her grandmother's hand. She too has remarked on the alcohol content of the sherry. Gradually she slumps down and stretches out on her side, covering Mrs Enwright's feet.

I took a gulp of my sherry which is no longer burning.

'I was a lonely, unhappy child,' I said. 'A dog would have comforted me after E.J. died. I wanted someone to hold me.'

'I'm sorry, Joan. No one should grow up alone.'

'I didn't really mind. My parents tried their best, but I couldn't stop them. I almost lost my mind.'

The big eyes on the sofa are moist, looking at me.

Because of the sherry, alcohol content 17.5 per cent by volume, I am saying things I have never thought and do not mean. In front of someone I do not like. I did not realise that ethyl alcohol could put a person so out of touch with true feelings.

I somehow pushed, pulled, and urged my body to the edge of the chair. I put my empty glass on the coaster. Jesus bustled through the swinging door carrying a tray which he set down on the table at the far end of the room.

'Hello,' he called out. 'It's all ready.'

'I've got to be going,' I said. 'I just remembered that time is passing.'

Jesus stared at me and ran from the room again. By now we must be too late for the movie anyway. Mrs Enwright held out her hand.

'Help me up, Joan, and we'll go to the table. I think Jesus needs our expert assistance.'

'Jesus said we will be having a lobster's bisque,' I remarked. 'Actually, I don't know what part that is.'

'Good heavens,' replied Mrs Enwright, waving her cane in the air. 'It's just a bunch of stuff all mixed up together.' She pulled herself up and sighed. 'Oh, my. I do love cocktail hour.'

We did the twenty-two steps to the dining-room table arm in arm. As if down the aisle in a wedding procession.

The table is an art gallery.

'I will get Jesus,' said Mrs Enwright. 'You sit down.'

I pulled out a chair and sat. How else can you make a decision? Simply go to the nearest one and do it.

Through the door I overhear Jesus and his grandmother.

'She doesn't like me,' says Jesus.

'Oh, yes,' whispers Mrs Enwright, 'she likes you. But she can't know it. You're the only one who needs to know, darling. Give her time. In my opinion it is too soon to meet Freddy and Lila and that other pair tonight. I never remember their names anyway.'

'Okay,' said Jesus.

'Now come in and serve the soup. You look so handsome.'

A kiss on the cheek. The door opens.

Jesus is smiling again. Mrs Enwright sits down.

I look away to indicate that what they have been talking about is of no interest.

'I was slow heating the soup,' said Jesus. He starts to hand me a bowl of mixed-up bisques. 'Oh,' he says. 'If you move to the other chair, a place is already set.'

I look down. Sure enough. I have made a hasty decision and picked the only place not prepared.

'Hasty decisions never save time,' I said.

I wobble around the table to the other side. Jesus puts the soup in front of me. He hands the next bowl to his grandmother. Finally he sits down and takes one for himself.

I note which spoon Mrs Enwright picks up. I do the same. Like her, I slide mine into the liquid front to back, just skimming the surface. This soup is a velvet.

The forks await. One for the lamb, which Jesus mentioned as he drove. And one, I suppose, for what he called the 'garney'. I am not familiar with that type of fish but will watch how Mrs Enwright approaches it.

'So I was saying,' comments Mr Perez, 'I suppose we have missed the movie due to my slowness. We will have to meet my friends another time. I hope you don't mind.'

'Not at all,' I said. 'I have to be going now anyway.' I took another sip of my soup.

Jesus looked at his grandmother. She looked at him. This I noticed.

I tried to stand up but could not push the chair out.

'I don't have any friends,' I said. I gave up on the chair.

I passed my bowl to Mr Perez for seconds.

'So you like lobster bisque,' said Mrs Enwright.
'I didn't realise it at the time,' I replied.

– chapter twenty-two –

Here come two children. One boy, age three. One girl,
age seven. One plus one equals two. They are riding
their bicycles down Sycamore Street. Unionville, New
Jersey. President Eisenhower.

Rather, the *girl* is riding a bicycle. The boy is riding a
tricycle. It might have been red. It has a small running-
board between the two back wheels. On to this running-
board the boy places his right foot. He reaches forward
to the handlebars, grabs on, and pumps himself along
with the left foot. 'You never able to catch me, Junie!'
He is, for his age, unusually coordinated.

The running-board is cracked, bent and rusty. His foot
might break through but does not. Other children have
loved this tricycle, but left it out in the rain. We made
our purchase from the Salvation Army. We do not leave
it in the rain. Else it will immediately be given to a more
deserving child.

The girl, on the other hand, has a real bicycle, a blue
two-wheeler. Schwinn, although they cost more. Even
second-hand. Larry's American Cycle Shop. Twelve
dollars. On her seventh birthday the father says: We'll

take it. You care more about her than me, says the mother.

The girl has long blonde hair which trails behind her like a jetstream as she whizzes along Sycamore. She may ride in the street, he may not. She is too thin, she is too pale. Mrs Gagliardi and the town librarian believe she has anemia.

The boy, shaggy dark blond with wide brown eyes, is a three-foot high bear cub with thick legs. He barges and charges, falls down, struggles up. A roly-poly Christmas bundle to squeeze and toss.

'You tickling me, Junie,' he says. 'Do it again more.' This would be when the girl pretends to be dressing him. Actually she is holding him close to her heart and slyly poking his sides. Waiting for him to squeak in mock surprise and nuzzle her neck. As if he didn't know the real point all along.

It is four p.m. this particular day of bicycle riding. An autumn day, a cool day. The mother has gone shopping, will soon return. Up and down the wide and gracious tree-lined street the children ride. 'Vroom, vroom,' growls the speeding baby bear, 'I can fly.' The leaves are changing colours, the day will end, all fall down. Thinks the girl.

Oh, dear. The boy has caught a stick in the spokes of his front wheel. He is standing by the tricycle. He is kicking this wheel. The girl tilts the big Schwinn with its fat tyres into a generous arc, slows down, and approaches the sidewalk. She dismounts, punches the kickstand down with her heel, and pats the bicycle seat. She goes to the boy.

'Don't kick your tricycle, E.J., Mama will beat you.'

'This tricycle not going,' he pouts.

'We just need to take the stick out. See?' She points. 'There is a big bad stick caught in the spokes of your wheel.'

They kneel down.

'There it is!' he cries.

'Let's pull it out carefully,' she says.

That done, the boy positions himself and prepares for take-off.

'Have a safe flight,' says the girl. She buries her fingers in the thick hair of the boy. He pushes her arms away.

'Junie, I busy.' Not so he can't turn his face to hers and pucker up his lips. 'But I have kisses.' The girl leans over.

'Bye, Junie,' and he is off.

The girl returns to her blue bicycle.

Then she sees the mother marching up the street in her brown Oxfords. A paper bag of shopping is cradled in one arm, her black handbag with the gold clasp held by the handle below the bag. In the other hand, pinched at the top between thumb and fingers is a tiny white paper bag.

'Come on, E.J.,' calls the girl. 'Mother is here.'

She pulls her bicycle on to the sidewalk. Gripping the

handlebars, she waits. The boy has abandoned his tricycle in front of the Motleys'. He is barrelling down the
sidewalk towards the mother, who by now is smiling at
her children. The girl can see without a doubt that her
mother is a thin woman, and too short. Wiry, one might
say. Or 'a bundle of nerves.' In the house her eyes dart
about like a sparrow's: what's that I hear? What's that I
see? What did you say, young lady? Pouring a cup of
coffee she explains the doctor says I drink too much
coffee.

Her chestnut hair, parted in the middle, is flat against
her head. A black bobby pin on either side keeps the
hair in place. From there it hangs down to just below
her ear lobes and splits at the ends. She is wearing her
dark brown shirtwaist dress from the Army-Navy stores,
heavy cotton, nearly oilcloth. It is bound at the waist by
a thin brown belt. Perhaps this was the uniform of a
lady colonel who jabbed her pointer at war maps in
urgent meetings with Churchill. Whether this is right or
wrong is another matter: the mother is fast
approaching.

'Don't jump on me, Edward! I'll drop the groceries!'
she roars.

'I just grab you!' he shouts. Which he does. Around
her legs. Locked together they rock precariously, teeter,
and plummet to the sidewalk.

'Edward!' screams the mother. 'I *told* you!' She is on

her rear, he on her lap. Somehow the packages and hand-bag are still in the appointed places.

'I want to see what did you buy me,' he says sweetly, kissing her on the cheek.

The girl leaves her bicycle and walks over to them. She keeps her arms at her sides and waits. She is a patient child.

'Joanie, honey, take the groceries.' The mother pushes the boy off her lap and groans. 'I'm going to have one sore behind. You kids are about as much as a person can take.'

The boy inches over to his mother and lays a plump hand in her lap.

'Time to open the white bag, Mama,' he says. She slaps his hand. He pulls it away.

'Have you been a good boy?' she says.

'Yes,' he replies, 'I have.'

'You didn't ride your tricycle in the street?'

He brightens. 'Oh, no!'

I am holding the groceries. I too wish to know what is inside the little sack.

'Was Joan Marie good?'

'Yes,' says the little boy. 'She have been good since school.'

'Nobody lost their tempers?' The mother wags her finger at the boy and smiles.

'No,' he says. Looking down.

'All right. Let's see what I have here.'

The girl sits down with them on the sidewalk. She sets the groceries carefully beside her.

The mother opens the white bag and looks in.

'Well. What a surprise.'

'Me see! Me see!' The boy is squirming.

The woman smacks his hand again. He curls it under his sweater.

'You may each have one item now and one item after your supper.'

She reaches into the bag.

'Joan Marie, would you prefer a Tootsie Roll now, or Necco Wafers?'

'Necco Wafers now!' cries the boy.

'Shut up, Edward!' shouts the mother. 'It's not your turn yet!' He lowers his head.

The girl says, 'I will have the Tootsie Roll now, please.' She will eat one section at a time. Only two sections before dinner. A package of Necco Wafers will also last. She will have some of both available for several days.

'Open your hand,' says the mother. On it she places the Tootsie Roll. The girl folds her fingers over the treat. She lifts her left thigh, places her fist underneath, and lowers the thigh.

'Now, Edward,' says the mother. 'Which item would you like before dinner?'

'Necco Wafers, please,' he says quietly. The boy opens a hand and receives the roll of candy. 'Will you open them for me, Junie Marie?'

The mother replies, 'What do you say, Edward? What do you say first? Don't touch those, Joan.'

'We say thank you, Mother.'

'Good boy!' She kisses his head. 'Now Joan Marie may open your Necco Wafers.'

Mrs Motley has come out of her house. What a lovely idea to have a picnic on the sidewalk, let me get a picture of that.

E.J.'s cheeks are packed with Necco Wafers, his eyes are heavy. The bear is ready to hibernate. Mrs Motley goes back into the house and returns with her Kodak Brownie.

Smile! Come on now! Aren't you just having a great time! Joanie, she says, put Edward on your lap for me. That's it! Now Ernestine, arm around Joan Marie's shoulder. Perfect!

Some people thought there were no more photographs. Some thought the books were all gone. But this particular photograph was slipped between pages four and five of *Snow White*. *Snow White* was then placed beneath a floorboard under the girl's bed with *Little Red Riding Hood* and *Wobble Dee and Squabble Dee, Friendly Creatures from Outer Space*.

One plus one children and the mother. Not present: the father and President Eisenhower.

– chapter twenty-three –

Afterwards in the bath he played more airplanes. The tub was another runway. Blowing in the water, he made the sound of engines. I am talking here about propellers, not jets. 'Pilot is ready for take-off,' he gurgles.

My job is to bathe my little brother, not to touch him. Certain parts of his body bob up and down under the water. I no longer wash him there because of what my mother said when she once found me. However, this was towards the end of her decisions about him.

Still, that afternoon here is what I did: soap my left hand until foamy. Ask Edward John to stop slipping around. How can I get you clean if you won't stay still.

He stops, puts down his B-52. He waffles his fingers through the water like fishes and lets me slide mine between his thighs. I float my hand around and under the soft sack and the limp knob of flesh. I cup them in my palm, bouncing them, churning up the waters. I rotate them in my hand until all the soap is washed off. By then the fleshy knob is firm, and slightly longer. E.J. giggles. I giggle. Gently grasping the sack and stubby little rod, I give them a few tugs. We giggle some more.

After the bath, E.J.'s wet arms around my neck. Beads of water roll down my back, inside the bathrobe.

Wrapped in a towel, he is carried by me to our room. He is groggy now, in a half-sleep. I open my bathrobe, lie back. His bed. He kicks weakly at the towel which I unwrap. I cover him with it as I pull him down on to my stomach. He buries his face in my chest. The bundle between his legs I position between mine. My two hands pat his bottom, pushing him against me. I sway hips until I am gently throbbing and the day slips by as if all is well.

– chapter twenty-four –

'How did it go?' asked Louie. 'You look exhausted.'

By now it is one a.m. The sherry has worn off and I am back to normal. Miss Forth and Jesus have just dropped me off. Jesus and I have decided on Thursday evening for him to begin the floors, Saturday night to go to the movie and meet his friends. Freddy and Lila, Bobby and Marsha. As I understand it, they all know each other. Freddy is studying Advanced Refrigeration, Bobby owns one tow-truck and a car crusher. They used to be in the industrial lighting crowd, which is how Jesus met them. When he and Benny needed a new supply of fluorescent bulbs. Lila and Marsha are the girlfriends.

Bobby, Freddy, and Jesus did not go to Vietnam because of Benny: he knew someone who knew someone. The second someone certified them as homosexuals and passed the papers to a contact in Washington. 'No sense wasting good white boys on a slant-eye war,' said the contact. Unionville lost many Negroes in Vietnam, which isn't entirely fair.

'Why are you up so late?' I asked.

'A re-run of *The African Queen*.'

There is a banging on the door.

'Christ,' says Louie, 'who could that be?'

'Maybe it's Mrs Cunningham-Freeman,' I reply. 'She has a dinner party next Friday. She gets insomnia about a week before.'

'Who's there?' shouts Louie down the stairs.

'It's me!' shouts Angela. 'I need another cup of sugar!'

'You were close, Joan,' says Louie.

He scuffles down the stairs in his slippers.

'Thank God you're up,' I hear Angela say. 'Daddy, he tried to kiss her.'

'Angela, what are you talking about?'

'That little spic tried to kiss our Joanie.'

Louie moaned. 'Are you ever going to leave us alone?' he said.

'I was parked down the street with my lights off. I just happened to be in the neighbourhood. Someone needs to take responsibility and as usual it's me. Is she awake?'

I heard Angela pounding up the stairs. Louie ascended slowly after her.

She rushed into the room.

'Joanie! Thank God you're all right!'

She threw her arms around me. Then she held me away.

'What in the name of Christ are you wearing in your hat?'

'It's an orchid plant,' I said. 'Jesus and Mrs Enwright gave it to me.'

'You went to that woman's house like *this*?' She looked me up and down.

'Yes,' I said.

'Daddy, you let her go out in this get-up? "Joan Marie Pardee, Associate Director" '?

'Angela, if she looks so bad, why did he try to kiss her?'

'He didn't,' I said.

'Oh, be quiet, Joanie,' said Angela. 'How would *you* know?'

'At least I don't think he did. I suppose it could have slipped my mind. When did you say it was?' I asked.

'As you were getting out of the van,' replied Angela. 'Don't lie, Joanie. There is too much at stake here. I saw him offer you his hand.'

'It was quite high up,' I said.

'Obviously it was high up. I have eyes.'

'So where did he kiss her, Angela?' asked Louie. 'On her hat?'

'Prophets have always been mocked, Daddy. So I am not surprised at your attitude. Did I say he actually kissed her? Did I? No. I said he *tried*, which means there is only one thing left for the next time. And we all know what that is.'

'The actual kiss would be next,' I said. I am going to have to start paying attention.

'Exactly, honey. Which brings me to my other point. Are you two fully aware of Perez' background?'

'We're not interested in your dirt, Angela,' said Louie. 'And I am sure that is all you have to offer.'

'Daddy, if you understood human development you would know that the apple doesn't fall far from the tree. That is a basic tenet of psychology. His mother and father were drug pushers. The father flew the coop and went into hiding. The mother died of a heroin overdose a year later. A couple of beatniks. There. Now you know.'

'What do we know, Angela? What?' said Louie. 'Did I miss something'

'I can also tell you that the grandmother was very big in Seniors Against the Vietnam War. She was one of the ringleaders.'

'She wears sandals,' I said.

'You see what I mean?' said Angela. 'See? Even Joanie here noticed it.'

'What did I notice?' I said.

'Her instability, honey. Her anti-American tendencies. No wonder you look tired, out with a known anarchist.'

'I think it's my turn to see Dr Plotz,' said Louie.

'She raised that boy, Daddy, so you can bet he's got problems. Big problems. It is a very suspicious history.'

'Like mine,' I said.

'Right. And look how you turned out.'

Oh.

'Joanie,' said Angela, 'I'll try to help you get over this if I can. But it won't be easy. What did you talk about with them? Just so I know. Pay attention, Daddy. Sweetheart, was my name mentioned?'

'Angela,' said Louie, 'it is almost two o'clock in the morning. I shouldn't be listening to anything except my own breathing.'

'Just give us an idea of the topics covered, honey.'

'Well,' I said, 'there would have been the topic of dogs. Then there would have been the topic of food.'

I had decided not to point out about the sherry.

'What did she serve?' asked Angela.

'Lobsters' bisques. Mixed up and made into soup.'

Angela groaned. 'You hear this, Daddy?'

Louie is leaning back in his chair, legs outstretched, hands folded on his stomach. He yawns.

'I hear it, Angela, I hear it. I only plug my ears when *you* talk.'

'Lobster bisque *is* a soup, Joanie!' she screamed. 'Bisque *means* soup, for Christ's sake! I can't believe how you disgraced me in front of this woman!'

'I thought you said she's a no-good anarchist,' said Louie. 'Since when do you care what Sacco and Vanzetti think?'

'But that's what I said,' I replied. 'Soup. I knew it was soup. I was positive.'

Angela sighed. 'Oh, never mind, Joanie. I give up.'

'Hallelujah,' said Louie.

'*And*, just to answer your question, Daddy: the *last* thing I care about is that woman's opinion of me. I just don't like to see anyone put us down. Joanie is family, aren't you, Joanie?' She put her hand on my leg and kissed my cheek. 'I hope she fed you more than a bowl of soup.'

'Oh, yes. Pieces of cold lamb and garney fish. Except she forgot to bring out the fish. I pretended not to notice so she wouldn't feel bad.'

'What kind of fish was that again?' Angela looked puzzled.

'Garney. A meat course followed by a fish course. But, as I say, we never had the fish.'

'This is the last thing I ever thought would happen to me,' said Angela, shaking her head. 'I am part of a complete social embarrassment.'

'But is hasn't happened yet,' I said. 'I'm sure Benny will come back.'

He always does. But each time she thinks he is gone forever, like E.J.

Now someone else is banging on the door. 2:15 am. It has got to be Mrs Cunningham-Freeman.

'Who would have the nerve to show up at this hour?' says Angela. 'Probably Perez and his pals, drunk. What else? He's been gloating over his "score" with you.'

Louie has dozed off. Angela shakes him.

'Daddy, there is someone here.'

He opened his eyes. 'No kidding,' he said.

'Someone *else*,' she said angrily. '*Who is it?*' she roared at the door.

Louie got up. He went over to the window, pulled it up, and leaned out.

'Hello?' he called.

'Louie, it's me!' cried Mrs Cunningham-Freeman. 'Let me in! Please!'

'We're closed, you no-good stupid bitch! It's two o'clock in the morning!' said Louie.

'2:15,' I said.

'2:15,' sobbed Mrs Cunningham-Freeman. 'I can't sleep.'

'She is crying,' I said.

'Crying? Crying?' screamed Louie. 'We got Niagara Falls out there, Joanie. Don't talk to me about tears.'

He slammed the window and went into the kitchen.

'I'll take care of this,' said Angela. She marched over to the window, flung it up, and propped herself out over the sill.

'Do you speak English, Mrs Fancy-Pots?' yelled Angela. 'Do you? The servants no-bake-a-pastry at two in the fucking morning! Comprendo?'

The crying got louder.

'Is Joanie up there?' she wailed. 'I need my Joanie!'

'What did I hear you say? What was that? *Your* Joanie? *Your Joanie?*'

She picked up the plate from Atlantic City and threw it down at Mrs Cunningham-Freeman. She missed. Oh, no. The plate lay smashed on the sidewalk. Louie came out of the kitchen holding a butter knife. He is making a snack.

'Angela! Shut up! You'll have the police over here!'

'Gimme that knife!' she screamed. 'I'm sick of her!'

She and Louie struggled over the knife, kicking each other and cursing. I went to the window.

'Hello,' I said.

Mrs Cunningham-Freeman was sitting on the curb in her bathrobe and slippers, crying into her hands.

She looked up. She took a tissue from her pocket.

'At least I thought to bring my hanky,' she said.

'That's good,' I said.

'I can't sleep,' she said.

'Is something on your mind?' I asked.

'Bruce is having an affair with Ermie.' She blew her nose again.

Ermie is married to Mr Cunningham-Freeman's boss, Duncan Marshall.

'Are they invited to the dinner party?' I asked.

'Yes,' she replied. 'And Bruce was invited, too.'

'Maybe you should alter the guest list,' I said.

Angela lunged towards the window, shoved me aside, and threw the knife at Mrs Cunningham-Freeman.

'Your aim sucks,' sniffled Mrs Cunningham-Freeman.

'I'll let you off easy this time, girlie!' shouted Angela, 'but watch out. I know your type.'

'Angela, the sandwiches are ready,' called Louie.

'Well,' said Mrs Cunningham-Freeman, 'I could always seat Ermie next to me, and Bruce next to Winston Smith. I don't think I could stand to see her cut his meat.'

'He doesn't cut his own meat?'

'I suppose I've spoiled him.'

'Who is Winston Smith?'

'Duncan's squash partner. He's a broker with Suds Fright.' She started to sob again. 'Long-term, high-yield securities.'

'Do you still want us to make the Monte Bianco?' I asked.

'No! It's Ermie's favourite. Make a *torta di pesche alla creme*. She hates peaches.'

Mrs Cunningham-Freeman stood up.

'Thank God that's resolved,' she said. 'I'll show her.'

'Joanie!' cried Angela. 'Get in here and eat your sandwich!'

'It's time for me to eat my sandwich,' I said.

'You don't have to put it that way,' said Mrs Cunningham-Freeman.

She scuffled over to her white Mercedes.

'You're a fine one to talk, Joanie,' she said. 'At least you have a life.'

She got in, slammed the door, and sped off.

Oh. Now I remember. I remember what she is talking about: Mrs Enwright kissed me good bye.

However, one must always define 'at least' in reference to both past and present conditions.

– chapter twenty-five –

There used to be a playground on top of the hill. This is the place, as I have said, from which one can view the Hudson River, its adjacent condominiums, and Manhattan beyond.

The playground was, perhaps, two hundred feet from the fence. Which was then a sparkling construction, bright green poles and silver chainlink mesh. What remains of this playground is a slab of concrete. This has heaved and cracked over the years. Grass and weeds push through.

After school this was where we went. Some to play. Some to stand politely with hands clutched behind backs wishing to play. If you don't bother us we might ask you.

But I didn't say anything.

That's what we mean, that's good.

Soon the sun will be going down. Children trickle away. The last two are leaving. Their mothers like them home. A faint glow of light is not enough for a child waiting patiently in an empty playground.

Are you just going to stand there?

You told me to.

We don't care what you do, we're going home.

See you tomorrow?

Maybe. Maybe not.

They are gone.

But wait a minute. Here comes Joey Haskell in his black high-top basketball sneakers. Old jeans and a navy blue sweatshirt. Carrying the ball under his arm. He is fifteen. He has a job after school. Which is why he comes late to shoot baskets.

Hello, Joey. I am Joan Marie Pardee.

I know who you are.

Tap, tap, whoosh.

I won't bother you.

You don't bother me.

Tap, tap, whoosh.

Why didn't you go home with all your friends?

I don't know really.

What grade are you in?

Fourth. Mrs Crocker.

You look older. Is she any good? I had Mrs Brent for fourth. A real dumbbell.

Mrs Crocker is very good.

Tap, tap, whoosh.

Wasn't it your little brother that got killed?

Yes.

What happened to him?

He drowned on our vacation.

Too bad. You kids ought to be more careful.

Tap, tap, whoosh.

Gosh. You're very good at baskets.

Thanks.

I guess it takes a lot of practise.

Oh, yeah. Did you see me in the game against Paramus?

No.

I scored eighteen points.

That's a lot.

Darn right. And Paramus is the best in the league.

Tap, tap, whoosh.

You want to try a shot?

Oh, I couldn't.

Sure you could. Here. Hold it like this.

It's heavy. Although it doesn't look heavy.

You get used to it. Of course, I have strong hands. Go ahead. Shoot.

I'm sorry. That wasn't even close.

Don't worry. Try again.

It's harder than you would think.

People don't realise. They figure anyone can do it. Not like me they can't.

Oh! I've missed again.

That's okay. It's getting dark. You have to be pretty good to make a shot in the dark.

Tap, tap, whoosh.

You did it! Great!

Thanks. I'm going for Player Of The Year.

You'll get it for sure.

I should. I deserve it. Billy Hartmann thinks he'll win because he sucks up to Coach Hayes. But he can't hit the basket and he can't run.

Tap, tap, whoosh.

You never miss.

Not if I can help it. Try another shot. Go ahead.

I should be getting home.

I'm serious, take the ball. You could be good if you practised. You move nice. You have the legs.

Well, I guess one more would be okay.

I'll help you hold it. Maybe if I put my hands on your hands from behind and stand in close like this.

Oh.

How's that?

Well, I suppose that will make it easier.

Now, shoot! Nice try, Joan! Not bad!

It was terrible! I'll never learn!

Maybe another time.

He put his right arm around my waist. He pulled me back to him. He began kneading me. He lifted my dress with his left hand, reached under, yanked my underpants down to my knees. His fingers pushed between my legs and inside.

You like that? You like that?

He held me tighter. He pumped faster.

He moaned. He leaned his head against my back. His hands and arms went limp.

All of a sudden he lifted his head.

I've got to go. You okay?

Oh, yes.

Don't tell anyone or you'll be sorry.

What would I tell?

You better not. Anyway, you did as much as me.

He picked up his basketball and left.

My thick cotton underpants, the band now torn, fall to my ankles. I fumble for them, pull them up. I go home.

Why are you late?

I went to Margaret's for supper.

Our supper isn't good enough for you?

Later: how did you soil those panties, Joan Marie? I saw those panties. Do not tell lies. I know when you are telling me lies.

In the playground, Mother: we sat in a circle on the basketball court. I was included! We held hands and sang songs.

That's my girl! That's what I like to hear! Participation!

– chapter twenty-six –

Jesus started work Thursday. We closed early, he laboured through the night. He finished by the time we opened on Friday.

One of the few things that will last forever in America, he said, is a good floor. Miss Forth slept in the van.

There was minimal disruption to customers. Even so, we put out lovely *ricciarelli*. Almond cookies are traditional for Christmas, but some situations call for a flexible approach, regardless of season.

The floors gleam. White is perfect. Angela took me to the big Woolworth's in Paramus. I bought new plastic table cloths. Pink roses with green leaves against a soft yellow background. We are getting pretty fancy, I said to Miss Forth. Next we'll be a nationwide chain. Who knows.

Early Friday morning Louie made a nice pot of coffee for Jesus. He drank one cup and fell asleep at the table. He just put his head down. When Benny is away he works hard. All the jobs, plus office details. I got a small cushion from upstairs. He never realised who lifted his head on to the pillow. Then again, it couldn't have been anyone else.

I woke him at eleven so he wouldn't be late for Zingo's Wine Bar, a well-known East Coast tax shelter. He was meeting three carpenters there because Frankie Zingo wanted to rip out his $20,000 ceramic tile floor. Frankie says suburban stockbrokers prefer wide, antique pine floors. So he bought boards for $50,000 from an inn in Virginia where Thomas Jefferson once slept. The part I believe is that he bought them. Jesus laughed when he heard the story. He said he'd have given Frankie our floor for nothing. 'Miss Forth Slept Here,' he said. One thing about the early Presidents: I bet they didn't mind a good joke on history. Louie said someone in Virginia was getting the biggest laugh of all.

Mrs Gagliardi came in for coffee just after Jesus left.

'Hello, Geraldine,' said Louie.

'Hello, Louie,' said Geraldine. 'Congratulations. Look at this place. You put us all to shame. You trying to drive out legitimate business?'

'It's all Joanie's fault,' he replied, going into the kitchen.

'Do you like the colour, Mrs G?' I said. I did a pirouette in the centre of the floor.

'It's beautiful,' she said. 'You can't do better than white.'

'I chose it,' I said.

'Good girl,' she said. 'I saw the Perez boy loading his van outside. I hear he's nice, never mind a knockout.'

'He is a punctual worker,' I said.

'Ah. I'll say no more.' She took my hand.

'Let's find the man with the coffee. Oh dear. My favourite cookies.' The powdered sugar on top is Geraldine's downfall.

Louie came out of the kitchen with a fresh pot of coffee. We sat down.

'So,' sighed Louie. 'This is our new floor.'

'Not exactly a ringing endorsement,' said Geraldine.

'It's nice,' said Louie, sipping.

Geraldine sipped. She put down her cup. 'I think someone is not so crazy about his shiny new floor. I know Louie Fusco a long time. And I know a faker when I see one.'

'Me too,' I said.

'So you understand what I mean,' she said.

'Yes,' I replied.

'You two seem to have a secret,' said Louie. 'Why don't you let me in on it?'

'The times they are a-changing, Louie,' said Mrs G. 'That's the big news.'

'You're telling me?' he said. 'Ford pardons Nixon and you're telling me? A couple of foxes in the chicken coop. That's what's happened to America, Geraldine. Slime in the Potomac. Clerks in the low standards department. It's downhill from here.'

He stood up and walked around the new floor with his hands in his pockets. Looking down at it. He tapped the floor with his foot. He did a few quick bounces perched on his toes.

'The Democrats are no better,' said Geraldine. 'You always say they are but they aren't. They fooled you. Kennedy and Johnson did the Vietnam thing, didn't they? "Just a few troops, just a little more money, in a couple of days we win." Every politician is a crook and a liar. Somebody should keep these cookies in another room.'

'Not Roosevelt,' I said.

'Don't you believe everything your Louie says, Joan. I'm sure Roosevelt did plenty when our backs were turned.'

'Like what?' said Louie. He took a hand out of his pocket and swept Geraldine's words away. 'You can't name one thing that guy ever did to hurt this country.'

He stamped his foot.

'This floor has no bounce. It's hard as rock.'

'Roosevelt must have done something, Louie,' said Mrs G. 'It's in the nature of the beast. He wasn't perfect.'

'To me he was perfect,' said Louie.

'Look,' she said, 'the whole point about America is you take the garbage with the flowers. This means any idiot can be President. If you want Roosevelt, then you have to take Nixon.'

'Not me,' said Louie.

'It's vinyl,' I said to Louie. 'There is no rock whatsoever. Vinyl is softer than rock. I was very careful to avoid anything like rock.'

'Of course you were, Joan,' said Mrs G. 'Louie is just having a nice juicy feast of sour grapes. It's not your fault.'

'Go ahead,' said Louie. 'Name one thing about Franklin Delano Roosevelt. You can't.'

'He neglected his wife,' said Geraldine. 'If you ask me, she was the saint in that marriage.'

'Baloney,' said Louie. 'Eleanor Roosevelt had a damn good life. Joanie, all I'm saying is the old floor, the wood, it had give. It had all the dips I was used to. It took in the smell of every piece of dough I ever baked. This vinyl won't wear. It won't even scuff.' He whacked it with his heel. 'You see what I mean?' He cocked his head and cupped his ear. 'No reply. And it smells like the dentist's. Next we'll have Musak.'

'It will get dirty,' I said.

'Not like wood it won't,' he said.

'I'm sorry for making such a big mistake,' I said.

'It's not your mistake,' said Louie.

'Louie,' said Mrs G., 'have you been sleeping? *New* is in. *Clean* is the latest thing. Fresh start is the name of the game. What are you – old fashioned? Unpatriotic?'

'Yeah,' he replied, 'that's right. I'm just an old fogey. I still like Benny Goodman.'

'It was my mistake because I picked it,' I said.

'He didn't stop you, did he?' said Geraldine.

'He encouraged me,' I said.

'So there you are,' she said. 'He's as much to blame as Nixon.'

'I thought he would like the vinyl,' I said. I got up, lifted my skirt ever so slightly, and skipped around the floor a few times.

'You do more for it than he does,' said Mrs G.

'The customers will have to put in their own bounce,' I said, sitting down again. 'The vinyl itself is not a living thing.'

'Joanie, the floor is fine,' said Louie. 'I don't know what's bothering me.'

'You miss Roosevelt,' I said.

'Let me ask you this,' said Geraldine. 'What do you do to these cookies?'

'A little extra orange,' replied Louie.

'Hmm,' she said.

'Less than half a teaspoon,' he said. 'A teaspoon would be more than you need.'

'I put the sugar on top,' I said. 'Not too much, not too little. I'm sorry about the floor, Louie.'

'The past is past,' said Geraldine. 'Louie will get used to the floor.'

'I will not,' he said.

'Come on, be a sport,' said Geraldine. 'We got used to our new neighbours here in Unionville, didn't we? Side by side with muggers and rapists. The great melting pot.'

'That's Nixon's fault, too,' said Louie. 'They cross the river from Manhattan in a recession.'

'You need direction, Louie,' said Mrs G. 'A new purpose in life. Pessimism is un-American. Myself, I've got a good idea where to begin.'

She licked powdered sugar off her fingers and reached for another cookie.

'Would you like a few more?' suggested Louie. 'Don't hold back.'

'She thought you'd never ask,' I said.

That Geraldine. She really perks up my sense of humour.

– chapter twenty-seven –

Two days later. Saturday. Angela has agreed to let me go out with Jesus.

On one condition: that I not wear my uniform, cap, and name badge due to her unresolved low self-esteem. I agreed and must therefore put these items on when she is not looking. When will Benny come back? This is day thirty-two. Angela has increased her sessions with Dr Plotz to seven per week, not including emergency phone calls. I am not sure who calls whom.

One other condition: no movie. And meeting the friends in a well-lighted public situation, preferably a baseball stadium. I tell her he did not invite me to the World Series. She calls him and says I do not see well in the dark. On doctor's orders I am not to go to movies. Or bars. Or discos. Or S & M parlours. 'I know what goes on in sub-culture, Perez.' She enquires: Where did you have in mind, what are their names, have they worked through their pre-oedipal conflicts. She hands me the phone.

'Hello,' I say.

'Hello,' says Jesus.

'How are you?' I say.

'Fine,' he says.

'How did it go at Zingo's?' I say.

'The boards were too warped to use.'

'Had you already ripped out the tiles?'

'Yes,' he said. 'And the boards were all labelled "Product of Brazil, 1970" on the back.'

'Oh dear,' I said.

'Frankie wasn't too pleased,' said Jesus.

'I thought Brazil was a military dictatorship,' I said.

'A lot of the trees must have been shipped to Virginia,' said Jesus.

'Thomas Jefferson would have died by then,' I said.

'Exactly,' said Jesus.

'What's Frankie going to do?' I asked.

'Will you get to the fucking point?' screamed Angela. 'Where and what time? Where and what time? We're talking about you going out! I don't have all day!'

'Where and what time?' I asked.

'Do you mean where and what time are we going out?' asked Jesus.

'I think so,' I replied. 'I'll just ask to be sure.'

I turned to Angela.

'Just to be sure,' I said, 'do you mean where and what time are we going out?'

'Good Lord!' shouted Angela. 'I'm in a looney bin!'

She grabbed the telephone.

'I want to know where he is taking you tonight so I can evaluate the situation!'

'Perez, listen up. This child is a nutcase. You dig? *I* decide what's what.' Pause. 'Oh. So you heard me. All right. Yes. I'm sure that will be fine. Good thinking, Perez. Pick her up at eight. I'll be here at 7.45 to iron out any last-minute details.'

She handed me the phone.

'He's taking you to grandmother's again. The friends will meet you there. I approve.'

'Hello,' I said. 'She approves.'

'Hello,' he said. 'She approves.'

'We're all going to your house,' I said.

'I'll ask everyone to meet at my house,' he said.

'Fine,' I said. 'I'll see you at eight.'

'I'll pick you up at seven,' he said. 'Is that all right?'

'Good-bye,' I said.

'I hope we have a nice time tonight,' he said.

'Fine,' I said.

'Would you like a corsage?' he asked.

'I already have one,' I said.

'So. I guess we've covered all the details. Can you think of anything else?'

'Give me a minute,' I said, and hung up.

Angela was sitting in the chair staring at me.

'The first thing I have to teach you two is how to communicate. You call that a conversation?'

'I understood everything he said,' I replied.

– 214 –

'Understanding is only one part of communication, Joanie,' said Angela. 'Saying something worth listening to is the other part.'

'Oh,' I said. 'I thought conversation could be about anything.'

'Christ no, Joanie. That's your whole problem. It has to be about *something*. No one would want to be part of that conversation you and Perez just had.'

'I thought we worked out the arrangements nicely.'

'No, sweetheart, it was dreadful. You thought it was nice because that is all you are capable of. For now anyway. Don't look so discouraged! I said for now. It will get easier.'

She put her arm around me and pushed my head on to her shoulder.

'I'm not discouraged,' I said.

'Yes, you are,' she said.

'Oh,' I said.

'You're discouraged because you see how far you have to go. But you've got to start somewhere, Joanie. It's just that most of us are lucky enough to be where we should be for our age. But, Joanie, it's not fair to begrudge others their good fortune. It's no one's fault but your own if you have so much catching up to do.'

'I try to be fair,' I said. 'I try to balance everything out in my mind and give equal weight to all possible sides. One-two-three here, one-two-three there.'

'You're not trying hard enough,' said Angela.

'I thought that was an actual conversation,' I said. 'I thought it actually occurred.'

'No, honey, I'm sorry. It didn't. It really didn't. It meant nothing. Neither of you said anything that mattered.'

'Maybe I shouldn't go,' I said. 'The whole thing will be about conversation.'

I relax my head on Angela's shoulder. Everything will be all right. She will explain the best way to proceed.

'Perhaps I could exchange ideas,' I said. 'But I'm not sure which ones.'

'No, honey. Ideas are out of the question,' she stroked my hair.

'I'm almost positive I'm not going,' I said.

'I think maybe you should just try to be yourself,' sighed Angela. 'I know that doesn't sound very appealing, but it's the only thing I can think of. Our real problem is what the hell to put on you. The only thing you ever wear is this nurse get-up.'

'I could always branch out,' I said. I smoothed the skirt of my uniform. 'But I'm used to this, I like this.'

'No, you don't,' said Angela. 'It's just a defence.'

'I like the way it feels,' I said.

'That doesn't mean it's good for you,' said Angela. 'You can't spend your whole life governed by feelings. If we are going to get you out on a date, then you are going to have to start thinking about what's *right*, not what you feel.'

'I don't think I should go,' I said. 'I'm almost positive.'

'You're going,' said Angela.

She kissed my forehead.

'Thank you, Angela,' I said. 'This means a lot to me.'

'Don't grovel, sweetheart. Nobody likes a loser.'

– chapter twenty-eight –

What with a special occasion coming up, I am suddenly remembering Angela's birthday last year. Benny took her out for lunch and invited me along. We went to a diner near a similar highway. 'Four Brothers Acropolis Family Restaurant.'

Benny and Angela had a couple of drinks in the car. No more than three apiece. Probably five. We pulled over frequently. They had to kiss. Once they got out and went to the bathroom beside the road. Angela couldn't stop laughing because Benny put some on her foot.

We sat in a nice booth. Benny sang Happy Birthday to You. Angela sang Happy Birthday to Me. In unison. I kept time with my hand. Then I took my cap off and placed it next to me on the bench. Angela and Benny sat opposite. So let's order, said Benny. I unfolded several sections of the huge menu. Propped this in front of me like a movie screen.

'Isn't the selection marvellous?' I said.

As there was no reply I peered over my menu.

Angela and Benny had placed their hands under the table. While kissing. Their mouths roamed across the faces, returned to lips, roamed. Then suddenly plunged into each other.

Benny smoothed his hands over Angela's breasts, cupping and squeezing them. Rolling his tongue around her mouth and down her chin. I couldn't decide whether to have the tuna salad platter or not. I slid down, looking under the table. Benny's hand was moving underneath Angela's skirt. She was rubbing and pressing between his legs. I sat up.

Angela, too, was using her tongue. Her eyes were closed. His eyes were closed. Close your eyes when you kiss.

Angela put her hand on the back of his neck. Pulled his face against hers. She bared her teeth, bit his tongue, lips. He moaned: Grab it, Grab it.

She kept shifting in her seat. I bent to the side. Looked under the table again. Her legs were splayed apart. Benny's hand up and down under the skirt, pushing, digging, slapping.

Oh, God, she said. Oh, yes. His legs too are stretched wide open. Between them Angela pulled and kneaded rapidly at a massive bulge.

I sat up. I realised two items, mentally: first, there is an insistent throb rising up between my legs, pushing doggedly at me whichever way I turn. A tightening, tingling sensation races down my thighs. I must have drunk some sherry without personal knowledge. Second, several waitresses are amassed behind the counter nearby. Four, to be exact.

'Do you think she's going to come?' says one.

'This is incredible,' says another.

'I've waitressed in a lot of places, Stella,' says the third. 'But this I've never seen.'

'To think I almost took the day off, Monica,' says the one called Stella. 'I'm never taking a day off again.'

'Do you recommend the tuna salad platter?' I asked.

'We're not taking any orders now, sweetheart,' said Stella.

Angela moaned.

'Christ, I think she's there, Stella,' said Monica.

Angela gasped, cried out, fell back against the seat. Benny pulled her into his arms.

'Lucky her,' sighed Monica.

The other two waitresses have run to the opposite end of the counter. They are wolfing down cheese Danishes and coffee. White as sheets.

'They don't like this line of work?' I asked.

'Would you believe,' said Stella, 'those two just got off the boat from Greece. First day on the job, they don't speak a word of English.'

'I have a feeling they're going back,' said Monica. 'They have a different culture over there.'

Stella pointed at Angela and Benny. Who are stumbling towards the Ladies and Gentlemen. They go into Ladies and slam the door. 'Friends of yours?' she says.

'Oh, yes,' I said.

'I figured,' said Stella. 'That's not the kind of thing you'd do in a booth with a stranger. Generally speaking.'

'Live and learn,' said Monica.

Angela and Benny came back and sat down. Benny was carrying his flask. They each took gulps. He put it back in his pocket.

'Well, now,' said Monica. 'Are we ready to order?'

'Happy Birthday, Angela,' I said.

'You're not kidding,' said Stella.

Angela took my hand. Kissed it, massaged it.

'It's really good to see you, Joanie,' slurring. 'It means a lot to us.'

'Let's order,' said Benny. 'Christ, I feel terrific.'

'No wonder,' said Stella. 'That was some hard-on you had, buddy boy.'

'You want to get us fired?' said Monica.

'I beg your pardon?' said Benny.

'We've been trying hard to get your order sir,' said Monica. 'That's what she meant. If you want my opinion, I recommend the hot turkey plate. Gravy, mashed, peas. The works. All homemade.'

'I doubt it,' said Benny. 'Next time mind your own business.'

'Yeah?' said Stella. 'Next time do it on on Forty-Second Street if you want privacy. This is a restaurant.'

'Restaurant?' said Benny. 'It's a fucking dump, you whore!'

'My, my,' said Stella. 'Hear how we talk to a lady.'

'I'll have the tuna salad platter,' I said.

'We're recommending the hot turkey,' said Monica. 'You heard me.'

'She wants the tuna!' yelled Angela. 'Get her the god-damned tuna! You're the waitress. Christ, Benny. What kind of place is this?'

'Too good for you,' said Stella. 'Beat it. Get your hot cunt out of my diner.'

'Benny!' screamed Angela. 'Did you hear what she said to me!' Angela burst into tears. Collapsed sobbing on to the table.

'Who's your supervisor?' yelled Benny.

'Bridget Bardot,' said Stella. 'Will I get her for you?'

Benny grabbed Angela's arm and pulled her out of the booth.

'I'm going to report you,' he yelled. Then swept the salt, sugar, silverware, and napkins off the table top.

'Temper, temper,' said Stella.

'I want to eat,' cried Angela.

'I'd like to cancel my order,' I said.

'Fine. Cancel one turkey, Stella,' said Monica.

Benny dragged Angela through the door. I slipped out of my seat. Put my cap on.

'Thank you,' I said. 'What a lovely lunch.'

'I'd find some new friends if I were you, honey,' said Stella.

'You're not me,' I replied, and left.

– chapter twenty-nine –

'Hello, Jesus,' said Louie.

'Hello, sir,' said Jesus.

As usual Louie is in his light blue cotton pyjamas with the dark blue piping. Plus bathrobe and slippers. This is how I know it is time for coffee, dessert, and the evening news. Thanks to Louie I no longer have to tell time, which is a relief after so many years. Louie's wife Mildred gave him the pyjamas in 1958.

Louie sits in his chair, head resting against the back. This, too, is typical, and why not. Stretching out. The robe falls just below his knees. The pants of the pyjamas, hiked up to mid-calf, float around his legs.

'So, my good man,' says Louie to Jesus, 'how about a nice cup of coffee and a little rhubarb pie?'

'Well, that's just great,' replied Jesus. 'A nice night we're having.' Cough.

'Are you sick?' I say.

'No,' he says.

'The boy wants food, Joanie,' says Louie.

'We won't be able to stay long, sir,' said Jesus.

'And what's that supposed to mean?' says Louie. 'You got something better to do?'

'Angela,' I said.

'Oh, yes,' said Louie. 'My charming daughter thinks you are coming at eight.'

'Yes, sir,' said Jesus. 'That is why I am here at seven.'

'So we will be going prior to that particular arrival,' I announced.

'Wise children you are,' sighed Louie. 'I'd leave too if I wasn't in my best pyjamas. Joanie wants to buy me a new pair for Christmas, Jesus. Do you think I need a new pair?'

'No, sir, I would hold on to the ones you have.'

'Thank you, Jesus,' said Louie. 'One thing I like in a young man is honesty.'

'I didn't mean you should throw this pair away,' I said. 'I don't believe in a course of action on all subjects.'

'As I say,' remarked Jesus. 'This certainly is lovely weather we're having, day in day out, simply day after day.' Cough.

'Are you sick?' I said.

'No,' he said.

'Louie, I think he's sick,' I said.

'He's not sick,' said Louie.

'Oh,' I said, 'I thought he might be sick.'

'He isn't,' said Louie.

'You're not sick after all,' I said to Jesus.

'That's a relief,' said Jesus. 'Because I was really looking forward to spending the evening with you.'

'I think I may be catching what he's got,' I said to Louie.

'No you're not,' said Louie.

'I'm almost positive,' I said.

'You're not sick,' said Louie.

'That's a relief,' I said, 'because I was really looking forward to spending the evening with Jesus.'

'It's beginning to sound like you two won't take me up on my offer,' said Louie.

'I guess we better not, sir,' said Jesus.

'I'll give you one more chance, Jesus,' said Louie. 'The best rhubarb pie in North America.'

'Maybe we will,' I said. 'We're in no rush. Maybe we won't even go. You never know.'

'We're going,' said Jesus.

'Louie,' I said, 'I've been thinking. Maybe we'll have the pie and coffee another time. If I'm ever in the neighbourhood again.'

That was a joke.

'Isn't she something,' Louie said to Jesus.

'Yes, sir,' said Jesus, 'that's why I'm here. I haven't laughed this much in years.'

'By the way,' said Louie, 'did I ever tell either of you about my first date with my wife, Mildred?'

'No,' said Jesus.

'Yes,' I said.

'Well, ' said Louis, 'we both lived in Hackensack. She was seventeen, I was nineteen.'

'We'd better sit down,' I said to Jesus. He looked at his watch.

'Her father had a scrap metal business,' said Louie.

I said to Jesus: 'Tell me when it is 7.25. We will leave promptly at 7.25.'

'Angelo Sorrentino was his name,' said Louie.

Jesus said: 'Freddy and Lila and Bobby and Marsha aren't coming over until 8.30. But my grandmother wanted a little time with you and me.'

'How much time?' I said.

'A small amount,' said Jesus.

'A big fat guy with a cigar,' said Louie. 'I should have known Mildred would be an eater.'

'Is your grandmother lonely?' I said to Jesus.

'She likes you,' he replied.

'That explains it,' I said.

We sat down.

'Mildred Sorrentino she was then,' said Louie. 'Soft chestnut hair in a nice little bob, deep brown eyes. Beautiful. Also she had other prominent features which I am too polite to mention.'

'Oh my God,' said Jesus.

'Even if you two won't have any of my pie,' said Louie, 'what about me? Have you forgotten about Louie?'

Jesus jumped out of his chair. 'No, sir!' he said. 'May I get you some pie and coffee?'

'How did you guess?' said Louie.

Louie watched Jesus go into the kitchen. He is wearing starched, stiff blue jeans and a yellow T-shirt, sleeves rolled up over biceps. Which bulge and flow under the sleeves due to the strenuous nature of the carpet business. On the T-shirt is a blue, red, and green abstract print of an oak tree. In an arch over the tree is written: 'From An Acorn The Mighty Oak.' The small gold ring in his left ear has been polished, his hair washed.

The pony tail rests softly between his shoulder blades. He is wearing work boots. Like a lumber jack he executes one large stride after another into the kitchen. Each will leave a lasting impression. The Mighty Oak is a bar in Trenton that caters to the demolition crowd (Bobby).

Suddenly Louie sat up in his chair, pulled his robe tight against his chest, and kicked straight the legs of the pyjamas.

'Get me that blanket over there, Pardee,' he said. 'All of a sudden I'm cold. How is he not cold with just that little T-shirt on him?'

I got a small quilt from the back of the couch. I walked over and started to drape it across Louie's back and shoulders. He took it from me.

'I'll do it,' he said, and laid the quilt across his knees. He tucked his white ankles into each other. Shielded by the quilt, they disappeared under the chair.

'That's better,' he said.

'I'm not going,' I said.

'Of course you're going,' said Louie.

'I know my own mind,' I said.

'And you know you're going.'

'How can you be sure?' I said.

'I'm not blind,' he said, smiling.

'Why are you smiling?'

'Because of you,' he said.

'I thought so,' I said, 'but I'm still not going. You can't make me.'

'All right, stay here and play cards.'

'No.'

'See what I mean?'

'Are you warm enough?' I asked.

'Yes,' he said.

'What are you going to do after we leave?' I said.

'Are you trying to pry into my personal life, Pardee?' asked Louie.

'Yes,' I said.

'If you must know,' said Louie, 'I am having a bunch of geisha girls up here to massage me.'

'I thought so,' I said. 'But I am staying in only if I want to, not because of you.'

'Good,' he said. 'But you'd be making a mistake to play cards tonight, seeing as how I'm on a winning streak the last three times.'

'You cheated,' I said.

'So? You never cheat?'

'No.'

'Only when I'm not looking, you mean.'

'I'm going out. I know my own mind. You can't stop me.'

'Where are the cups?' called Jesus.

'Second cupboard east of the stove,' called Louie.

'I don't see them,' said Jesus.

'Should I stay or go?' I asked Louie.

'Behind the tomato paste and Corn Flakes,' called Louie.

'Oh,' called Jesus. 'I was looking in the cupboard with the plates and saucers.'

'I keep the cups separate,' called Louie.

'No one can do anything about it,' I yelled.

'I thought you just said you know your own mind,' replied Louie.

Jesus came out of the kitchen carrying a tray. 'Here we go,' he said to Louie. 'You can put this right on your lap.'

'Well, well,' said Louie. He sat up and held the tray on his lap, both hands gripping. 'Just what I had in mind.' He took a sip of coffee. 'You do all right for a mere sapling,' said Louie.

'I'm good at coffee,' said Jesus, sitting down again.

'So Mildred Sorrentino worked in her father's scrap metal business,' said Louie. 'She had a high school diploma, I had a high school diploma. In other words we were big shots.' He took a bit of pie.

'I drove a truck, odd jobs, mostly fruit and vegetables. Delivery all around. I could lift and haul anything. For example, look at me hoist this cup.' Held high. 'You get the picture.'

'How did you and Mildred meet?' I asked.

'I thought he told you the story before,' said Jesus.

'That was before,' I said.

'Oh, in that case,' said Jesus.

'Some guy had a load of junk he wanted me to sell for him,' said Louie. ' "No problem," said I. Because everyone had heard of Sorrentino. So I knew where to go. What I didn't know was he had this beautiful daughter running the place.'

'What a surprise,' said Jesus.

'You're not kidding,' said Louie.

'7.15,' said Jesus.

'Ten minutes,' I said.

'I am really looking forward to spending the evening with you,' said Jesus.

'Don't interrupt,' I said.

'Is Mr Sorrentino around, I say to this girl. Who, I didn't know at the time, is actually my wife. "I've got some stuff in my truck I want him to look at." So she says, "He's out, I'll look at it for you." "But I need a price today," I said. "I'll give you a price right now," she says. I say to myself, a woman can give me a price on a heap of scrap? It wasn't like it is today. There was no such thing as the Modern Woman.'

'So imagine my surprise when this young girl says to me, "We won't give you much for that." How much, I said. "Ten dollars," she said. Ten dollars! I was sure what I had there was worth twenty-five. "Forget it," I said. "I'll wait for Mr Sorrentino." "That won't do you any good," she said. "If I say ten, it's ten." "You're telling me ten?" I said. "Right," she said, "you heard me." "This stuff is worth twenty-five minimum," I said. "I don't care what it's worth to you," she said. "To me it's worth ten." Can you imagine?'

'That's amazing,' said Jesus. '7.20.'

Louie chewed some pie and took a gulp of coffee.

'Five minutes,' I said.

'This is probably boring you kids to death,' said Louie.

'Oh, no,' said Jesus.

'Oh, no,' I said. '7.21.'

'Good,' said Louie. 'Because I'm going to tell it anyway. Those are my chairs you're sitting in. Which gives me certain rights.'

'Did you ask her out right away?' I said.

'Hell no!' he said. 'I had my pride. Ten dollars and I'm going to ask her out? I couldn't stand her! Later I found out that's the first sign of love.'

'Yes, sir,' said Jesus. 'Love at first sight.' Cough.

'So I said, "Forget it, I'll take it to someone else." "Suit

yourself," she said. "But you won't get more than ten."
And you know what ? She was right.'

'Amazing,' said Jesus.

'I went to two other guys. One offered me eight, one
offered me ten. And I thought I was smart.'

'You were just starting out,' I said.

Louie took the tray off his lap and placed it on the
floor. He took his feet from under the chair, covered
them with the blanket, and stretched out.

'Well, I guess it's that time,' said Jesus. He began to
get up.

'That's how it all started,' sighed Louie. 'I went back
to Mildred and took her ten dollars. "You're not much
of a business man," she said. "You drive a hard bargain,"
I said. She said, "So ask me out." Let me assure you she
was the only girl who talked like that in 1920.'

'7.25,' said Jesus, sitting down.

'Is your watch fast or slow?' I said to Jesus.

'In between,' he replied.

'Then we're fine,' I said.

'Maybe if you get up slowly and get your coat,' he
said.

'I'm not wearing a coat,' I said. 'Don't be ridiculous.'

'Oh,' said Jesus.

'My friends told me to forget her,' said Louie. 'Pure
poison, they said. She'll want to wear the pants. You'll
never be able to do anything right by that girl, that girl
has no respect for the way things are between a man

and a woman. They had in mind I should date Mary O'Leary. An Irish immigrant! Whoever heard of such a thing! She'll listen, they said, she'll take orders, she'll keep quiet. With Mary O'Leary you'll be boss! Irish? I said. You must be kidding!'

'That's nice,' said Jesus.

'Very,' I said.

'They knew what they were talking about, I'm sorry to say.'

'So,' said Jesus, slapping his thighs. '7.28. Off we go.' He stood up.

'After you,' he said.

'After you,' I said.

'I did everything wrong,' said Louie. He shook his head. 'Would you believe on that first date I tried to put my hand down her blouse?'

We sat down.

'Maybe if you gave a few more details I could picture it,' said Jesus.

'The details aren't important,' I said.

'Boy. Did I feel sick,' said Louie.

'Take your time, sir,' said Jesus. 'Just say whatever comes to mind.'

'I'm a basically nice guy, right?' said Louie. 'So I take her to the pictures. Such as they were in those days. Then I take her for an ice-cream soda. No booze whatsoever. A pleasant, respectable evening. Mind you, that didn't stop her being obnoxious all evening. In the pictures we changed seats three times. "This one's too close, this one's too far away, this one's too hard." Okay, so around we go. Who am I to say shut up on the first date? No. I was saving my talents for the end of the night.'

'Then what happened?' gagged Jesus.

'At the soda fountain she orders a chocolate ice-cream soda. I order strawberry. The chocolate's too rich, she says, after one sip. You should have taken me to Ferrara's. They make it nice. I ask Jimmy behind the counter, can you make this with a little less chocolate for the lady? Off he goes. Then she turns to me and says, I changed my mind, I'll have strawberry. Here comes Jimmy with the chocolate. Jimmy, I said, she wants strawberry. Are you trying to be funny? says Jimmy. Jimmy, I said, this is not funny. Now, you kids have to remember I'm paying for all this. I was no fancy chief executive in those days like I am now.'

'I am getting a headache,' I say.

'So,' said Louie, 'she took a sip of the strawberry and said, "In Ferrara's they use real strawberries." '

Jesus buried his face in his hands. 'Oh, no,' he moaned.

'Yeah,' said Louie. 'Can you believe it? I swore I'd never take her out again, to hell with her. It's Mary O'Leary for me.'

'Then what happened?' asked Jesus. 'Just relax as you are talking, Mr Fusco, and you'll be all right.'

'You want to know what happened, Jesus?' said Louie. 'The same thing that happened for the next forty years.

We got outside Jimmy's. She took my arm, put her head against my shoulder, and said, "I've had a wonderful time. Thank you, Louie." I nearly died! Naturally I said it's been wonderful for me, too. I kissed her hair. Don't ask me to explain it. But at that moment she was all I wanted in the whole world.'

Jesus and I said: 'We know what you mean.'

'Are you going to faint?' he asked me.

'No,' I said. 'I'll just close my eyes for a little while.'

He put his hand on my head. 'I'll be right here,' he said.

'We walked to her house like that,' said Louie. 'Arm in arm, not saying much. I told her all about the mark-ups on fruit and vegetables, how it works, the whole system. Isn't that interesting, she'd say. Aren't you something, I never knew what went on. That type of comment. By the time we got to her house I was on the moon. She loves me, she loves me! I was shaking like a leaf. We stood under the glare of the bare bulb on her porch. "Thank you for a lovely evening, Louie," she said. "I really mean it." She held her hands together behind her back and kind of bowed her head. All of a sudden she looked shy. Unbelievable! Mildred Sorrentino shy! She's standing there in this beautiful cream-coloured blouse, ruffles on the sleeves, ruffles up and down the front, gaga for *me*, Louie Fusco. A very expensive blouse, mind you. Even I could tell that. Sorrentino was a shrewd operator, plenty of bucks.'

'Then what, then what?' asked Jesus.

'So then I threw myself at this blouse, Jesus. Just like that. I tried to jam my hand down into the high ruffled collar of this $20 blouse. I nearly choked her. And ripped off the top button in the process.'

'Oh my God,' said Jesus.

'I can't look,' I said.

'Oh my God is right,' said Louie. 'She screamed bloody murder and hit me so hard I had a black eye for two weeks. All the lights upstairs went on, her father opens the window and yells, "What's going on down there, who's down there?" She's screaming at me, "You Italian scum, what do you think I am, you stinking bastard, I never want to see you again, I hope I die first," etc., etc. Then she kicks my legs, bursts into tears, and runs inside the house.'

'And you were married for forty years?' gasped Jesus.

'Forty-three,' said Louie. 'You have to start somewhere.'

'Anywhere,' I said.

'Yes,' said Louie. 'Forty-three wonderful years.'

He raised his face to the ceiling. 'Oh, Mildred, weren't those the days.' He laughed. 'And in no time we worked out the particular area in question.'

'I can't imagine how you got together after that,' said Jesus.

'I went out once with poor Mary O'Leary. Already a pale old bore at sixteen. Well, I suppose anything would

– 237 –

have been pretty dull after that night with Mildred. I reached the conclusion that no one would ever love a big oaf like me. I decided to concentrate on saving for my own truck. I couldn't eat, I couldn't sleep.'

'She'll come back,' I said. 'Don't give up.'

'Sure enough,' said Louie, 'a month later I'm loading crates of oranges from Florida to go to Connecticut. I turn around and there's Mildred. "Mildred!" I said. "You're damn right, Louie Fusco," she said, standing bold as can be with her hands on her hips. "Why haven't I heard from you? You think I'm going to wait forever? You look like you could use a good meal." So that was that. I never had a dull moment with Mildred Sorrentino for the next forty-three years. Mind you, most of the time I couldn't stand her. But I always loved her.'

Jesus collapsed back into the chair.

'This is exhausting,' he said.

The room was spinning.

'Are you sick?' asked Jesus.

'No,' I said. 'I'm just having such a wonderful evening.'

'Me, too,' said Jesus.

'I suppose you two want to be on your way,' said Louie.

I looked at Louie. 'I've decided to go, no matter what you say.'

'Mildred and I won't wait up. We trust you,' he said.

'Thank you, sir,' said Jesus.

When we got outside we looked both ways but Angela was nowhere in sight.

Jesus took my hand. 'I think you are beautiful,' he said.

My heart raced. 'I think you are, too,' I said. 'Well, handsome, I mean.'

Then I told Jesus I forgot something and went back up.

Louie didn't hear me because of tiptoeing and pausing on each step. He was in the chair with the photograph album opened on his lap. A box of Kleenex on the arm of the chair.

I closed my eyes again, and felt the way down our darkened staircase into the night.

– chapter thirty –

'Hello,' I said to Mrs Enwright. 'I am Joan Marie Pardee.'

She has taken my hand in her hand and smiles with those grand saucer eyes.

'Yes,' she said. 'I remember.'

'How charming,' I said.

'I suppose you want another glass of my Spanish sherry,' she said. 'No doubt you have waited all week for this moment.'

Still holding my hand she leads me carefully into the bright room. Windows are open, summer softness floats through like a genie from his lamp. Jesus has disappeared into the kitchen. I do not see Miss Forth.

'I do not see Miss Forth,' I say.

'Nor do I ,' says Mrs Enwright.

'We have been left alone,' I say.

'Phooey to them,' she replies. 'They don't know where the fun is. Sit over there. I'll get the libation.'

I tumble into the chair.

'Perhaps there is such a thing as hope,' I say. 'It is always possible.'

Grasping the bottle of sherry, Mrs Enwright turns to me.

'Why do you say perhaps?'

'Verisimilitude,' I say. 'This is my biggest problem.'

'Quite,' says Mrs Enwright. 'In my experience there is nothing else worth worrying about.' She ambles toward me. She places the bottle on the coffee table and returns to the cabinet for glasses.

'I should have gotten up to help you,' I say.

'Not at all,' she replies, sitting again. 'I'm only eighty-four and only half blind.'

'In that case I'll pour,' I say.

'Thank you.'

No more delicate stemware. Tonight we have copious crystal goblets, sparkling, radiant, shimmering. Which put me in mind of Henry VIII. Mrs Enwright is wearing a floor-length sleeveless cotton dress with high collar. Short slits on either side. An African print in brown, gold, orange and black. We are in a jungle.

'Yet I fear not the hidden dangers,' I remark.

'Bravo,' says Mrs Enwright. She lifts her glass.

We sip. We put the glasses down. She settles into the sofa. She looks at me. This is my chance to turn away.

The sherry descends into my blood on a mission of mercy, spreading hands of condolence. And I didn't even know I was upset. Isn't it amazing how the simplest thing can slip your mind.

'This conversation makes me think of an experience I

once had,' said Mrs Enwright. 'In 1918 I was jailed for two weeks for my role in advocating the right of women to vote. I was involved in demonstrations which the police and politicians considered a threat to social order.'

'Oh, dear. Social Order,' I said.

'Precisely.' She took another sip of sherry. 'They were right, of course. We were indeed trying to haul down the proverbial scaffolding. I thought I could do anything. What a fool. As for courage, I am ashamed to say that where courage should have been lay a huge crater.'

I held my arms above my head in a circle. Then let them fall.

'Now you're making sense,' I said.

We sat holding our glasses.

'What are we having for dinner?' I asked.

'Pizza,' she replied. 'I love pizza.'

'Me too,' I said.

'At the time everyone said how brave I was to spend two weeks in jail, as if I had a choice. You'll never guess what I did to get arrested.'

'You were in a demonstration.'

'No, I mean what I actually did in the demonstration.'

'I don't know.'

'I stomped on policemen's feet as we marched by.'

'Oh,' I said. 'Well.'

'Extraordinary, isn't it?' she said.

'On purpose?' I asked.

'Yes. Absolutely.'

'Then. Violence with intent,' I said.

'These days it doesn't seem like much. But I was considered quite a radical for that.'

'So you did have courage,' I said. 'I wouldn't dream of stepping on a policeman's foot.'

'Of course not,' laughed Mrs Enwright. 'Who in their right mind would? Stupidity is not courage. I showed my true colours in jail.'

'What do you mean?'

'I wept like a big baby every night. I was miserable! Homesick, hungry, cold. I never went to another demonstration again. So much for principle. I wouldn't have made it in Siberia, I can tell you.'

'No pizza,' I said.

'I do like my creature comforts,' she said.

'Sherry is political,' I said, taking a generous sip to ward off the cold of the jail cell.

'But I was damn glad when we got the vote,' she said.

'My parents never drank,' I said, 'but Benny is an alcoholic.'

'I've heard that,' said Mrs Enwright.

Her eyes are swimming toward me. Or is my head swimming away?

'He was teaching me to drive,' I said.

'Where is he?' she asked.

'This is one of my questions. He is in love with a

prostitute named Candi Jones who works at the Paradise Lounge. Angela suspects but doesn't know.'

'And you're not telling,' said Mrs Enwright.

'Do you think I should?'

'No,' she said. 'Stay out of it.'

'That's what I thought. Angela thinks he is in Puerto Rico on business when he is actually drinking or staying with Candi. Candi is wonderful.'

'Someone is going to get hurt,' said Mrs Enwright.

'Who will it be?' I asked.

'Candi,' she said. 'Well, all of them I suppose.'

'That's what I thought,' I said.

'Benny isn't going to leave Angela, Angela isn't going to leave Benny. They'll just stay on and make each other suffer. And poor Candi has no claim on anybody. When I was in jail one of the guards called me a whore. I was so pleased with myself. I thought I was the height of sophistication. Absolutely no notion of the real world.'

'You should see the Paradise Lounge. I wet my pants the day Benny took me there to meet her.'

'That must have been upsetting. And you're already nervous,' she said. 'Just an observation, not a criticism.'

'Usually,' I replied.

'Yes,' she replied. 'I would have said you are usually nervous.'

'My father was a worrier, too, so I don't mind. It's not so bad when someone else knows the situation.'

'That's true,' said Mrs Enwright.

'He killed himself,' I said. 'So he doesn't worry much anymore. Just occasionally.'

'I wasn't aware of that, Joan. I am so sorry.'

'I'll just drink the sherry, thank you.'

'I hope it helps,' she said. 'Because for some reason it is quite painful for me to think of you suffering.'

'You must have someone else in mind,' I said. 'My little brother E.J., perhaps?'

'No. I was thinking of you.'

I stood up.

'Well, I'll be going then. Thank you for the charming drinks.'

'Of course,' said Mrs Enwright, 'it might work out well if you stay.'

Jesus came through the kitchen door.

'I got the pizzas,' he said. 'The gang should be here any minute.'

'Why don't you sit down, Joan?' said Mrs Enwright. 'Just for a minute. You'll be more comfortable when the others arrive.'

'Is everything all right?' I asked Jesus.

'Oh, yes,' he said. 'We've got plenty of pizza, coke, wine, the works.'

'I mean with me.' I smoothed my skirt and adjusted my cap.

'You look wonderful,' said Jesus. 'Oh yes.'

Mrs Enwright worked her way off the sofa and came over to my chair.

'Just for tonight,' she said, 'give me the name badge. You don't want to give away all your secrets at once.'

'I'll introduce you,' said Jesus. I unpinned the badge. I try to believe in the future. Mrs Enwright took the badge.

'Actually,' I said, 'I'll keep the badge in my pocket just in case. Then again, why don't I hold it.'

'Now the cap,' said Mrs Enwright. 'Everyone will think you're leaving if you keep the cap on.'

'Is she leaving?' groaned Jesus.

'Joan will have to answer that herself.'

'I'm staying,' I said.

'So it's off with the cap,' said Jesus.

'Can you pull the pins out?' said Mrs Enwright.

'Yes,' which I did. 'Jesus, I'm staying after all. I thought I'd let you know in advance.'

He replied, 'You are everything I have ever wanted or needed and try as I might I cannot imagine living my life without you. I am filled with gratitude that you will be joining us for pizza. I have never known such happiness, such carefree abandon.'

'Are you talking about pepperoni pizza?' I asked. 'I don't eat pizza without pepperonis.'

'Yes,' said Jesus. 'One large mushroom, two large pepperoni, and two large everythings. Lila and Marsha are on diets so they won't eat much.' He went back into the kitchen.

'Am I on a diet?' I asked.

'No,' said Mrs Enwright, 'but a lot of the girls are.'

'I thought I might be because I am not a big eater.'

'Not the same thing,' she said.

I put the name badge in my pocket. I spread my fingers and placed my hands over my head to hold the hair in place. I doubt I can keep this up all night, however.

'I can't keep this up all night,' I said. 'For circulatory reasons.'

'No,' she said, 'you couldn't possibly. What are you worried about?'

'My hair.'

'What about it?'

'Will it stay down.'

She strained her neck and head forward to take a good look.

'As far as I can tell, the pins are holding it in place quite well. You did it that way to put under the cap. Nice job, too.'

'But now the cap is in your closet.'

'Why don't you try taking one hand down for a moment and see what happens.' Which I did.

'Did anything happen?' I asked.

'No,' she replied. 'Not at my level.'

'Yours seems to stay in place with no problem. I can see it.'

'So you worry because you can't see your own hair. I have an idea. Why don't I keep an eye on it for you? One less thing to think about.'

'You'll let me know if anything changes.'

'Yes. If I kick the floor twice that is your signal to go and look in the mirror. If I tap my glass, all is well.'

'Meanwhile I can just do conversation.'

'That's right,' she said. 'Enjoy yourself. Get to know everyone.'

'Not that I care, but where will you be?'

'Right here. I've known this crowd for a long time. They indulge me, let me hang around. I like to keep up with the customs of local tribes.'

'I too am planning to stay right here,' I commented. 'What a coincidence. Perhaps Miss Forth would need to sit by someone all night. Miss Forth!' I called.

'She must be outdoors,' said Mrs Enwright.

I got up and opened the front door to look.

Four people, two young men and two young women, were standing. Miss Forth was with them, wagging her tail and smiling.

'Hiya,' said one of the women. 'I'm Lila.' She was chewing and snapping gum. 'The bell must be broken. See? I keep pushing it and nothing happens. Are you the new maid? Look, Freddy, Mrs Enwright got a maid. Pleased to meet you.'

She held out her hand. '*Parlee view Fransay*?' she yelled.

'God, Lila, not so loud,' said the man who must be Freddy.

'Oh, there you are, Miss Forth,' I said. 'Come now.' I

slapped my hip and in she ran. I closed the door. Miss Forth was waiting by my chair so I sat down.

'Was there someone at the door?' asked Mrs Enwright.

'Yes,' I said. 'Two young men and two young women.'

Suddenly there was a loud pounding.

'Maybe we should let them in,' said Mrs Enwright.

Jesus came running through the kitchen door.

'Right with you!' he called. Grinning, he said to us, 'They're here!'

He flung open the door. Bobby and Freddy pumped his hand, banged him on the back, grabbed him around the shoulders, and punched his ribs.

'Hey, Zeus, man, good to see ya,' said Freddy.

'The one on the left is Freddy,' said Mrs Enwright.

'Thank you,' I said.

Bobby felt Jesus' biceps, flexed his own, held them up for comparison. 'What are you taking, Perez – steroids?'

'Oh, cut it out, Bobby,' said Jesus shyly.

'Hey, Mrs Enwright,' said Bobby, 'you see this? You got Adonis for a grandson.'

'I know,' said Mrs Enwright. 'How about a drink?'

'So introduce us around,' said Freddy. 'Hiya, Mrs Enwright. Looking younger than ever. How you gettin' along?' He grasped her hand and kissed it.

'What a gentleman,' said Mrs Enwright. 'I'm just fine, Freddy. Still bumping into furniture. Can hardly see a thing.'

'Way to go,' replied Bobby. He waved to Lila and Marsha. 'Come in here, ladies.'

They are still by the door. They hold hands and move cautiously into the room, giggling. Jesus sat on the arm of my chair and leaned gently against me. I leaned into him, patted his tummy, and said, 'What a lovely evening we are having so far.'

Lila and Marsha are wearing tight mini-skirts. Lila's is red cotton, Marsha's brown leather. Lila has white high heels, Marsha black. Lila wears a white halter top over which is draped a short-sleeved red jacket to match her skirt. Four gold chains around her neck. Long curly blonde hair showers down her back, on to her shoulders. Bright red lipstick.

Marsha is wearing a loose black overblouse, open collar, more gold chains. Long sandy hair is pulled into one braid which drapes over her shoulder on to her chest. Large brass earrings with different parts, some beaded, hang down.

The two women wobble in their high heels to where Mrs Enwright, Miss Forth, and I are sitting.

Mrs Enwright holds out her hands to them.

'Hello,' she says. 'Come here to me. Just look at the two of you.'

They tip themselves down to Mrs Enwright, each kissing a cheek. 'It is wonderful to see you,' she says.

'Thank you, Mrs Enwright,' they say.

'Are you both well?'

'Yes, Mrs Enwright.'

'Good. Now you want to meet our guest.' She nods to Jesus.

'Oh, we met her at the door,' says Lila. 'I didn't know you were getting a maid.'

Jesus groaned.

Lila turned to me. She bowed.

'Bone swear,' she yelled. *'Wel – come – to – America. We will help you learn English.'*

'Good girl, Lila!' said Freddy. 'Hey Mrs Enwright, did Jesus tell you Lila is taking a course in international relations?'

'And French,' she said, blushing. 'You probably noticed. It's not difficult, thank God.'

'How wonderful,' said Mrs Enwright. 'But you flatter me to suggest I could interest Joan in being my house-keeper.'

'You never asked,' I said.

'I guess Lila noticed how quickly you have become one of the family.'

'Wait a minute,' said Bobby. 'Is this the Joan we've been hearing about? Zeus, man. Little did we know what you have been holding back from your best friends! Hello, Joan. I am pleased to make your acquaintance. I can't imagine how you put up with him.'

'Hello, Bobby,' I said. 'I am pleased to make your acquaintance, too.' We shook hands and he slapped Jesus on the back.

'It's about time, old buddy. Nice work.'

'Well, everyone,' coughed Jesus. 'I guess you know by now: this is Joan Marie Pardee. I am pleased to say.'

'Hi there,' said Freddy. 'Nice to meet you.'

'Nice to make you, too, Freddy,' I said.

'I'm Marsha,' said Marsha. 'Sorry about Lila calling you a maid. I knew you weren't the maid.' She smiled. 'But that's Lila.'

'Thank you for smiling,' I said.

'So when did you get over from Paris?' said Lila. 'Jesus never mentioned you were French.'

'Well,' I said, 'let me just think for a moment.'

'Oh, God,' said Jesus, and ran from the room.

I put my hands on my head.

'I'll help you, Zeus,' said Bobby, and ran after him.

Mrs Enwright tapped her glass. I took my hands down.

'Poor thing,' said Lila. 'The sound of the airplane is still ringing in her head. *Restay View. Go lie down.*'

'Lila,' said Freddy. 'Joan is not French. You're embarrassing me.'

'How do *you* know?' said Lila. 'I'm the one studying about other nations.'

'Now, now,' said Mrs Enwright. 'There is no need for anyone to feel embarrassed. We're all just getting to know each other. That takes time, doesn't it. Actually Joan is not from Paris. She lives right here in town.'

'I told you,' said Freddy.

'Oh, God,' said Lila. 'Sometimes I can be such a jerk.'

'Don't worry,' said Marsha. 'It's just your basic nature. We love you anyway.'

'*Really*,' said Lila. 'I'm so disgusted with myself. The minute I concentrate on practising my French I do it at the wrong times. The teacher hasn't covered application yet.'

'When I opened the door earlier,' I said, 'I thought you were Marilyn Monroe.'

Lila blushed. 'Why, thank you. Did you hear that, Freddy?'

'Do you really think so, Joan?' he asked.

'Oh, yes,' I replied.

They embraced.

'But when I remembered that Marilyn Monroe had died, I decided she probably wasn't at the door after all. So I went back inside. Which was ridiculous because here you are.'

'Wow!' said Lila. 'And me thinking you were the maid.'

Freddy furrowed his brow. 'Uh, well. I think the guys probably need my help in the kitchen.' He ran out.

'A lot of running going on around here,' said Lila. 'It's very rude. Men. They're all alike. Anyway, now we can really talk.'

She and Marsha sat down. Marsha next to Mrs Enwright on the couch, Lila on the other chair.

'So how long exactly have you and Zeus been going together?' asked Lila. 'Tell us *everything*.' She giggled.

'*Lila*,' said Marsha. 'Sorry about that, Joan.'

'What's wrong with asking a question?' said Lila. 'Quit apologising for me. You always think you act better than everyone. It's a free country. If she doesn't want to tell, she won't tell. But I hope she does.' More giggles.

'I've always admired your honesty, Lila,' laughed Mrs Enwright. 'It's refreshing.'

'That's my policy, Mrs Enwright,' said Lila. 'Put the cards on the table. Joanie, I have a lot of integrity. What you say here tonight won't leave this room. Isn't that so, Marsha? Don't I keep my word?'

'Absolutely,' replied Marsha. 'You're very good that way.'

'In other words, I'm not as flighty as I might appear. By the way, Joan, do I seem flightly to you? I don't mind, whatever you say.'

'Oh, no,' I said. 'You seem fine.'

'It's just that Freddy likes me to put forward a certain appearance so people will respect him. We've been working on this Marilyn Monroe look for months and and you're the first person who's noticed. Well, except for Marsha.'

'I noticed right away,' said Marsha. 'It was that good.' She rolled her eyes.

'She's just jealous, Joan,' said Lila. 'Don't mind her.

- 254 -

But seriously I guess Zeus likes you to dress down, pale colours and so forth. You really do look French.'

'Well,' I said.

'I'm afraid of pale colours myself,' said Lila.

'Why?' asked Mrs Enwright. 'What is there to be afraid of?'

'The whole idea,' replied Lila.

'What do you mean, the whole idea?' asked Marsha. 'You're not making any sense. Think things out first, like I told you.'

'I mean, let's ask the person herself,' said Lila. 'Joan, are you nervous in that outfit?'

'Oh, yes,' I said.

'There. She knows what I'm talking about. But those clothes are all right for her because she's the quiet type whereas I am the noisy type.'

'So red suits you,' I said. 'Whereas I would faint if I had to wear red. Sometimes I even faint in white.'

'Right. And Marsha likes black, which to me is sick.'

'Why is it sick?' said Marsha. 'For God sake, Lila, all the best designers use black. It is a very expressive colour, very bold and dynamic.'

'You know what I mean,' said Lila. 'Don't make me say it.'

'Let's not hold back on my account,' said Mrs Enwright.

'Death,' said Lila. 'There. I said it.'

'Why does everyone associate black with death?' said Marsha. 'It's a purely arbitrary symbol.'

'Not to me,' said Lila.' 'I want to think about life. Life is colour.'

'So go ahead,' said Marsha, 'think about life. No one is stopping you. But don't blame black.'

'Or white,' I said.

'So, Joan,' said Lila, leaning forward, 'how is it with Zeus? Confidentially I mean. And don't you say anything, Marsha. I know you're just as curious as me.'

'It's true,' laughed Marsha. 'I am. But Lila's the one to say it.'

'I love your earrings,' I shouted.

'God,' said Marsha, 'I guess you do. What brought that on?' She looked at Lila and rolled her eyes.

'Marsha makes jewellery,' said Mrs Enwright. 'When she isn't taking my blood pressure and heart rate. She is studying for a certificate in gerontology.'

'I thought if I mentioned your earrings I would get to know you,' I yelled.

'It's no big deal,' said Marsha. 'I'm not trying to hide anything. All you have to do is ask.' She whacked the side of her head. 'It would save my hearing.' To Lila she said, 'Quiet type nothing.'

'Sorry, sorry,' I said.

Lila winked at me. 'You just don't want to tell us about you and Zeus, isn't that right.'

'Well, let me see,' I said.

'Lila, can't you take a hint,' said Marsha. 'She doesn't want to talk about it.'

'By now we're probably ready for the pizza anyway, aren't we?' said Mrs Enwright.

'Listen, Joan,' said Lila. 'I'm just trying to be friendly. Please accept my apologies if I have been, well, personal. Everyone accuses me of prying. I am taking international affairs to try and branch out.'

'You didn't do anything wrong,' I said. 'I want to say something. But nothing comes.'

'And to be honest, Joan,' said Lila, 'that quality in a person makes me nervous. I like people who say things. Sitting right here right now with you I feel nervous. Not that I want to hurt your feelings. Are you nervous, Marsha? She's very nice but that way of hers, plus the white, it makes me edgy. Listen to me chatter. Does it make Zeus nervous? Your personality I mean. I guess not.'

'Lila, you're the one making us nervous,' said Marsha. 'Who can relax with you talking all the time?'

'I don't want to make anyone nervous,' I said. I turned to Mrs Enwright. 'Are you anxious?'

'Not at all,' she replied. 'No one has done anything wrong as far as I can tell. You're just not used to each other. I am sure this is the first of many evening together.'

'Marsha,' said Lila, 'I was trying to be friendly, relax the situation. Jesus really likes her.'

'Each to his own,' said Marsha.

'Maybe I do make him nervous and that's why he hasn't kissed me,' I said. 'At least I don't think he has.'

'Oh, God!' screamed Lila. 'He hasn't kissed you? Marsha, did you hear that? He hasn't kissed her!'

'You mean, she doesn't *think* he has,' replied Marsha.

'I guess I would know,' I said.

'I don't believe this,' said Marsha.

'Be quiet, Marsha!' said Lila. 'You're making her shy! Just let her talk! Joan, tell me all about it. I'll help you.'

'Should he have kissed me?' I asked.

'You're damn right!' said Lila. 'There's got to be something in it for you! All they do is take take take. Don't you go all the way until he produces that ring. I'm telling you. And if he pressures you, tell me first.'

'So far there's no pressure,' I said.

'That's good, 'said Lila, 'because frankly I don't think you can take it. What do you think, Marsha?'

'She can't take it,' said Marsha.

Mrs Enwright smiled at me. 'I think she'll do fine.'

Bobby, Freddy, and Jesus came dancing and singing through the kitchen door with aprons on, each holding pizza.

'When the moon hits your eye like a big pizza pie that's amore,' they blared.

Jesus was embarrassed because on the one with pepperoni Bobby and Freddy had put a card with our names, Jesus and Joan Marie, written underneath silver embossed wedding bells. You aren't supposed to take those cards from the florists's unless you buy something.

At the end of the evening Marsha took everyone's blood pressure. Mine was sky high due to the spicy food. She made me lie down.

Lila put a cold cloth on my forehead. She told Jesus to get out of her sight, he caused the whole situation in the first place.

– chapter thirty-one –

Eventually Benny came home. He was sober. He sold the Cadillac and told me further lessons are out of the question. Angela is happy now, we hardly see her.

Jesus said he would teach me to drive. Lila replied: no man can teach a woman how to drive, Marsha and I will handle this. Bobby and Freddy had to hold their sides. They said they would put the tow truck, the car crusher, and the State Police on red alert. See what I mean about men, said Lila.

Benny has promoted Jesus: he now handles major corporate and private clients in New York, New Jersey, and Connecticut. Contract, installation, supervision. Everything. Some people are so proud of him. Mrs Enwright bought him a tie. Black swirls against a rich burgundy background. Once every three weeks, on his day off, Jesus removes his tie from his dark blue denim shirt so Mrs Enwright can send the tie to be cleaned. Have it ready in an hour, she tells them. Jesus sits at home waiting.

One day Benny asked me out to lunch. I didn't realise he wanted me to see Candi again. He picked me up in his new Ford station wagon. We sat in the car, in front of the shop.

'There is something you and I have to talk about,' said Benny.

'What?' I asked.

'Candi,' he replied.

'Candi who?'

'Cut it out, Joan.'

'I don't want to talk about Candi who.'

'We have to,' said Benny, 'because I should never have allowed you to go there with me. And now we have to figure out what you are going to do if Angela browbeats you. I can't expect you to carry this on your own. What will you say if Angela asks you for information?'

'She already has,' I said.

'She already has?'

'When you were away.'

Benny took a deep breath and rubbed his chin.

'What did she say?'

'She said she knew you were with one of those whores on your anniversary and if I didn't tell her where you'd gone she wouldn't let me live in the house anymore.' I pulled my cap down due to the cold light flashing behind my eyes.

'She said Mildred left her one half of the house,' I added. 'But Louie said we will go to Italy before he'll let Angela take over. So I am in an excellent position.'

Benny slammed the dashboard with his open hand.

'Jesus Christ,' he said. 'That bitch. How could she say that to you?'

He shifted in his seat and folded his arms across his chest.

'It wasn't difficult,' I said.

'I don't know if I can take this,' he said.

'It happened,' I said.

'Angela told me she knew I had been in Puerto Rico,' said Benny. 'How did she figure that out?'

'Everyone knows about you, Benny.'

He banged the steering wheel.

'Shit, Joan!'

'It wasn't me who told,' I said. 'People know things.'

'I'm sorry,' said Benny, taking a deep breath. 'I shouldn't blame you. We care about you. Candi was very upset the day we all met. She feels I shouldn't have brought you there. She feels she should have protected you. Now she has the idea we should sit down together and help sort out your confusion about all of it. She suggested we have coffee this morning.'

'But I'm not confused, Benny,' I said. 'Everything is clear. Where would confusion enter into it?'

'Joan, you know something you shouldn't know. You found out because I was drinking and because I used extremely poor judgement. And now we have to help you handle that information.'

'What is it you feel I need to hear?'

Benny sighed. 'Just come along. Let's have a rational

- 262 -

conversation, the three of us. Not like last time. Candi likes you.'

'I like her.'

He started the car.

'I almost forgot to ask where we are going,' I said.

'This time to a real diner, a restaurant even. For a proper cup of coffee and some lunch.'

'Candi likes tea.'

'Right. She'll have tea.'

'Sometimes you make me sick, Benny,' I said.

'Imagine how I feel when I look in the mirror,' he replied.

Suddenly we are on a hectic four-lane highway. I have completely lost track of where we are or might have been. Although I feel I know this place. Factory outlets, muffler shops, Japanese car showrooms, bowling lanes, and fast-food ranchettes whirl into one as if we are being whipped around a metal tub into cotton candy no matter how much I care about and maintain distinctions. Cars are rushing back and forth, turning in, pulling out, screeching to a halt. Lurching forward, honking each other into oblivion.

'Why did we have to come this far?' I asked.

'Because nobody in this area knows Candi or me. If we go out we can't go where we're known.'

'By whom?'

'Certain people. Leave it at that.'

'I was just looking for someplace to put my finger on.'

– 263 –

'We're there in a jiff.'

A hundred yards beyond this intersection I see a flashing sign in red, white, and blue: 'Four Brothers Acropolis Family Restaurant.'

'We've been here before,' I said. 'They'll know you.'

'What are you talking about?' said Benny. 'Candi suggested it. I've never heard of the place.'

'Maybe we could go somewhere else,' I urged. 'You don't remember. We have been here. I am sure of my own mind.'

'Sometimes I get the impression you think I was in a perpetual blackout. I didn't drink all the time, for Christs' sake. Even an alcoholic knows more or less what's going on around him.'

Nausea rolls my stomach into my throat. I am jelly in a tube being squeezed.

He parked the car and we went in.

Candi is sitting in a booth far from the door, in the corner by Ladies and Gentlemen. She is wearing a wide straw hat from the trip to Puerto Rico, and dark glasses. A deep rose cotton dress, open at the neck, a string of coloured beads. She raises her hand to beckon us. She smiles, we walk forward.

My legs ache, my head is light. Someone is facing me into wild storms. A plastic pinwheel, I whirl but do not split. I take charge. Holding the stick of this pinwheel I tilt back and forward on my own authority to test resistance and possibility. Benny is already seated.

Suddenly Candi is beside me. She has my hand.

'Hello, Joan,' she says. 'Come and sit. It's wonderful to see you again. This time we won't make you wait to eat.'

Candi is soft to look at.

'Nevertheless,' I said, 'that is my hand you are holding.'

I took back what is rightly mine and sat down.

– chapter thirty-two –

'Isn't it fantastic,' said Candi, 'to see this guy sober?'

She put her arm around his shoulder and gave him a hard squeeze. Benny pushed back her hat. They kissed deeply.

Stella and Monica rushed down to our end of the restaurant and plunked themselves on two stools behind the counter.

'Take a load off your feet, Monica,' puffed Stella. 'The show is about to begin.'

'God, Stella, it's a different girl!'

'Variety is the spice of life, Monica. The last one was only his wife.'

Pointing at me, Monica said, 'I guess he brings the dental hygienist along with all of them.'

'You would, too,' said Stella, 'if you put your mouth in all the places this guy does.'

'You're disgusting,' said Monica.

'Believe it, baby, believe it,' said Stella. 'I've lived a beautiful life.'

'Why, hello,' I said to them.

'Hi, honey,' said Stella. 'What's the occasion this time?'

'Just a little get-together,' I replied.

'Isn't that sweet,' said Stella. 'You dental assistants sure clock in a lot of free hours.'

While I thought about this, Benny and Candi slid away from the embrace. Benny removed Candi's sunglasses. They looked carefully at each other. Then Candi re-adjusted her hat, took the glasses back, put them on.

'Maybe he's the dentist,' whispered Monica. 'Did you ever think of that? Which would explain all the time off he gives the hygienist.'

Candi smiled at me.

'Are you ready to order? The waitresses are right here.'

'I can't decide,' I replied.

'In a few minutes,' said Benny.

'I guess we're not quite ready,' Candi said to Monica and Stella.

'Too bad,' replied Stella. 'I was really in the mood.'

'Boo-hoo,' said Monica. 'No action.'

They popped off their stools and strolled down the counter filling the sugar bowls, polishing, straightening, whistling. They'll soon be busy with the lunch crowd.

'Joanie,' said Candi, 'I guess you know why Benny and I wanted to see you,' said Candi.

'No,' I said.

'She knows damn well,' said Benny. 'She likes to be difficult lately.'

'I'm sorry, Joan,' said Candi. 'That's not a very cordial

way to begin after all this time. I've thought about you so much.'

'Why?' I asked.

'Because of everything that happened the last time I met you.'

'That was actually the first time you met me.'

'See what I mean?' said Benny. 'Joan, cut it out right now.'

'She's angry, Benny,' said Candi. 'What do you expect?'

'Benny told me,' I said, 'that you and he are worried someone will find out about you. But I haven't said a word. So the whole situation does not concern me in the least.' And what I say to Mrs Enwright doesn't concern them.

'I think it does,' said Candi. 'You and Angela are friends. And unfortunately it turns out Angela and I know some people in common.'

'Candi,' said Benny, 'Joan told me on the way over here that Ange really pumped her while we were in Puerto Rico.'

'I have no doubt about it,' said Candi. 'What do you think is giving me ulcers lately?'

'She even threatened to kick her out of Louie's if she doesn't tell.'

'God, Benny, that's terrible! She said that?' Candi shook her head. 'Joanie, I am so sorry!' 'But there is no way in hell it'll ever happen,' said Benny. 'I'll get her to sign her half of the house over to me.'

'She won't,' I said.

'Benny,' said Candi, 'I must say that does sound like fantasy.'

'She will,' said Benny. 'I know Angela. I know how she feels with me home and sober. Don't worry. I'll figure something out. The important thing is that Joan has protection once Ange gets going.'

'You should never have been in this position in the first place, Joan,' said Candi. 'That's our fault.'

'Despite your selfishness, I already knew,' I said. 'Everyone knows. I told Benny but he won't believe me. I keep trying to bring this idea forward.'

'*Everyone* knows?' said Candi. 'Who is this everyone?'

'No one in particular,' I answered. 'Everyone in general.'

'Benny, what is she saying? How can this be?'

'Candi, it's beyond me. We have been as careful as two people can be.'

'That's the point,' said Candi. 'There are two of us. And all of a sudden I have this very frightening feeling that one member of this team hasn't been looking out for the other.'

'I'm getting nervous,' I said.

'Candi,' said Benny, 'that's not fair. Why in God's name would I tell a living soul about being in love with you? That would destroy the only thing I ever wanted. And by the way, you're a fine one to talk. As if Gino

Stromboli thinks I'm just another one of your customers.'

'But he doesn't talk,' said Candi. 'He is paid to keep his mouth shut.'

'In other words,' I said, 'lots of people have seen you.'

'The average person doesn't take any notice, Joan,' said Benny.

'Never mind average,' said Candi. 'At this moment I am sick to my stomach about what you have said and to whom.'

'Me, too,' I said.

Benny banged the table with his fist. He turned to Candi and growled, '*Candi*. How many times do I have to tell you? If anyone knows about us it isn't from me. I have as much to lose as you.'

'Benny, please,' she said.

He took a deep breath.

'I'm sorry. This is no time to argue. No time for me to lose my temper. I'm sorry. I don't want to treat you that way.'

Candi took his hand.

'Your temper is the least of our problems,' she said. 'Thank God you're sober.'

'Maybe you said things you don't remember,' I merely suggested. 'To people you don't remember. In the past. Which of course you wouldn't remember.'

'You mean when I was drinking?' said Benny. 'Oh, hell, I never got that bad. Part of what is upsetting me now is that I know what happened, Joanie. I *know* what a pig I was.'

'You didn't remember being here on Angela's birth-day,' I said. 'Which would be forgetting. Not remember-ing is the same as forgetting.' I had to mention it, it had to be done.

'Being where?' asked Candi. She looked puzzled.

'Benny brought Angela here a few months ago for her birthday,' I replied.

'I did not!' yelled Benny. 'Jesus Christ, Joan. There's no end to the trouble you cause.'

'What do you mean, "here"?' asked Candi. '*Here*?' She pointed at the table top.

'It was actually that table by the door,' I said.

'Dear God, Benny,' she said.

'Is this what you were referring to in the car, Joan?' said Benny. 'This is what you were talking about?'

His voice is a high-pitched whine, like a jet engine.

'I don't know what's the matter with you lately, Joan,' he went on. 'All she can seem to do, Candi, is trash the people closest to her. Embarrass them, shame them. The difference is this time she had to resort to an out-and-out lie. Why are you doing this?'

His voice, a fingernail on the blackboard, is trapped in his throat. I know the feeling. His teeth are clenched.

I am going to throw up. I close my lips as hard as I can and roll them tightly together.

'Don't you realise,' he said, 'I can't take any more

pressure. I can't take accusations. I am beginning to think Angela has a point about you, Joan. Jesus has somehow twisted your mind, hasn't he? Somehow he's convinced you to hurt the people who care most about you. Candi, this whole thing is ridiculous. I trust I don't need to say it to you, of all people.' He takes another deep breath.

She just stares at him. Then slowly nods.

'Now I get it,' she says.

'Get what?' snaps Benny.

'You were having blackouts, ' said Candi.

'Candi, I wasn't! I honestly wasn't! I wouldn't lie about a thing like this!'

'No, you wouldn't be lying because you don't remember. The times you repeated yourself. The times you were late or didn't show up or forgot things I told you. I thought you were just being selfish.'

'When was I ever late meeting you?' he growled. Sticking his mouth up to her ear. 'When? Name one time, you bitch.'

'Benny,' said Candi, 'keep this up and I am going to walk out. The way I see it, we have a big problem on our hands.'

'Sorry, sorry,' he said stiffly. 'It won't happen again, sorry. But you understand what this is like for *me*. I'm the one being falsely accused. I never kept you waiting. I never forgot things.'

'Oh, yes. You did,' she replied. 'But good old me, I didn't complain. Don't sweat the small stuff, I said to myself. I thought I had to be patient. I still do. A real dope, Candi Jones.'

'Then it's your word against mine,' he said triumphantly. 'Joan's little provocation proves exactly nothing. Fucking nothing.' He folded his arms defiantly in front of his chest.

Suddenly he brought his knee up against the bottom of the table top with such force that sugar spilled from the bowl, the salt and pepper fell over with a bang. Silverware clattered. Hinges holding the table to the wall screeched and loosened.

'Benny!' yelled Candi.

'You think you're a goddamn saint, Joan Marie Pardee, don't you? Don't you?' he shouted.

He hurled himself across the table. Clutched my shoulders, jerked me backward, jerked me forward. 'You think you're God's gift to the world, the Virgin Mary! Well, you're not!'

Outside observation would suggest that I am undulating from this force. Head unlocked at the base of my neck, shoulders flopping like the wide brim of a felt hat in contradictory breezes. I see this film in slow motion: Benny's strong fingers digging in, the pain shooting down my arms, my neck muscles swollen with tension. Mouth stretched open in a grimace of restraint, eyelids shivering. Each detail slips naturally into the story as a whole. I myself prefer slow motion so you get the sequence exactly. Which, subsequent to events, can be re-played without danger of error in recall.

'Benny!' screamed Candi. 'Let go of her! She's shaking! Stop it!'

Candi pulled at Benny's arms, but he wouldn't let me go. She beat his arms with her fists.

'You're going to save the world from sin, aren't you?' he said to me. 'Not off my back, you moralising, superior little cunt! So pure and innocent!'

When he spat into my face, I realised just how difficult it would be to capture individual drops of the spray, even in slow motion, for future recollection. In the dispersal they fanned out rapidly across the terrain of skin on tiptoes, short hops with a quick, delicate brush like a kiss from E. J. Yet a bolt of danger unlike that sweetness pierced me now. I realised I was having a nightmare and tried to wake up. But the shocks kept coming, pushing me back.

'Help me, Mama!' I cried, silly girl.

Candi slapped Benny hard. He released me. Lighter, I rose approximately four centimetres off the seat. The bruises on my shoulders showed up the following day.

'That's enough, that's enough!' screamed Candi.

I opened my handbag. Mother's old one with the gold clasp. Threw up and snapped the bag shut.

'It's all right,' I said. 'I'm fine now.'

Benny buried his face in his hands and sobbed. Candi rubbed his back slowly.

'Benny, Benny,' she whispered.

By now there are other customers in the restaurant.

Monica and Stella stroll down to the end of the counter.

'Hello again, Mr Manini,' said Stella. 'Let me just give you a little hint about things in the real world. That table you just bashed with your leg. It's private property. Right? And what you did to your hygienist, that's assault. As I believe I mentioned to you when you brought your charming wife in here, this place is known to most people as a restaurant. Monica and me, we're called waitresses. Customers eat food in these booths. They don't fuck, they don't beat each other up. And most of the time they don't puke. Get it? But when they do, my bosses tell me to throw them out. Or worse yet phone up and *they* will throw you out. Believe me, Manini, one thing you don't want is to meet my bosses. Take my word for it. So I'm giving you exactly thirty seconds to clear out. And after that I am not going to see you, your wife, your girlfriend, or your assistant in here again. Starting from now.'

'That's right,' said Monica. 'You heard her.'

'I'm sorry,' Candi pleaded. 'He's been sick.'

'So go to a hospital,' said Stella. 'This isn't Bellevue. Although I'm beginning to wonder.'

'We're leaving,' said Candi. 'Please don't call the owners. Please. It's very important. You don't need to tell anyone about this, do you?'

'Who's telling?' said Stella. 'Did I say a word? It's not

my fault if other people come in here thinking it's a diner. Listen, honey. I got no need to talk to anyone about anything. But other people? Who knows. They do what they want.'

'It's not our problem,' said Monica.

They walked away.

'Get up, Benny,' said Candi. Benny slid out from behind the table. He hung his head.

'I'm sorry, Candi,' he mumbled. 'I don't know what happened.'

His voice limps away. He is pressing his temples, rubbing his forehead.

As we walk out, the chalk faces of the real customers turn to us. The mouths are chewing. Each eye is a hard, flat surface which throws back my reflection. I open my own mouth to call for them. But Benny has closed the door behind us. There is no point trying to penetrate a slab of glass.

Outside, Candi says, 'You brought Angela here in a blackout. There's no great mystery. The waitresses recognised you and Joan. You just don't want to admit it.'

'I want to admit it,' whined Benny. 'I just don't remember.'

'That's the point,' said Candi. 'You refuse to admit anything unless *you* remember. To hell with me, to hell with Joanie. What am I supposed to do now? What else have you forgotten? I'm petrified. I can't stand the sight of you.'

'Don't leave me, Candi,' sobbed Benny. 'Please don't leave me.'

'You really are a selfish bastard, aren't you,' she said. 'But no. I won't leave you. Of course not. I'm not that smart.'

'Let's go,' said Benny, trembling. 'I'll drive you home.'

'No, said Candi. 'I'll go by myself. We shouldn't be seen together for a while. Don't come to the Lounge, don't phone.'

'That's ridiculous!' he cried.

'You know it isn't,' said Candi.

'I need you,' said Benny. 'Please. I love you.'

Candi sighed. 'I feel the same way, Benny. I probably always will. So much for common sense.'

They looked at each other. They watched carefully what was occurring on each of their faces. How the lines were re-routing, the curves and contours shifting.

'I'll call you,' said Candi.

'Okay,' said Benny.

Candi smiled at me.

'Maybe one of these days you and I can meet someplace where it doesn't end up a disaster.'

'I doubt it,' I said.

'Jesus Christ, Joan,' said Benny.

'At least we know The Paradise Lounge and Four Brothers Acropolis Family Restaurant are out,' said Candi.

'Next time we'll diversify,' I said.

As she kissed me good-bye her eyelashes fluttered with longing against my skin. A trapped butterfly. I turned my face into hers, placing my lips against her cheek. The warm softness of this experience, I pulled away.

Candi walked from us down a narrow footpath. Was soon devoured by voracious neon, a thrashing heartless speedway. And evaporated.

My handbag was starting to smell, so I dropped it into a trash can. In any case, it was too small to be practical.

– chapter thirty-three –

When we went to Seaside Heights for our first vacation, my father's supervisor Bob took us in his car. And was supposed to pick us up when it was over. As a favour to my father. I was eight.

Not being a driver, my father took two buses to work: the number six from South Main and Poplar to the corner of Elm and Barker. Then the number forty-seven from there to the field office of Nick Delmonico Construction Company. This on a link road between the New Jersey Turnpike at Secaucus and the site of a proposed government office complex. A project which went on for seven years, abandoned in the eighth after a court order. My father had been on this job six years when he jumped off the scaffolding for the new water authority, so naturally he was known and liked. Mr Delmonico sent a big wreath worth at least $20.00.

Not that we never had outings. Picnics or the zoo. But this was an actual summer vacation in a bungalow by the sea. To tell about in September. Given over to us by Bob's cousin Henrietta who had rented it for those two weeks in July. In June she developed complications with her uterus and couldn't attend. Shut up, Hal, said my mother. She is too young to hear bad words. E. J. was four.

He was allowed a new pair of red sneakers for the trip. He held these in a plastic bag on his lap during the car ride. For me my mother bought a padded Playtex Starter Bra due to the boys who would be ogling me on the beach. She knew I needed it because when I was bad the week before we left, she slapped my breasts. On the beach I wore the bra and my yellow flowered underpants. Not one of the boys bothered me.

Bob was to come for us at eleven a.m. Saturday. E. J. and I got ourselves so excited the night before that we stayed wide awake until midnight. Scooting illegally in darkness between the two beds. Discussing Seaside Heights in sign language. Which can be heard by touching fingers and paying close attention. I can see the clock by shining my Penlite. I am not allowed Penlites.

At seven a.m. Saturday my mother woke us. Singing. In her nightgown. Juggling a box of Corn Flakes.

'It's time to get up, it's time to get up, it's time to get up in the *MORNING*! We want to get up, we want to get up, we want to get up in the *MORNING*! Because it's VACATION for us this MORNING! Come on you two!' she cried. 'Today's the day!'

She jumped on my bed, then E. J.'s. Pouring Corn Flakes over the children.

'That's really something funny, Mama,' said E. J., not moving.

'Breakfast! Breakfast!' she roared. 'Anybody for breakfast? Shake a leg! This family is going on a VACATION!'

E. J. and I looked at each other. 'Yay!' we whispered.

'Quiet down!' yelled Mama, jumping off E. J.'s bed. 'You'll wake up the whole neighborhood!'

She whacked the cereal from Edward's face, gripped his neck in her hands, and growled, 'I love you kids so much. I can't believe how lucky I am.'

'I love you, too,' we said. E. J. gagged. She let him go. Pushed his head on to the pillow.

'Bouncy-bouncy,' he said.

'Straighten this place up, Joan Marie,' she chirped. 'And get the two of you packed, lickety-split. Everything folded, your things on the bottom.' She opened my closet and threw a large red Woolworth's shopping bag at me. From last Christmas.

Then she skipped out of the room, leaving the box of Corn Flakes tipped over on the floor. E. J. and I collected bits and pieces, munched these while we sorted, folded, and piled the various items into the bag. We do not worry about bathing suits in this family – one less thing – because none of us can swim. You have to belong to a country club.

E. J. lay sideways on the floor next to the box of cereal, peering inside. He rustled his hand through the flakes.

He brought out a fistful which he crushed and showered on himself.

'Where is the prize?' he asked.

'There is no prize in that one, E. J.,' I said. 'Now look at the mess you've made.'

'This is the best day of our whole lifes,' he said, sitting. 'Where's Daddy?'

I went to the doorway and listened.

My mother was downstairs in the kitchen. Humming and banging pots and pans to the tune of 'The Battle Hymn of the Republic'. I could hear water running from behind the bathroom door. An occasional clink-clink: the razor being tapped against the inside of the sink. After rinsing, preparation for another slow stroke from chin to cheekbone, mouth wide open to the hollow.

'He is shaving,' I said.

'Is he tired?' said E. J.

I laughed. 'You think ears have eyes.'

'But is he? Is he?' asked E. J. again. 'Just say, Junie. Say is he too tired today.'

'E. J., I can't say. I can't *see* him. I can only hear him shaving. He's fine.'

E. J. went to our door and cupped his ear. Then he called out: 'Hello, Daddy! Are you there?'

Silence.

'You are right, Junie. He shaving. He feeling just wonderful.'

A moment later, sure enough, there he was. All

dressed. Shiny face, khaki pants, white sneakers, navy blue T-shirt. Wet blond hair slicked back. Hands on hips. Smiling at the two children.

'Did I hear someone calling me?' he asked.

'Nobody in here,' I said.

This is a joke. E. J. covers his mouth, trying not to laugh.

Daddy opened his hand and blew me a kiss. I opened mine and caught it.

'Well, isn't that strange,' he said, 'because I was sure I heard someone shouting.'

'You must be mistaking,' giggled E. J.

'In fact,' said Daddy, 'the voice I heard sounded just like my favourite little boy, E. J. Pardee. Just like *you*.'

E. J. burst out squealing and threw himself on his bed. He wobbled to his feet and tossed himself up and down.

'You are right! That was *me*, Edwid Padee! I fooled you!'

Daddy held E. J.'s hands while the boy ricochetted up down to and fro on the bed. Finally the same boy bounced to a halt on his rear. The father surveyed the room.

'Well,' he said, 'I see you've managed to destroy everything in sight. Nice place for the Corn Flakes,' as they crunched under his feet. 'All you need now is the milk.'

'Heavens, we would never pour milk on the floor,' said the girl.

I rolled E. J.'s blue socks into a ball. Tucked them down the side of the bag.

'Mama did it,' said E. J. 'Mama said here your breakfast and pour them down.'

'Oh, I see,' said Daddy.

'Oh, I see,' said E. J. Man to man, shaking his head at the Corn Flakes. 'What terrible mess this is.'

'Are we ready to hit the road?' asked my father. 'How about it? Our first summer vacation. Not bad if you ask me.'

'Yay!' we yelled.

'That's what I like to hear. Now I'll have my coffee,' and down he went.

I tiptoed to our door. E. J. came, too, and stood behind me. Arms around my waist. Head resting on my back.

'Don't you look like something in your new summer sundress,' we heard my father say to my mother.

'Oh, Hal,' she replied.

I closed my eyes. I could see her moving towards him although she would protest.

'Come on, cut that out,' she said. 'How are we going to be ready for eleven o'clock?'

'We'll be ready,' he said. 'You didn't worry about the time last night.'

Kiss.

'Not that I recall,' he added.

'Last night was last night. Now it's down to business. Look at this kitchen.'

'It hasn't been like last night since I don't know when.'

'Move that wandering hand of yours, Hal Pardee. You have no sense of reality.'

'How about a cup of coffee then,' he said.

Smack!

The children jumped.

'Ouch!' yelped my mother. 'That's my bottom, if you please.'

'I should take you on vacation more often,' said my father.

'You're not kidding,' said my mother. 'If you were man enough to stand up to Delmonico we'd have everything.'

'Why are you bringing that up, Ernestine? Now of all times.'

'What's wrong with now? It can't be denied, Hal.'

'You know I've said my piece to Delmonico. A dozen times. And a dozen times I've been told to keep my mouth shut or look elsewhere.'

'What *you* mean by talking to him and what *I* mean are two different things.'

'If I said what you want me to I'd be fired. That's the only difference. Come on, let's have a nice day. Everything is going so well for us.'

'Get your hands off me, Hal. Fired? Never! You'd be *respected*. He'd know this family meant business. He'd know we're not dirt. The way you go about it he thinks he can step on you.'

'He *can* step on me, Ernestine. He can step on anyone he wants. Which he does regularly.'

'So tell him! Tell him: "I'm different, you stinking wop! You won't use me for a doormat! I'm a *man*! You'll pay me what I deserve or I quit! I know things about you, by God, that could blow the lid right off this place!" That's what I mean, Hal. Your idea of standing up to someone is getting down on your knees. Begging like a dog.'

'Ernestine. Stop. Please.'

'I know what I'm talking about! I'm the one who suffers because you're a coward. Because you've sold these kids down the river. How do you think *we* feel? Someone else's car takes us to someone else's vacation. Huh? In front of the whole neighbourhood. Think of *me* for a change!'

'We're going down the river on our vacation!' whispered E. J.

'We're going to the ocean,' I said.

'Then why are they fighting?' he asked.

'I don't know. Be quiet.'

'I want to go to the river,' said E. J. 'Let's tell them I changed my mind about Seaside Heights.'

'Shhh.'

'If you've finished,' sighed my father, 'I'll go upstairs and get my bag.'

'You see what I mean?' said my mother. 'You won't even argue with *me*, will you? What happened to that stiff thing you had on you last night? Huh? Who's the woman around here?'

Crash.

'That's it!' she yelled. 'Fight back!'

'Be quiet, Ernestine,' said my father. 'Look what you made me do. And this was supposed to be a nice day.'

'Be quiet, Ernestine,' whined my mother. 'Look what you made me do.'

Crash.

'Go ahead,' she said. 'Wreck the place. Be a big he-man. See if I care. A lot of good it does me to keep a decent home.'

'I think they having a nargrament,' said E. J., leaning in tighter.

'It's okay,' I said.

'I'm hungry,' he said.

'Me, too, E. J., but there won't be time for any more breakfast.'

My father is coming up the stairs. Pots and pans are banging around the kitchen. Cupboard doors slamming. E. J. and I move away from the door. We sit on my bed, feet flat on the floor. Our thighs and hips touch. Little children's hands are crumpled up in little children's laps.

'Hi,' says my father. 'Bob will be here pretty soon.'

'I'll clean up the floor,' says E. J. 'I lied. Mama didn't do it. I did it.'

'It doesn't matter, E. J.,' said Daddy. 'I'll help you.'

'I made this big mess,' said E. J., 'and now you'll be all tired out.'

'No, I won't. We'll have a great vacation. Don't worry.'

'I want to go down the river,' said E. J.

'What's he talking about? asked my father.

'I don't know,' I said. 'He's hungry.'

'Are you packed?' said my father.

'Yes,' I said.

'Are you guys okay?' he said.

'Yes, Daddy,' we said.

'I have new red sneakers,' said E. J., clutching the plastic bag. 'Keds.'

'I'm sorry, Princess,' my father said to me. 'That's no way to start a vacation.'

'It's all right,' I said.

'Are you tired? asked E. J.

'No,' sighed my father. 'No. I'm all right. Everybody has arguments, E. J.'

'I don't like them,' he said.

'It's over now,' I said. I hugged him because he is still young. 'Everything is over sooner than you think, E. J. Then something new starts up.'

'That's my girl,' said Daddy. He left the room.

'Daddy needs a nice rest,' said E. J.

'That's why we're going on vacation,' I said.

'Goody,' said E.J.

I carried the Woolworth's bag, E.J. carried the sneaker bag. We are both wearing new blue shorts. Both children also have new rubber sandals. My father had gone into the bathroom again. We tiptoed past the closed door and down the stairs.

My mother was sitting in the living room on the sofa.

One hand was on the brown cardboard valise we save for special occasions. This is because the surface looks like real alligator skin. And the two clips which secure the top look like real gold. Her legs are crossed at the ankles.

The other hand is at peace in the lap of her new green and yellow sundress. She is wearing new white sneakers which match my father's. She is holding a packet of marigold seeds. One bag with sheets and towels sits lopsided by the front door. My mother is staring straight ahead, not blinking.

'Look, Junie,' whispered E.J., 'Mama is in a coma.'

'Good boy!' I said ruffling his hair. He had just learned that word and already knew how to use it.

I sat next to Mama with the bag tucked between my legs on the floor. E.J. sat next to me with his bag also on the floor. I put my arm around E.J.

'This is the best day,' he said solemnly.

'Are you kids all packed?' asked my mother. Not moving.

'Yes, Mama,' we said.

'Good. I don't want to keep Bob waiting.'

'What time is it?' said E.J.

'Joan Marie, go look at the kitchen clock and tell your brother the time.'

When I came back, I said: 'It is 10.15.'

'Thank you, Joan Marie,' said Mother.

'What's 10.15?' asked E.J.

'Forty-five minutes until Bob comes,' I said. 'Sit still.'

'Junie,' he moaned, 'that's too long. I can't wait.'

'Yes, you can,' I said 'Think of all the fun we're going to have at Seaside Heights.'

'I thought about it already,' he complained. 'I want to do something else. I want to play a game.'

'We're not having any games now, E.J. We are going to wait patiently for Bob.'

'He might be early,' said my mother. 'You never know.'

E.J. gritted his teeth and sat up perfectly straight. Palms pressed down on the sofa next to his knees. His legs dangling over the edge of the sofa. His feet swinging back and forth.

In a moment he reached down and picked up the sneaker bag.

'Did you pack his blue socks, Joan Marie?' asked my mother.

'Yes,' I said.

'Good. I like those blue socks. They go with every-thing. E.J., are you playing with your new sneakers?'

E.J. stuffed them back into the bag and threw it on the floor.

'No, Mama,' he gasped.

'You better not. If you get those sneakers dirty I'll throw them away.'

'They will stay clean, Mama,' said E. J.

'You're allowed to wear them in the bungalow. Not outdoors. Do you understand? Not on the beach, not on the boardwalk. In the house only. Your sandals are for outdoors.'

E.J. stared at mother.

'Junie,' he whispered. 'Mama's head don't move.'

'*Doesn't*, E. J. "Mama's head *doesn't* move." Shush now.'

Mother said, 'Henrietta told Bob there will be some of the same people from last year down there now.'

'That's nice,' I said.

'Don't be so sure, Joan Marie. Who knows what kind they are. We'll be friendly all right. But we're not going to throw ourselves at them.'

'Oh, no,' I said. 'We wouldn't do that.'

'I promise not to throw anything,' said E.J.

'I don't know what I'm worried about,' sighed my mother. 'It will probably be fine. I want you and E.J. to mix in with the other children. No standing back. You'll hurt their feelings. Do you hear me? Just act natural.'

'What's a boardwalk?' asked E.J.

'Just like it sounds,' said my mother. 'A long walk made of boards. For strolling up and down the beach.'

'How many boards?' asked E.J.

'Oh, millions,' answered my mother. 'More than even I could count.'

'That's a lot,' said E.J. 'I can't walk that far.'

'You won't have to,' said my mother. 'We'll just stay on the part nearest our bungalow. The beach will be right there.'

'What's a bungalow?' said E.J.

'You don't shut up for a minute, do you,' said my mother.

'He's hungry,' I said.

'I'm not hungry any more,' said E.J.

'You had Corn Flakes, for God's sake,' said my mother.

'I guess he's extra hungry because of the vacation,' I suggested. 'Actually, I'm hungry myself.'

'Well, then, go in the kitchen and take two cookies from the tin. *Two*. And no drinks. I'm not asking Bob to make a stop just because one of you kids has to tinkle.'

I came back and slipped E.J. both cookies. He put one cookie in his pocket. He broke off and chewed small bits of the other.

'I wonder,' I said, 'whether it might be possible to bring the tin of cookies with us in the car. Bob might enjoy a treat along the way. I wouldn't mind holding it on my lap.'

'Isn't that a thoughtful idea, Joan Marie. Yes. Certainly. Go and get the tin. And you may take two more for being so polite.'

By then E.J. had started in on the cookie from his

pocket. This one was going quickly due to all the excitement. When I came back from the kitchen I snuck the other two into his free hand.

'Did you notice the time, Joan Marie?' asked Mother.

'10.30,' I replied.

'We're getting there,' she said. 'Any minute now.'

My father came down the stairs with an old duffel bag slung over his shoulder.

'Everybody ready?' he said. He plopped the duffel on the floor.

'Of course we're ready,' said my mother. 'What does it look like?'

My father sat next to E.J.

'Hello, Daddy,' said the boy.

All in a row we waited until eleven o'clock. I suppose each person had his or her own thoughts.

At 11.05 my father got up to look out the window.

'Are you sure he said eleven?' asked my mother.

'Yes,' said my father. 'He's probably on his way. It's only five after.'

'I'm not waiting like this all morning,' she said. 'I can tell you that.'

'Why don't you make some more coffee?' said Daddy. 'We can sit for a minute when he comes and have another cup.'

'I've had enough coffee,' said my mother. 'Make it yourself.'

My father folded his arms across his chest. He looked at my mother.

'What's that you've got in your hand?' he asked.

'Flower seeds,' she replied. 'Marigolds.'

'Oh,' he said.

She leaned forward, looked past me and E.J., and shook the packet at my father.

'Ernestine,' he said, 'that's not necessary.'

'Aren't you going to ask me why I am holding a packet of marigold seeds?' she said. 'Aren't you even interested?'

'Of course I am. Don't be ridiculous.'

'So ask,' she said.

'Why are you holding a pack of marigold seeds. There. Now can we please relax?'

'I thought you'd never ask. I bought these for Henrietta because Bob said she loves flowers. I thought they might cheer her up. Bob can pass them along.'

'But we've never even met Henrietta,' said my father. 'And we're not going to. She's in the hospital. She might die, Ernestine.'

'We are *using* her house. She is *giving* us her house. Houseguests bring gifts, Hal. Something to say thank you to the host and hostess. A social gesture. Not that you would know about such things. For Bob we have cookies.'

Silence.

Then: 'It's a nice idea. I'm sorry I jumped on you,' said my father.

'It's all right,' said my mother. 'Something is bothering me, God knows what. Maybe I haven't shown you enough appreciation for arranging this.'

'I know you appreciate it. This is the kind of thing Bob and I do for each other.'

'I hope you don't let him take advantage,' she said.

'Not Bob. You know him.' My father leaned forward so he could see my mother. 'Let's take it easy today, Ernestine. Okay? I'm sorry if I hurt your feelings. I'm sensitive about the thing with Delmonico.'

'I can't keep my big mouth shut,' said my mother. 'That guy positively makes me see red. I know you've tried. So let's all keep trying. Right, gang?'

'Right,' I said.

They sat back again. We waited.

Then my father jumped up and went to the window.

'Bob's here,' he said.

– chapter thirty-four –

To reach Seaside Heights in the modern day you take
the New Jersey Turnpike to the Garden State Parkway.
Connection at Woodbridge. Where cars line up for miles.
Blaring their horns and overheating.

However, what I am talking about when I talk about
E.J. is the historical era. Before the Garden State Parkway.
Therefore when the Pardees went to the Jersey Shore
they took local roads. Bob knew his way. And told us
all about Seaside Heights as we hummed along in his
1952 Chevy. Which had an actual radio and windows
down.

Bob and my father sat in front. Bob said things like,
Are you comfortable back there, Mrs Pardee. My mother
smiled. She looked out the window at every possible
thing. She said, I can't thank you enough for this, Bob.
Feel that warm breeze on your face, kids. And we did.
Isn't this something, Hal. A dream come true.

Bob refused to take more than one cookie. He insisted
E.J. and I eat the rest. Oh, go ahead, said Mother. A few
more won't kill you. We gorged ourselves.

Then all of a sudden from a small cooler hidden under

his feet Bob produced bottles of Coke! The children each had two, very fast. Thank you, Bob. Thank you, Bob. Just let me know, he said, if you need anything and we'll stop. No problem. This we did. Once for me to go to the bathroom, once for E.J. Even my mother agreed to try it.

Soon after the second toilet stop, Bob supposed we were hungry again. He pulled the car up to a Dairy Queen and got us each a large. Chocolate all around. E.J. said this is fabalous and dripped everywhere. It's bound to happen, said Bob, and handed me a towel.

Finally E.J. collapsed into Mother's arms and fell asleep.

She leaned back against the seat. Hair swirled around her face. She closed her eyes. She let it happen. Give me your hand, Joanie. This is a happy moment.

Bob told us that up and down the boardwalk are games, rides and refreshments. Here, Joan Marie, he said reaching over his shoulder. Take this dollar bill for some fun. The way you look, Mrs Pardee, Hal will have to get the police to protect you from all the lolly-gaggers. Oh, Bob! No, I'm serious, Mrs Pardee.

The bungalows run along the road which is behind the beach and the boardwalk, below sand dunes. These bungalows are one-room wooden frame structures, weatherbeaten, white, raised slightly on four heavy wooden stakes in case of floods. Pointed roofs, a little uncovered porch platform out front. Two steps down to a skinny dirt path which leads to another wider dirt path. This one runs parallel to the line of bungalows and facilitates visiting.

All have a patch of grass behind, approx. eight by ten. That was Bob speaking. There are poles in this grass which support a clothes line. Children may play on this grass. Some people bring folding chairs and tables and eat outdoors. Each cottage has one tin garbage can located against the back of the house. There is one door only, in front. With a mat for wiping sandy feet. Two windows, on either side of the door, with curtains. Some red, some blue, some yellow.

Inside on the right is a small icebox, larder, hot plate, sink. Table and four chairs. Toilet and shower in a cubicle in the far right corner. Two sets of bunk beds against the left wall. A double bed in the far left corner. A light bulb hangs from the centre of the ceiling. I think this covers everything Bob told us.

And, he said, you'll meet a nice crowd. Policemen, firemen, that type. Construction guys, school teachers, a few politicians. No niggers. A solid group.

Then he said, I almost forgot. You probably want to hear about the beach. Here I am going on and on about the bungalow. The beach stretches for miles. Now, you need a pass to get on each particular section, to show you're a summer resident. I took care of that. Hands pass to my father. Sticking out from the beach into the water are concrete piers, jettys, different people call them different things. You can sit out there. Sun yourself, fish, run up and down, get away from the sand. Vendors in bare feet hawk ice-creams, popcorn, and candy bars up and down the beach. On trays held by long straps around their necks, just like at the ball park. It is a very good time.

Bob helped us get settled in the bungalow. Everything he had said was correct. The table had a thick green waxy cloth over it. Our elbows and wrists stuck to it when we ate. E.J. and I did not trust the top bunks so Mother made up the two on the bottom. After discussion in the bathroom with my father, she made the double for them. Four of the five nights we were all there she slept by herself above me. Except the last. When she and my father slept together. A special occasion, I suppose.

My father saw Bob to his car and then ventured off over the dunes to the boardwalk. He was gone about an hour. He took long walks every day, in fact. When he came back he would bring a chair and a cup of coffee on to the porch and sit. E.J. at his feet with two tow-trucks and a bulldozer. I on the porch steps reading a book. Mother indoors.

That first day E.J. and I helped Mother put the groceries away. E.J. lined up the cans of fruit, beans, vegetables, soup, and spaghetti. Perfectly. On the bottom shelf of the larder. I took care of the sugar, coffee, cereal, crackers, potato chips, Wonder Bread, and jam. In the icebox, of course, went the milk, margarine, eggs, Velveeta, apples, hot dogs, and a jug of grape Kool-Aid. Mother mixed it up first thing so we wouldn't get dehydrated. That night we had a lovely meal of macaroni and cheese. I am surprised I can still taste it.

Neighbours said hello the second day and invited us for a cookout. But we didn't like them so we stayed home.

We loved the beach. Our section had a magnificent jetty where children kicked beach balls at each other and leaped into the water to retrieve them. Played hopscotch. Lay on towels. Listened to radios. E.J. and I sat on the edge, wriggling toes, holding hands. We decided not to play with the others. I wasn't used to my new bra and E.J. was too young. We had a great time.

Monday and Tuesday were cool and cloudy. We put sweaters over T-shirts. Light rain predicted for Wednesday.

Daddy suggested we try the boardwalk Tuesday afternoon. We were sitting at the table eating spaghetti for our lunch.

'It will be too crowded,' said my mother. 'On a lousy day like this.'

'I don't care,' said E.J. 'I want to see games and take a ride!'

'E.J.,' I said. 'Put your spaghetti back in the bowl.'

'Okay, Junie, but they got a airplane ride over there, you know.'

'I know,' I said, 'but we aren't allowed if you make a mess on the table.'

'Anyway, he's not going on any airplane,' said my mother.

'He'll be all right,' said my father. 'It doesn't really go in the air.'

'It does too!' said E.J. 'Like this!' His hands sweep across the table. Crashing into my glass of milk.

'E.J.!' I said.

My father got up, milk dripping off his legs.

'I'll get a towel,' he said.

My mother smacked E.J. across the face. 'Bad boy. Bring me some Kool-Aid, Hal, if you don't mind.'

'I sorry!' wailed E.J. 'Please let me go on the airplane!'

Tears stream down his face. I wipe them away with my hand.

'Let me think about it,' said my mother. 'We'll see what happens.'

E.J. rubbed his nose. Straightened himself in the chair.

'May I have some more milk, please.'

My father poured his milk and Mother's Kool-Aid.

'Are you okay, Tiger?' he said to E.J.

'Yes, Daddy. I fine.'

'Good boy. We'll go to the boardwalk after lunch. We'll do something nice.'

E.J. gulped his milk.

'I just told him we'd see what happens,' said my mother. 'Why do you always go against me?'

'He didn't do anything wrong, Ernestine. It was an accident. He's excited.'

'But it's bad for them to have parents disagree. You've got to follow suit.'

'But I say it's not serious, he should have a ride on the boardwalk. Why don't *you* agree with *me* if agreement is so important?'

'I'd like to go, too,' I said.

'Of course, Princess,' said Daddy. 'I assumed you were coming.'

'Oh. So that's it,' said my mother. 'Three against one. I'm supposed to stay here and clean up. Worry about the practicalities while you have a ball.'

'I'd like you to be with us, Mama,' I said.

'Me, too,' said E.J. 'I would enjoy your company and be quietest could be.'

'Make up your own mind, Ernestine,' said my father, clearing away the bowls. 'Obviously it's nicer if we all go.'

He took his chair and his coffee out to the porch.

'Shut the door,' said my mother.

'I don't have to be told to close the door,' answered my father. Leaving the door open.

'Finish your Kool-Aid, Joan Marie,' said my mother. 'That's the girl. Oh, why not. I'll try it out. See what's supposed to be so great about this board-walk business.'

'Yay!' we yelled.

'Put on your jackets,' she said. 'And calm down.'

When we got outside, she said to my father, 'Who's paying for all this?'

'I have money for E.J. and me,' I said. 'The dollar bill from Bob.' My father handed me another.

'There,' he said. 'That should do it.'

By now E.J. and I are positively thrilled down to the bones.

As we walk I review over and over the best way to spend our money: half this first week, half the second. Rides are ten cents apiece, most games three for a quarter. The House of Horrors is fifty cents, out of the question. Cotton candy, fifteen; popcorn ten and twenty; drinks, twenty; ice-cream, fifteen and twenty-five. My heart is pounding.

The amazing thing was that my mother did the airplane ride. Suddenly opened her bag, paid her ten cents, squeezed into a little red shell behind E.J.'s yellow one.

'Follow me, Mama!' yelled E.J. 'Pay attention!'

As the operator eased the lever forward, E.J. spun his fake steering wheel like mad as he and my mother bobbed around in a perfect circle. My mother gripped the sides of the plane, sat erect, and bared her teeth. Only later, when she said how much fun it was, did I realise she had been smiling. My father and I leaned on the fence.

This was Tuesday. All in all I spent only sixty cents from Bob's dollar, nothing from my father's.

E.J. and I still have the other dollar-forty.

– chapter thirty-five –

Wednesday. Without a doubt the water was high and rough that day. No one on the beach, or nearby. It would have been the perfect opportunity for Parcheesi. E.J. and Daddy's favourite game. I never thought of it.

But at four o'clock a break in the clouds. The day seemed to clear. My mother said, 'I'll go to the market and buy corn for dinner.'

'Oh, boy,' said E.J. He loved corn on the cob.

Off she went. My father got up from the table, stretched.

E.J. stood on his bed, punching the springs of the bunk above him.

'Careful,' said my father. 'You'll break the bed. Or your hands.'

I finished washing out the clothes. Squeezed them and piled the wet balls in a pyramid in the sink.

'It's no day to hang those out,' said my father, sitting down again.

He opened his newspaper, flipped through it, yawned.

E.J. said, 'Let's play traffic, Junie.'

This was a game. I had invented it two days before:

running up and down the long path in front of the bungalows, we pretend to stop for traffic lights. 'Red light,' I would call. 'Green light,' E.J. would say immediately. People on their porches enjoyed us. Would shout: 'No speeding,' 'Next stop Peoria,' or 'Here they come, Florence.' Just to pass the time in a leisurely way.

The whole problem was: on Wednesday I didn't feel like it.

'Maybe later,' I said. I sat at the table eating an apple.

E.J. came over and tickled me. 'Pretty please, I love traffic.'

'Well, in a few minutes then.' I was hoping he would forget, move on to something else. I felt tired. Parcheesi never entered my mind. I can be so selfish.

Instead, my father suggested we go for a walk on the beach.

'Come on,' he said, dragging himself up from the table. 'Let's clear out the cobwebs.'

'Oh, Daddy,' said E.J. 'Don't be silly. I not a *spider*.' Wasn't he something.

'You're too quick for me, E.J.,' said Daddy.

He got up and opened the door.

'Perfectly fine day,' he said. 'Cloudy but no rain. Man the spacesuits.'

I got our jackets and started to slip E.J.'s rubber sandals on to his feet.

'You never wear your new sneakers, E.J.,' said my

father. 'How about it? Your feet will be chilly in the sandals.'

E.J. and I looked at each other.

'He's not allowed to wear them outside,' I said.

'Of course he's allowed. Where else would he wear them?'

'Inside,' said E.J. 'I allowed wear them inside only.'

'Where did you get an idea like that?' said my father. 'Look at my feet. Look at your mother's. We wear our sneakers everywhere. That's what they're for.'

'I don't think so,' said E.J., watching me.

I said: 'Mama told him he can't get his sneakers dirty. I think he should wear the sandals.'

'Baloney!' said my father. 'The whole point about sneakers is you can *wash* them, E.J. You see how Joanie was doing clothes in the sink? Well, you clean sneakers the same way. You wet them down, scrub them with a little brush, and tie them on to the clothesline by their laces to dry. Simple.'

'Oh!' cried E.J. 'You can wash them, Junie!'

'Daddy,' I said, 'I don't think it's a good idea. Maybe we should wait until Mama comes back. You could ask her.'

He laughed. 'For goodness sake, you kids are a bundle of nerves. Get your sneakers, E.J. Let's give them a try.'

The boy dashed to his bed, fell on his knees, and reached under. He produced the plastic bag.

'There!' he cried.

'Now you're talking,' said my father.

Daddy tied the bright white laces in a double knot. Snug on alabaster feet, the sassy sneakers tossed the little boy across the bungalow.

'They are *great*, Junie!' he cheered.

'You look like a pony,' I laughed.

'I a bird!' he said. Charging up and down, flapping his arms.

'More like a tank,' said my father.

'A tank bird!' said E.J. 'Open the hanger, Junie!'

I spread my arms. He plowed into me. I swept him up. I twirled him. As Louie would say: Such a thing as this there never was.

'Come on,' said my father. 'I'll leave your mother a note telling her to meet us at the pier.'

He wrote the note. Then went outside with E.J. On the porch he turned around.

'Why are you standing there like that, Joanie? Come along and close the door behind you.'

I stared at the plastic sneaker bag left behind on the table. I decided to fold it twice to make it a perfect square. I am not a sloppy girl. I looked around the room for a place to hide this bag, knelt at my bed without knowing the possibility of splinters. Put the plastic sack into the red Woolworth's shopping bag which is under the bed.

'Come on, Joan,' called Daddy. 'We're on our way!'

I hesitated still. The Woolworth's bag was, perhaps,

not in hiding. Mother could discover that sneakers have been removed and taken outdoors against policy. I put the red bag under two towels. But what if Mother decides to bring a towel to the beach? Details cry out.

I tucked the bag between the springs and the mattress and put the towels on top of the bed, accessible and unassuming.

A deep breath. Relieved but not prideful. I went out the door, shut it firmly, walked gingerously down the steps. I turned around. I mounted the steps and opened the door approximately one inch only. Resulting in a condition known as 'ajar'. I skipped across the road to meet Daddy and E.J. Everything is fine!

I am perched atop the dunes. A tight sky of grey and cool breezes, thick green sea in a tantrum. These meet me. The beach is crouched under all stillness.

The pier, being to the other side, is of course on my right. E.J. and Daddy are running in that direction. Daddy pretends he cannot catch E.J., a game. My little one is stomping and charging a path through the sand in his new red sneakers which flash across the beach like radar.

I looked back at the cottage. Not that I was afraid Mother might be coming. No sign of her, I ran down the dunes. There is no question I might be enjoying myself immensely. Unfortunately, not having accurately gauged the angle of the dunes, I stumbled, poor thing. I spread my hands out in front of my face to brace the fall. This gesture is successful: I have eaten only a few grains of sand which I grind between my teeth. Much the same as sugar if you have an open mind.

I stand up. My legs are stiff. Another amazing thing when you consider how wobbly they were a minute ago. E.J. and Daddy are now at the base of the pier chasing each other in a circle. I run towards them in my usual high spirits, shouting, I'm Here, I'm Here, which I was. We played Ring Around The Rosie, Tag, and Blind Man's Bluff.

All of a sudden I saw a figure on the dunes. A whole body out of the corner of my left eye. It is Mother. Isn't that just great. And she is carrying a plastic bag. A snack, no doubt, from the shopping, for good little children.

Mother descends the dunes more cautiously than I had done. She digs in with the sides of her feet, her body on a slight angle against the hill. One step, stop. Another step, stop. And so on until she reaches the ground. I did not, unfortunately, get a chance to compliment her on this technique because my little brother drowned a few minutes later. I suppose I should have mentioned it another day.

I said to Daddy and the boy, 'Here comes Mama and she is bringing us a lovely treat from the shopping, wouldn't you know it.' E.J. shouts against the wind, 'We are here, Mama!' He tackles Daddy around the knees. They fall down. What a good time.

Mama is getting closer. She is beginning to come into

focus. I realise: 'That mother looks angry.' Perception is no guarantee, however. Thus, I say to myself, 'Isn't it lucky she is in a good mood.' Then I looked at her again. 'What a relief. I thought she might be carrying the plastic sneaker bag with E.J.'s sandals inside.' Nevertheless, hoping to clinch the situation for all time I turned to E.J. and said, 'E.J., take off your sneakers.'

'But I want to show Mama them. I explain to wash them off.'

'No, E.J. Be a good boy for me. I'll hold them for you until later.'

Of course he wouldn't do it.

'Hello, Mama,' I said. 'Is that a treat from the shopping?'

'You bet it's a treat, you moron,' she said. 'You hid the plastic bag but you forgot to hide the sandals. Ha! And you think you're so smart. What did I tell you kids about those sneakers?'

The plastic bag containing the sandals rose in the mother's left hand. This hand with the bag then slammed against the right side of the girl's face. It must have been a clip on one of the sandals that made the cut near her eye. On the other hand, there was that clumsy fall on to the sand some moments earlier. The second blow made the inside of her ear groan like an old door. Still, there is no excuse in an aftermath for not hearing out of both ears.

This girl placed one hand over the right ear, the other

over her eye. To ease their likely discomfort upon top-
pling with her body to the sand following the mother's
second application of the plastic bag with sandals. This
effort, thank goodness, was effective. The eye, the ear,
and the self felt nothing. Then E.J. was near me.

'Junie didn't do something, Mama!' Sobbed the boy
and quaked at such a sight.

The father was beside the mother now, too. He grabbed her arm. 'Stop it, Ernestine! Stop it.'

'It's you,' she snarled at Daddy. 'Every time they're
with you,' which isn't true. She struggled free.

'Give me those sneakers, you little bastard,' she said
to her handsome young son.

'I can wash them! They're my *own ones*!'

'You won't wash anything.'

'Ernestine, leave him,' said my father. 'I'll buy new
ones tomorrow.'

'On what you earn? Get those sneakers off him this
instant, Hal Pardee. This is a family.'

'They *belong* me!' cried E.J., and he ran. In huge circles
in the sand. Chased by Mother up on to the dunes. She
chased by Daddy. I was, well, unable to mobilise.

Daddy stopped. Panting, he bowed his head and
rested his hands on his knees. He looked up, took a large
breath.

'Give Mama the sneakers, E.J.,' he called out. I noticed
he and Mother were getting tired from so much running
in the one day.

'I won't!' howled E.J.

He raced down the dunes. Mother was stopped, owing to breathing difficulties. Suddenly Daddy was beside me, examining my face with his fingertips. Having fallen so to speak into a cave, I was not available. But did look up and from my place in the darkness saw that my mother had started running after my brother again. He was going towards the pier which was being lapped up by waves of the biggest type. The sight of these shot the girl with motive. She jumped up.

'Don't go near the pier, E.J.!' I screamed.

I too began to run. My legs were rubber. My open jaw, voice ripped out, was crammed with gauze and mounted like a trophy. E.J. arrived at the pier. Mama was on her way.

'Now we'll see who gets those sneakers,' she panted.

I knew my father was somewhere close by and would take things in hand. I stretched out my arms. Conducted a breast stroke against wind. Impossible under the laws of physics to gain momentum in this manner. E.J. stumbled on to the concrete. Crawled, stood up, ran down this pier.

The girl, in her ignorance, still believes she heard the following: 'Junie Marie, Junie Marie!'

This memory, this ridiculous contraption, is of that actual boy crying out for help *where no help is*. So how could he have said it! The pier is perhaps two hundred feet long. Who knows how to gauge length or breadth any more. Mama stepped on to it and pursued.

Thank goodness, there he is. Daddy. I made up my mind. I will come, E.J. That is the thing to do and I will do it. E.J. looked over his shoulder, still running like mad the way he always did, that little devil.

'Ernestine, I'll get the sneakers! E.J., it's all right now, honey! Give them to Daddy, you can have them back tomorrow! Ernestine, stop. I'll get them.'

Unfortunately, E.J. bumped off the end of the pier just then.

'Oh, my God, oh, my God,' said Daddy.

'Where is he?' cried Mama. 'Get him, Hal, get him!'

'I can't see him!' Daddy charged from one side of the pier to the other, carving out a lack of direction. Mother ran a circle around the same spot on the pier, her head swivelling like a periscope.

Finally the girl in the story arrived.

She stopped running. She stood nicely with her hands folded in front, looking out at the ocean. Where nothing came alive to her. Still, an arm went up and the index finger pointed.

'What is it?' screamed Daddy. 'Do you see him, do you see him?'

'Get him, Hal, there he is, I see him, there he is! We're coming, honey! Mama is here!'

Daddy jumped off the end of the pier. He fumbled for a place to hold on. These piers are not meant to be climbed at from inside the ocean. Which is why they finish off the top in a smooth way, to encourage staying above. Water rushed over him.

'I can't do it, Ernestine,' he gasped. He clung to a jagged bit of concrete.

'But he'll be cold,' sobbed the mother. Which is true, even today. Especially at bedtime, as previously mentioned, I find he needs extra blankets.

Daddy flopped himself up on to the pier like a sack.

The next morning we took the bus home because no trains run through Seaside Heights.

– *chapter thirty-six* –

Just a few more points, Mr Fusco, and then
my last will and testament are finished.
Bygones are bygones. In my experience they
seek their own level. Good riddance.

5. I should say more about item one, Joan
waking in the night. Just to prepare you for
the worst. Joanie has nightmares. These have
frightened me for many years. Of all the
selfish acts a child can inflict on a parent,
nightmares are the worst. How do children
expect parents to cope without sleep? Why
don't they just talk about what is on their
little minds?

Joan had a brother. His name was Edward
John. Luckily he and Joanie did not get along
well and she has no memory of him. He died
of meningitis, due to medical neglect, at the
age of four.

Now, I don't want to go blowing my own
horn here, but it is mainly because of me that

Joan has been able to forget him. They shared a room. Edward died on a Sunday afternoon following three miserable days in a hospital. Joan went to stay with Hal's sister. The woman has since died and that is the best thing I can say about her. How could I be jealous of a low-class, meddling spinster?

It is impossible to describe the pain of a mother as she watches her innocent child suffer for no reason. Yet, despite my own pain, I knew Joan would need help. I rushed home from the hospital that Sunday, and with my husband, who was also upset, we threw Edward's possessions into the back of a neighbour's pick-up truck and took them to the dump. If I do say so myself, I was the one who thought to get rid of the photographs. Pictures are liable to trigger off a memory, you never know.

By the time Joan came home from her aunt's that evening, we had the room completely re-arranged to suit her needs. I had even painted on the door in gold lettering, 'Joanie's Own Room'. She appreciated her new privacy so much she could barely speak when she saw the room. All she said was, 'I am all alone.' Wasn't that sweet? She never mentioned

Edward again. I had been mature at her age myself, so I wasn't surprised.

I am telling you all this, Mr Fusco, because in her nightmares Joanie imagines she is struggling to save a little boy. Then she imagines that it is someone she actually knew. Occasionally upon waking she used to remark, for example, 'I thought I heard a small boy cry out for me last night,' or 'Last night I read a book to a sweet little boy.' These ideas are of course nonsense. I am holding you under strict instructions to put Joanie in the direction of reality, Mr Fusco. There are to be no non-sequiturs. You may laugh, but I've learned a big word here and there myself.

6. One final comment about Edward. It has become clear to me that Joanie believes she killed him. I have told her she is taking on a burden which really belongs to the American Medical Association. You have probably noticed that she has a tendency to protect higher authority at her own expense. I have told her many times they don't deserve it. What they need is justice. I have written to my Congressman to complain, and told him you would be following up the situation.

I can't think of anything else at the moment.

Good luck. Have a pleasant time. I hope the weather improves.

Signed:
Ernestine Pardee

– chapter thirty-seven –

'Benny is acting funny,' I said.

  'What do you mean funny?' asked Mrs Enwright.

  'Edgy,' I said.

  'He probably misses Candi,' she said.

  'Angela says he doesn't want to face reality.'

  Mrs Enwright laughed. 'Who does?'

  'There could be no other explanation,' I said.

  We sat.

  'Louie thinks AA is making Benny unstable,' I said.

  'You don't agree?'

  'Well.'

  'Have some more cocoa,' said Mrs Enwright.

It is Saturday. Lunchtime. Jesus went to work at eight. I walked over at 11.30. He is due back for his sandwich at 12.00. This would be typical. If the shop isn't busy, I eat lunch with Jesus and Mrs Enwright Monday, Wednesday, and Saturday, 11.30–1.00. Jesus takes me back in the van. I tend to business while Louie eats and naps. 1.15–3.30. From 3.30–6.00 we work together happily. Who would want to leave an arrangement like this just to get kissed.

'I don't think he is even going to AA,' I said.

'Possibly not,' said Mrs Enwright. 'Maybe he's drinking again, or about to drink. Tricky business.' She sipped her cocoa.

'I can't tell,' I said. 'He doesn't have that certain look.'

'You would know,' replied Mrs Enwright.

'It must be what you said. He misses Candi. They're apart for weeks. At least I think they're apart.'

'Either way makes no difference,' said Mrs Enwright. 'They're never really together, are they?'

The door opens. Miss Forth trots in ahead of Jesus.

'Hello, you two,' I call out. 'Right on time.'

Jesus cradles a cornucopian armload of long-stemmed yellow roses. Resting against biceps.

'Hi, Gram,' he says.

'Hello, darling,' she replies.

He stands in front of me and holds out the flowers.

'I suppose these are for me,' I say. 'I suppose you think I'll accept them, just like that.'

Mrs Enwright pulls herself up. 'Time for me to exit. Peanut butter and cucumber on whole wheat coming right up. House special.'

'Delicious,' I say, after she has gone.

'You are delicious,' says Jesus. 'I brought you these flowers in honour of a special occasion.'

The chair sags beneath the weight of roses on my lap.

I ask: 'And what might that be?'

'It is my birthday,' he replies.

'Oh, now,' I say.

'Thank you,' he says.

'I should have known,' I said.

'I wanted it to be a surprise.'

'The day you are born. My.'

'Twenty-eight years ago,' he reminded me.

I put my face to the rose petals. I shut my eyes against them. The powdery down fondled my forehead, my cheeks, my nose.

'I was born the day I met you,' said Jesus Perez.

I looked up. He was standing near the chair. Beads of sweat gathered on his temples. He brushed them away with the back of his left hand.

'I don't know how to say this,' he said.

'I am sure I won't be able to add a single word.'

'That is why I love you,' he said. 'Because you just said that. Plus your dynamic personality. Your imagination.' He lowered his head. 'I am so boring.'

I almost leapt out of the chair and dumped the flowers off my lap.

'Oh, no!' I cried. 'Don't ever say such a wrong thing!'

He shifts from one foot to the other and back again.

'I asked Bobby and Freddy,' he says. 'They said I am a little dull. Not a lot, thank goodness. I don't know what to do about it.'

'Would you like to sit down?' I said.

'They didn't think I would lose you, though. That was a relief. I believe I prefer standing.'

'The last word I would use to describe you is boring. But I could be wrong. Maybe you are.'

'I asked them something else. This is the hard part.'

'I don't know about that. I like you because you are continuous.'

He brightened. 'Really?'

'It's your rhythmical nature. You do the same things at the same time every day. I know how you will act and what you will wear. It is so exciting.'

'This is the best birthday I have ever had,' said Jesus.

'You are sweating,' I said. 'Lean over.'

I wiped his forehead and the sides of his face with my hand. What delicate, scratchy.

'I didn't shave this morning,' he said, straightening himself. 'Will you marry me?'

'No.'

'Maybe we could go to the movies.'

'That's a nice idea.'

'As I said there was one other point I mentioned to Bobby and Freddy. Did you ask Lila and Marsha anything?'

'No. It wasn't necessary. They will decide what I need to know.'

'I want to say how sorry I am not to have kissed you as yet.'

'They told you to say that?'

'Yes,' he replied. 'How did it sound?'

'Excellent,' I said.

'This situation will not persist much longer,' he said.
'Which one?'
'The one Bobby and Freddy said to apologise for.'
'Oh. That one.'
'They're helping me with it,' he said.
'When will you know how it is working out?' I asked.
'Soon.'
'I can think out my parameters if I know your pace. The way the world is these days, no man is an island.'

At lunch Mrs Enwright surprised Jesus with a black T-shirt. He absolutely adored it. Miss Forth gave him another tie, just like them one he already had. He couldn't thank her enough. This way he'll have a spare if the cleaners run into a problem.

– *chapter thirty-eight* –

I remember it was a Tuesday. Angela came by the shop for a free cup of coffee. On her way back to work from lunch.

I was making stuffing for *cannoli*. A small batch at a time insures freshness: enough to fill eighteen shells only. A wooden spoon handles the job. No mixers, no metals. If we run out, the customers understand.

What most people do not realise about *cannoli* stuffing is the glazed fruit and rosewater. We sneak in extra cinnamon, Louie's trademark. Never mind dry Marsala in the pastry shells, which must never be stuffed ahead.

I was tending the ricotta mixture in the kitchen. I had simmered water and confectioner's sugar to just the right thickness and was about to mix it in a large crockery bowl with fifteen ounces of ricotta. The bell went ding-a-ling, indicating door opening. Louie said hello to someone. I mixed, added the remaining confectioner's sugar and cinnamon, mixed again, refrigerated.

Then I cut the fruit, orange and lemon, into small pieces. These, the superfine sugar, and rosewater, will be added in about two hours. If at that point I like the look of the refrigerated mixture. Louie whips up the shells, naturally. These *cannoli* are the finest, plus more, that money can buy.

When I came out of the kitchen, Angela and Louie were huddled over their mugs of coffee, staring grimly into the black liquid. Angela had been looking and feeling marvellous so I was surprised to see circles under her eyes, hair not washed. Maybe it was just the careless way she had it bunched up on top of her head. Or that she had not bothered to take off her coat.

'Hello,' I said. 'The *cannoli* stuffing is in the refrigerator.'

They did not look up.

I went behind the counter, filled the sink with tepid soapy water, and washed some cups and trays. Wondering. Suspecting.

I did not have to wait long. A moment later Benny raced through the door. Flushed, agitated.

'There you are,' he panted. 'Christ, I've been looking everywhere.'

Angela watched him. Said nothing, wearily. He is unshaven. One, perhaps two days' growth. She turned to her coffee and took a sip. She pulled her coat in tight, hunched forward against the table.

'Get out, you fucking bastard,' said Louie. 'We're not buying.'

'What's your problem?' said Benny.

'*My* problem?' sneered Louie. 'You must be kidding.'

'I came to see *my* wife, if you don't mind,' said Benny.

'From now on, buddy,' said Louie, 'you want her, you talk to me first.'

Benny shook his head. 'Unbelievable. You'll never let her grow up, will you?'

'Why don't you just make your little speech and go,' said Angela.

'No speech, Ange,' he replied. 'Really, just to tell you something's come up. Very important, very big deal. Priority stuff. I have to be away, a few days, not much, possibly longer. Short notice, the usual.'

His chest is heaving, great waves, he can't seem to get enough air. Eyes dart around the room.

'Where's Joan?' He is so busy looking he can't see.

'Hello, Benny,' I said.

I dried my hands with the green dish towel and stepped forward. Still behind the counter. I tucked the towel into my white apron.

'Thank God,' gasped Benny. 'I was afraid you wouldn't be here.'

'That's not possible,' I said. 'I am standing on firm ground.'

He leaned over the counter. Put a finger to his lips. His eyes are bloodshot. Flooded with tears.

'Joanie,' in a hoarse whisper, 'Gino is dead. Candi is missing. Gone, nowhere. I can't find her.' Tears start to spill on to his rough face. 'You've got to help me.'

I turned to the sink. I plunged my arms into the now cool, thick water. I felt it edge up beyond my elbows like filmy plastic. Clinging to bits of skin and tiny hairs. Encasing each arm. Stumps of meat wrapped in a styrofoam tray in a supermarket cooler.

'So you'll be leaving town then,' I shouted.

'Now what have you said?' yelled Louie. 'Now *she's* all upset! Get out of my shop, get out of my sight, you sick crazy bastard!'

'Thanks for nothing!' screamed Benny. 'A man can't go on a business trip once in a while?'

Angela let out a feeble laugh.

'Listen, babe,' he said, 'I'll see you. Hopefully it won't be too long.'

'You'll *see* me?' she said. 'No, Benny, you won't see me.'

Silence.

'I hope you don't mean that,' he said.

She did not answer. He left.

'I can't get the wrapper off my arms!' I bawled. 'Take off this wrapper, Louie!'

From what I could see, I was waving my arms in the air, trying to shake away the soapsuds. Louie held me. Brought my arms down one at a time, dabbed them gently with the towel.

Somehow I had the ridiculous idea I was being embalmed.

– chapter thirty-nine –

Main Street from Sycamore to Louie's is dotted with traffic lights, intersections, clumps of bedlam.

On the other hand, it is relatively straight and open. No hidden dangers or sudden twists.

Lila told me: take your pick. It's that or the country roads in Monmouth. Bobby, against his better judgement, loaned us his father's 1970 Chrysler Imperial. Automatic gearshift, electric windows. After this, said Freddy, the Army will want it for a tank.

Marsha sat in the back seat taking inventory of the medical response system: blood pressure gauge, stethoscope, thermometer, sterile bandages, ear plugs. This is a portable, all-purpose kit which Marsha takes everywhere. She did not remove the eye patch, pregnancy test, or tourniquet. You never know, she said. Just because it's a driving lesson. Stranger things have happened.

She keeps an up-dated list of poisons, as well as emergency phone numbers. Including the County Morgue. This detail she contends has nothing to do with her preference for black. Lila argues that the County Morgue is of absolutely no use in an emergency, besides being disgusting under any circumstances. Thus illustrating how different two people can be.

Lila and I are wearing high heels. She insisted I copy her as a mark of self-respect. Marsha read her the riot act for supporting cosmetic change.

'Not to discourage you, Joan,' said Marsha, 'but frankly you need a lot more than a good pair of shoes.'

'Shut up,' said Lila. She is in the driver's seat, fumbling through a set of keys. About to give me a demonstration. 'We are out here today to build confidence. She needs to believe in her strengths, Marsha.'

'I won't hold my breath while you look for them,' replied Marsha, putting the thermometer in her mouth. 'I'm a naturalistic realist, Joan. I want the best out of each person. That means facing facts.'

She checked her stopwatch, took out the thermometer, and entered her temperature in the medical log.

'I only talk this way to people with potential. It's a compliment.'

I turned and smiled at her. 'I know. And I like you, too, Marsha. Even though you are depressing.'

'Now you're talking,' said Marsha.

'Cut it out, you two,' said Lila. 'I'm concentrating.'

Lila was trying one key after another in the ignition.

'That dumb boyfriend of yours gave us the wrong keys, Marsha.'

'It's usually the one with the name on it,' I said. I

picked out a key with a square top embossed 'Chrysler'.

'Well, aren't you a clever one,' chirped Lila. 'A little potential showing already.'

'Look who's calling who dumb around here,' said Marsha. She was carefully cleaning the thermometer with rubbing alcohol.

'The first thing,' said Lila, 'is to start the car. Put it in Park, like this. Make sure the brakes are on, like this. Then accelerate gently as you turn the key. Are you paying attention?'

'Yes,' I said. 'I am excited already.'

'Didn't I tell you, Lila?' complained Marsha. 'I knew she'd get excited.'

'She's not *that* excited,' said Lila. 'Just how excited would you say you are anyway, Joan?'

'Not very,' I said. 'Would you like me to stop? I don't mind.'

'Not me,' said Lila. 'Morticia back there doesn't trust anyone who isn't half dead. You get as excited as you like, Joanie. Let it all hang out.'

'Okay,' I said.

'Now watch me carefully,' said Lila. 'I'm going to start us up.'

I heard the click of Marsha's stopwatch. She was taking her pulse.

The engine roared, the car shook. Smoke spewed out the exhaust.

'You said gently,' commented Marsha. Click.

'Oh, well,' giggled Lila. 'It all depends.' She released the hand-brake. The car chugged contentedly, reminding me of Miss Forth.

'Here comes the tricky part,' said Lila. 'You put your foot on the *foot*-brake *before* you shift into Drive. See? Foot on brake. Car still in Park.'

'I'm sorry, Marsha,' I said, 'but I find I am getting very excited.'

'How is your breathing?' she asked.

'Frequent,' I replied.

'Are you seeing double?'

'How do you tell?' I asked.

'First you feel faint,' she said. 'Lack of oh-two. It's a chemical problem. I'll just make a note.'

The stopwatch clicked again.

'Go as far as the first intersection, Lila,' said Marsha. 'Then Joan will take over.'

'I am about to engage the gears,' said Lila. She pulled the gearshift on the side of the wheel down one notch. 'Remain mindful at all times of other vehicles. Notice my foot is still on the brake. I am going to let it up slowly, like this. Very slowly.'

The car shot forward into the street. Lila jammed on the brakes. The car screeched to a halt and stalled.

'Eight seconds,' said Marsha.

'Thank God I had presence of mind,' gasped Lila. 'That was a close call.'

'Yeah,' said Marsha. 'You were nearly going.'

'I think you should turn off the ignition and put the car into Park,' I said.

'Yes,' said Lila. 'Like this. Then pull the hand brake. You get the idea.'

'Nice job, Lila,' said Marsha. 'Some lesson.'

'It is no harm for Joanie to see an experienced driver handle a typical emergency,' answered Lila. She took a deep breath. 'See? Nothing to it.'

Other cars were driving cautiously around us.

'Joanie's turn,' said Marsha.

'You said to the first intersection,' whined Lila.

'No way,' said Marsha.

'Damn!' said Lila. 'She needs more exposure, Marsha.'

'Not to you she doesn't.'

'It's all right, Lila,' I said. 'I am very well exposed already.'

'Quit stalling, you two,' said Marsha.

Oh, dear. As usual one item reminiscent of another.

How could I have forgotten the most important point.

It was a *car* that took the boy E.J. on his vacation.

I was there. I was in the very car. No one can say otherwise, I will dispute with every bone. Me: in that car just going along like a moron. With that very boy to his destination. This is fact.

To the extent even of pleasure at the blop-blop of Bob's limp rubber tyres. As we lurched over seams in the concrete on old forgotten roads because he didn't have time to put in air. And said anyway the sound was like a song we would enjoy more than full tyres. I thought this was *fun*.

'Stop the car,' I said. 'We're not going.'

'I stopped us already,' said Lila. 'It's your turn to drive. Scoot over here.'

'She's not listening,' said Marsha. 'To put it mildly.'

'Joan, do you read me?' called Lila. 'Yoo-hoo? Come on over and let's see you drive this baby.'

'Forget it, Lila,' said Marsha. 'Never-Never Land. Turn the car on. Then off. Maybe she can't tell it's off until it's been on.' She rustled through the pages of her *Complete and Definitive Guide to First Aid*.

'On second thoughts,' she added, 'don't do anything. Let's just go home. This is getting to be a nightmare.'

'Thank you, Marsha,' I said. 'For a moment I couldn't find the word. Please stop the car. We are not going. This is the correct answer.'

Lila agreed. Marsha wanted to know where we weren't going and the answer to what. All of a sudden I wasn't sure. One minute to the next.

I cancelled the driving class. I felt my mind, to some extent, slipping. One ought to be in top form for any lesson, in life or otherwise.

What happens is this. At a point of difference, known to some as 'forward motion', there become particular moments. Certain times and places. Miseries impart, memory spills. The stain spreads. I cannot exude the required hopefulness.

I asked Lila could she possibly delay the finer points for a few years. She said waiting was ideal in terms of her own schedule, and would not in any way debilitate my knack for catching on.

'It is scientifically proven, Joan,' she said, 'that human potential is a constant.'

'Right,' said Marsha, pressing an icepack to her forehead. 'A constant pain.'

To this day I am trying to figure out which science she meant.